DEADLOCK

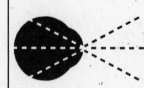

This Large Print Book carries the
Seal of Approval of N.A.V.H.

DEADLOCK

AL AND JOANNA LACY

THORNDIKE PRESS

A part of Gale, Cengage Learning

GALE
CENGAGE Learning™

Detroit • New York • San Francisco • New Haven, Conn • Waterville, Maine • London

GALE
CENGAGE Learning

LIBRARY OF CONGRESS CATALOGING-IN-PUBLICATION DATA

Lacy, Al.
    Deadlock / by Al & Joanna Lacy.
        p. cm. — (Thorndike Press large print Christian historical fiction) (Return of the stranger ; bk. 2)
    ISBN-13: 978-1-4104-2465-5 (alk. paper)
    ISBN-10: 1-4104-2465-0 (alk. paper)
    I. Lacy, JoAnna. II. Title.
    PS3562.A256D44 2010
    813'.54—dc22   2009048784

Published in 2010 by arrangement with Multnomah Books, an imprint of the Crown Publishing Group, a division of Random House, Inc.

Printed in the United States of America
1 2 3 4 5 6 7 14 13 12 11 10

*This book is affectionately dedicated
to our dear friend Alice Crider,
who is our acquisitions editor at the
WaterBrook Multnomah Publishing Group.
We very much enjoy working with you,
Alice! We love you.*
2 Timothy 4:22

FOREWORD

The Return of the Stranger trilogy is a follow-up to the Journeys of the Stranger Series and Angel of Mercy Series written for Multnomah Books by Al Lacy between 1994 and 1997. In 1997, Multnomah's president hired JoAnna Lacy as coauthor with her husband, and they began the Hannah of Fort Bridger Series that same year. Since then, JoAnna has coauthored every book with her husband that has been published by Multnomah Books and the new WaterBrook Multnomah Publishing Group.

Since Al ended the Journeys of the Stranger and Angel of Mercy Series, which centered on John "the Stranger" Brockman and Breanna Baylor, who married in the second series, Al and JoAnna as well as the publisher have received repeated letters, e-mails, and calls asking that Al write another Stranger series. This trilogy is in

pleasant response to those welcome re-
quests.

Al and JoAnna hope that fans of the
Stranger will enjoy this new trilogy and that
many new Stranger fans will as well.

ONE

It was almost nine fifteen Sunday morning, June 24, 1888, when chief United States marshal John Brockman — known in his early life in the West as "the Stranger" — put his two-horse team in motion and steered one of the family wagons from the corral at the Brockman ranch to the front of the ranch house. His wife, Breanna, their fifteen-year-old son, Paul, thirteen-year-old daughter, Ginny, and nine-year-old adopted daughter, Meggie, were chatting happily about attending church in Denver that morning.

The Colorado sky was clear, and the sun was shining brightly on the open range to the east. The towering Rocky Mountains just west of the ranch were brilliant, their awesome peaks standing jaggedly against the beautiful azure blue sky.

Paul, who was tall, quite strong for his age, and clearly resembled his father, lifted Meggie up onto the driver's seat. She quickly scooted close to her adoptive father and looked back at Paul as he climbed up and sat beside her. Paul grinned. "I'd let just you ride up here with Papa all by yourself, sweet stuff, but since we're picking up Uncle Whip and Aunt Annabeth, I have to leave some extra room on the benches in the back."

Meggie smiled, flashing her dimples, and said, "I think it's neat that even though we're not related to the Langfords, they let us call them Uncle Whip and Aunt Annabeth."

"So do I," Paul said, and he hopped down to help his mother into the rear of the wagon.

"Me too." Ginny smiled up at Meggie as she followed her mother into the wagon.

Breanna and Ginny sat together on one of the cushioned benches in the bed of the wagon.

Paul hurried up to the driver's seat. "Okay, Papa. Let's go."

"I appreciate your being a gentleman, Paul, and helping the ladies into the wagon."

"I learned from the most polished gentleman in the world, Papa. You!"

"Amen!" Breanna said.

"Yes." Ginny patted her mother's hand

and turned her eyes on Paul. "Preach it, brother!"

Meggie giggled and looked at Paul. "Yeah. Preach it, brother!"

A smiling John Brockman put the team to a trot and headed up their short, tree-lined lane toward the road. As they drove toward the Langford cabin, the Brockmans talked about the wedding that had taken place the day before at First Baptist Church in Denver between John's favorite deputy U.S. marshal, Whip Langford, and Breanna's closest co-worker at Denver's Mile High Hospital, Annabeth Cooper.

Paul looked back at his mother. "I'm sure glad we're having Uncle Whip and Aunt Annabeth over for dinner after church. Uncle Whip told me that since they wouldn't be able to go on a honeymoon, they would call Sunday dinner with us today their honeymoon."

Breanna's blue eyes twinkled. "Oh, he did, eh?" She chuckled. "Well, the girls and I will make dinner as nice as we can for the newlyweds."

Ginny said, "I'm sure glad they're riding to church with us today. It's neat that their first time at church as husband and wife will be with us."

Paul looked past Meggie. "Papa, it must

be a special blessing that you had the joy and privilege of leading Uncle Whip to the Lord."

"You're right about that, son. It *is* a special blessing to see the changes in Whip's life — an outlaw who became a deputy U.S. marshal."

Breanna adjusted herself on the bench. "It is also a special blessing that Annabeth, who was already a Christian and had been widowed, has found happiness with the man now known as the Outlaw Marshal."

Paul chuckled and looked back at his mother. "The *Rocky Mountain News* sure made a big thing by calling Uncle Whip the Outlaw Marshal over and over when Papa hired him, didn't they?"

"They sure did, honey."

The wagon was approaching the Langford place, and John guided the horses off the road toward the cabin. Whip was on the front porch, Bible in hand. As John pulled the team to a halt a few feet from the porch, Whip stepped down and greeted his friends. "My beautiful bride will be out shortly."

John nodded and looked over at the small fenced-in shed where Whip kept his pet wolf, Timber. "Since we've got a few minutes, I'll go say hello to my buddy Timber."

The tall, broad-shouldered chief U.S.

marshal hopped down from the wagon seat and made his way through the gate. The large gray wolf greeted him with friendly whining and licked John's hand. "John," Breanna called out, "Annabeth is coming out now!"

John turned and saw Annabeth step onto the front porch and shut the door behind her. A purse that John knew contained her Bible hung from her left shoulder.

John patted Timber's head, then pivoted and walked back to the wagon.

When the door had clicked shut behind her, Annabeth faced her friends, a smile gracing her lovely features. Paul had moved to the rear of the wagon next to Ginny, knowing that Whip would want to ride on the driver's seat with his father and Meggie. Paul, Ginny, and Meggie waved at the dear lady they loved to call Aunt Annabeth. Breanna returned Annabeth's smile, and a radiant glow beamed from Annabeth's face.

"Good morning, Annabeth," Breanna called out as the new bride descended the front steps.

"Good morning, everyone," Annabeth said as Whip stepped up to his wife's side, took her white-gloved hand, and walked her to the rear of the Brockman wagon, where he tenderly helped her to her seat. "Thank you, dear," Annabeth said, looking into Whip's eyes. She turned and hugged Breanna, Paul, and Ginny in turn. She then stepped up behind the driver's seat and hugged Meggie. Whip was now on the driver's seat as well.

John climbed up to the driver's seat from the other side. "Good morning, Annabeth."

She returned the greeting. Meggie looked up at her. "You look very pretty today, Aunt Annabeth."

"Why, thank you, dear," she replied. "It must be the happiness I'm feeling now that I'm Mrs. Whip Langford!"

Whip's eyes shone as he smiled at his bride and let out a big sigh. Annabeth smiled at him as she sat down next to Breanna.

Grabbing the reins, John turned and ran his gaze over his passengers. "Time to get rolling if we want to make it in time for Sunday school." He put the team in motion and headed toward Denver.

As the wagon bounced along the road, Breanna noticed Whip turn around and smile at his bride. Breanna glanced off to the side of the road, a satisfied smile on her lips. *I did a good job matching this couple,* she thought to herself. *A very good job!*

Whip looked past Meggie to John. "Chief,

Timber really likes you."

"Well, I really like Timber — especially because he has helped you capture so many outlaws when you've pursued them without another deputy along."

"Yes sir. That big gray wolf has been a tremendous help to me."

As the wagon rolled along, the conversation transitioned to the Sunday sermon, which Pastor Robert Bayless had announced at last Wednesday evening's service he would be preaching. It would be given in two parts — this morning and next Sunday.

John told Whip and Annabeth that his family would miss out on the sermon next Sunday because he was scheduled to preach both morning and evening services at Riverton Baptist Church in Riverton, Wyoming. He had preached there many times over the years. Breanna and the children were going with him.

Whip looked at John. "I want you to know I've really enjoyed your preaching at First Baptist. Of course, I like Pastor Bayless's preaching very much, but I wish Annabeth and I could go along with you to Riverton and hear you preach." He looked back at his wife. "We both have duties here though."

From where she sat next to Breanna, Annabeth said, "Darling, maybe we can go to Riverton with them some other time when Chief Brockman will be preaching. Right now we both have obligations to our jobs and a brand-new life to get used to."

Whip smiled at Annabeth. "Yes ma'am. A beautiful, new, and wonderful life to get used to."

About a mile ahead, outlaws Kent Fortney and Calvin Seidler were at the Platte River, due west of Denver. They were hiding in the dense trees near a bridge, on horseback, waiting for one of Chief Brockman's deputies to ride out of a nearby settlement of cabins on his way to Denver.

Deputy U.S. marshal Barry Sotak had trailed Fortney six years earlier on the Colorado plains toward Kansas and caught him, taking him to Denver for trial. Fortney had been sentenced to twenty years at the Colorado State Penitentiary in Cañon City and had been Seidler's cellmate since then. They had broken out two nights before, stolen two horses from a ranch near Cañon City, and ridden northeast toward Denver.

Fortney held a grudge against Deputy Sotak, not only for outmaneuvering and capturing him, but also because on the entire trip to Denver after his capture, Sotak had quoted Bible passages and tried to get Fortney to become a Christian. This angered him deeply and made him hate the lawman with a passion. When Sotak talked about Kent's need for salvation, he mentioned where he attended church in Denver and where he lived.

Fortney was determined to kill Sotak before he and Cal rode hard for California.

As they sat on their horses watching for Sotak, Fortney came to a resolution with the headlong willfulness of a mad killer haunted by a fixed determination. Turning to his partner, he said with burning hatred, "Cal, ol' pal, Deputy Sotak dies today!"

Seidler looked at Fortney's bitter, scowling face. "Yeah, Kent. He dies today. I'll help you see to it."

Fortney clenched his teeth. "*Only* if I need you, Cal. Otherwise, yours truly will be taking him out."

As the Brockmans and the Langfords drew near the Platte River, where they would cross the bridge and head for downtown Denver, John pointed up ahead and said to Whip, "Hey, there's Barry. If he sees us, I guarantee he'll pull rein and wait to ride to church alongside us."

Suddenly John and the others in the wagon saw two men on horseback come gal-

17

loping out of the woods by the bridge, both gripping revolvers. They were headed straight for Barry.

One of the riders shouted something and raised his gun, clearly indicating his intention to fire. Barry, who was lightning fast on the draw, whipped out his gun. As he fired at the man, his horse stumbled, and his bullet struck the other rider, who buckled and fell from his saddle.

John pulled rein, drawing the wagon to a sudden halt. He leaped to the ground and drew his gun. Whip Langford hopped off the driver's seat on the other side and pulled his own gun. Whip was glad Pastor Bayless never objected to the lawmen wearing their guns at church.

John shouted to those in the wagon. "Everybody get down on the floor of the wagon bed right now! Meggie, go to Mama!"

As the family scurried to safety on the wagon bed, John said, "All right, Whip. Let's go!"

John and Whip ran toward Barry, who was now off his horse, hunkered low behind a fallen tree.

Kent Fortney was firing at him from his saddle. The escaped prisoner suddenly saw the two lawmen running his direction. "One time or another, Sotak, I'm gonna kill you!"

Barry rose up from behind the tree and aimed at Fortney. Unaware that his right knee was leaning on a knotted, broken branch, Barry flinched as sharp pain shot through his leg. The bullet missed Fortney by some three feet.

The outlaw fired as well, hitting Barry's left shoulder before putting his horse to a gallop and heading into the thick forest toward the mountains. Drawing within firing range, John and Whip quickly fired in Fortney's direction, but the man who had just shot Barry had already disappeared into the dense woods.

As John and Whip ran toward the fallen deputy, two men on horseback galloped up, Ford Harper and Del Todman, neighbors from the nearby settlement of cabins. Paul Brockman had taken the wagon's reins and skidded it to a halt where Barry Sotak had fallen.

The chief U.S. marshal told Barry's neighbors what had happened. Both men slid from their saddles, thanking John for the update. Breanna and Annabeth jumped from the wagon bed and followed John as he led Ford and Del to Barry's side.

As the two nurses knelt beside Barry and began examining him, John ran to the spot where the second outlaw lay. Dropping to his knees, John quickly saw that the man was dead. He alerted Barry and the group.

While Breanna and Annabeth worked on Barry, he looked up at John and Whip standing over him.

"Chief," Barry said, his voice strained, "the outlaw that got away was Kent Fortney. I trailed him some six years ago onto the eastern plains of Colorado and caught him and brought him back to Denver."

"I remember Fortney, Barry. I believe he was sentenced to twenty years at Cañon City, so he must've escaped. That other outlaw you killed probably escaped with him."

"That's what I figured, Chief."

John looked at Whip. "We've got to go after Fortney right now."

John turned to Barry's neighbors. "Can Whip and I use your horses to go after the other outlaw?"

"Of course," Ford replied.

"Go get him!" Del said.

"We'll do our best."

Barry looked up at his chief. "Yeah, boss. Go get him."

The nurses had almost stopped the bleeding. Breanna looked up at her husband. "Barry isn't hurt real bad, but the slug must be removed from his shoulder. We've got the bleeding under control, so we'll take him to the hospital immediately."

"I'll drive the wagon, Papa," Paul said.

"Okay, son." John turned to Whip. "Let's get Barry in the wagon."

With the help of the two neighbors, the chief and his deputy picked up their wounded friend and placed him carefully into the rear of the wagon, gently laying him on the floorboards.

Paul helped both his mother and Annabeth into the bed of the wagon. John and Whip made Barry as comfortable as possible. Ginny and Meggie climbed up on the driver's seat so they could ride with their brother.

John and Whip quickly hugged their wives. Then John moved to the front of the wagon and hugged his daughters.

Paul took the reins in hand. "Papa, I'll be praying that you and Uncle Whip catch up with the outlaw real quick."

As Paul steered the wagon toward town, Ford and Del watched the two lawmen mount their horses and gallop away, heading west toward where they had last seen Kent Fortney.

When John and Whip reached the forest, they quickly saw fresh hoofprints. The outlaw was headed straight toward the mountains.

"Chief, since we have to go relatively close to my place to trail Fortney, let's stop and take Timber with us."

"Sounds good to me, Whip. Let's go!"

A few minutes later, a happy Timber ran through the opening gate of his small yard and joined the horses as they headed into the mountains. Soon they were climbing the steep slopes of the Rockies.

On the dusty road that led to Denver, Paul Brockman snapped the reins to keep the team at a full gallop.

Breanna and Annabeth knelt over Barry, doing what they could to make him as comfortable as possible in the bouncing wagon.

Breanna smiled at the wounded man. "As fast as my son has this wagon going, we'll be at the hospital in no time, Barry."

Barry managed a lopsided grin. "Don't worry, ma'am. I'm doing just fine, thanks to you and Mrs. Langford." The wagon jolted, and Barry grimaced. Seeing worry touch the nurses' faces, he said, "It's all right, ladies. I'm fine."

When they arrived at Mile High Hospital, Breanna stayed with Barry while Annabeth hurried inside to find a couple of orderlies who could come with a padded cart on wheels and take Barry inside. A few minutes later, Annabeth returned with help.

Breanna told the children to wait in the wagon until she and Aunt Annabeth came back, then hurried away beside the wheeled cart.

The two nurses stayed with Barry, though nurses on duty would actually help one of the surgeons remove the slug from his shoulder. In one of the surgical rooms, Dr. Harrison Riggs, whom Breanna and Annabeth had assisted many times, had another nurse at his side. Barry was soon under anesthetic. When the slug had been removed from Barry's shoulder and the ladies knew that the young deputy would be all right, they both praised the Lord.

A short time later, Barry had awakened, a heavy bandage on his wound. Breanna patted his hand. "Dr. Riggs told us you'll be just fine, Barry. Now that you're in good hands, we'll go on to church. Pastor Bayless will appreciate knowing what has happened so he can have the whole church praying for you, and for John and Whip. And I'm sure Pastor will be here to see you as soon as he possibly can."

His eyes still a bit dull from the lingering

effects of the laudanum, Barry slurred, "I'll l-l-look forward to seeing Pastor, ma'am. I appreciate what you and Mrs. Langford have done for me. God bless you. And . . . and I'll be praying for Chief Brockman and Deputy Langford."

Two

As the Brockman wagon left the hospital, Meggie's eyes drifted ahead, watching for the street where they would turn to go to the church.

Paul slipped his pocket watch from his pocket as he guided the horses in the direction of the church. He glanced at it and looked quickly over his shoulder at his mother and Aunt Annabeth. "Mama, it's already five minutes after noon. Unless Pastor preached longer than normal this morning, the service is just about over."

"You're right, son, but I'm sure Pastor and Mary will still be there so we can tell them what has happened."

Pastor Bayless and his wife, Mary, were standing on the front steps of First Baptist Church, shaking hands with the last few people leaving the sanctuary. At the end of the line was a silver-haired, elderly man, who walked slowly toward them. While her husband shook his hand and visited with him, Mary looked over at the people in the parking lot climbing into their buggies and wagons. A wagon swung off the street and headed up the angled drive toward the building.

Mary turned to her husband, who had just said good-bye to the elderly man. "Honey, look! It's Breanna Brockman with her children and Annabeth Langford. I wonder what's going on."

While the pastor concentrated on the approaching wagon, Mary shook hands with the elderly man and told him how nice it was to see him back in church since his recent illness. After the man turned away, Pastor Bayless said, "Mary, I wonder where John and Whip are."

Paul steered the wagon into a parking spot and pulled rein.

"I think we're about to find out," Mary said quietly, waving at the occupants of the wagon.

The pastor and his wife stepped toward the wagon as Paul hopped to the ground and hurried to help his mother and Aunt Annabeth. Ginny slid to the ground from the driver's seat and helped Meggie down.

The pastor frowned slightly. "I know

something must have happened to make you late to church, especially without John and Whip. Is everything okay?"

"Yes, Pastor," said Breanna. "We're here to tell you all about it."

Pastor Bayless and Mary listened closely as Breanna told them the whole story of what had happened on the way to church.

When she finished, Pastor Bayless said, "Well, Mary and I will be praying for John and Whip as they pursue that outlaw. We'll do that right now while we head for the hospital to see Barry."

Breanna smiled. "I told Barry you'd be there as soon as you possibly could, Pastor. And I want you to know that we'll be at the service this evening for sure. We were anxious to hear your sermon this morning. I hope John and Whip will be back with that outlaw in handcuffs in time to come to the service tonight too."

Kent Fortney was making his way up the winding Rocky Mountain roads, passing men on horseback as well as people in wagons and buggies. Since galloping away from the scene at the Platte River, he had been riding hard in case he was being followed. He glanced over his shoulder periodically, and twice in the last half hour he had caught sight of two men on horseback behind him. The first time, they were about a half mile behind him. The second time, when they were only a hundred yards back, he guided his horse into a stand of evergreens.

Peering at them from behind a tree, he saw badges on their chests flashing in the sunlight. They looked like the two lawmen who had shown up at the Platte River and run toward Deputy Sotak. Fortney was sure it was them, but he didn't think they had actually seen him. Somehow they'd saddled some horses and without a doubt were after him. He swung into his saddle and trotted his horse amid the trees to keep from being seen. From a spot where the lawmen certainly couldn't see him, he hit the trail and pushed his horse harder than ever.

As Chief John Brockman and Deputy Whip Langford rode the trail, they surmised that Kent Fortney was likely taking higher to the mountains. They paused and asked people along the way if they had seen a horse and rider that fit the outlaw's description. The first few had not seen such a rider and horse, but soon they came upon a rancher and his wife in a wagon who both described Fortney and the horse precisely. As the lawmen rode on, following the same trail, they soon met two men on horseback. They signaled the riders to stop and asked about the rider and horse they were after. Both riders had definitely seen Kent.

Encouraged that they were on the outlaw's trail, John and Whip continued the pursuit, keeping the borrowed horses at a fast gallop, Timber running beside them. They didn't catch sight of Fortney again but twice paused to ask people if they'd seen him. The outlaw had been seen riding due west.

As the sun set over the high peaks in front of them, John and Whip thought they caught a brief glimpse of Kent Fortney ahead of them but weren't sure it was him. They rode hard, trying to get closer to the rider they saw, but did not see him again. "We'll catch him, Whip. I can feel it."

Dusk settled over the mountains. The men pushed the panting horses as much as possible up the steep trail.

John pulled his horse to a halt and pointed up to a wide ledge that wound its way upward on the side of a mountain. "Look up there, Whip," he said in a low voice. "It's him!"

Whip focused on the horse and rider. "It sure is!"

Just before Fortney passed from view, he

looked down at them, quickly turning his horse. Within seconds, horse and rider vanished around a curve on the ledge.

"He knows we saw him, Chief!"

"He sure does," John replied. "We'll have to be careful he doesn't ambush us. Let's get up there!"

The lawmen pushed the horses hard and finally reached the ledge as darkness fell.

As they headed the same direction Fortney had vanished, the stars began twinkling in the night sky. "Like I said, Whip, we'll have to be careful. But we don't dare let him get away from us now."

"Right, Chief. Let's stay after him!"

Moments later, a full moon rose into the star-bedecked sky, and suddenly, through a wide space between the towering pine trees, they saw Fortney dismount. They quickly and quietly guided their horses into the deep shadows among the trees, remaining hidden from the outlaw's view.

The moonlight made it possible to see the outlaw lead his horse into a thick stand of trees, tie the reins to a bough, and dash into a cave about a hundred feet from there.

"Now's the time, Whip," John said, eying the relatively narrow opening of the cave.

"It is, Chief," Whip said, "and I've got a plan."

"Okay."

"I've had several situations like this one before, and I've trained Timber to go after outlaws who are in hiding. Is it okay with you if I send him in there to disarm and capture Fortney? Believe me, he knows how to do it."

By the light of the moon, Whip saw his boss's white teeth shine in a big grin. "Absolutely. Send Timber in!"

"All right. Let's get closer to the cave."

Timber stayed close to Whip's horse as the two lawmen rode to a spot some fifty feet from the cave. Both men dismounted, and John watched as Whip knelt down and patted the wolf's head, pointing to the mouth of the cave. "Timber," he said in a low voice, "there's a bad guy in there."

Timber's eyes showed that he understood what his master was saying to him.

As Whip petted Timber and told him exactly what to do, John marveled at how Whip had trained the enormous wolf. Timber stood thirty-four inches high at the shoulders and measured nearly six feet from the tip of his nose to the tip of his tail. Whip had weighed Timber some months previously and told John that the wolf weighed one hundred eighty pounds. Timber's gray coat shone in the moonlight, and his eyes glowed the color of the moon.

Inside the cave, a jagged split in the center of the ceiling some eight inches long and four inches wide allowed moonlight to enter. Deep shadows around the cave's narrow opening that spread several feet into the cave were dissipated by the moonlight.

Kent Fortney knew the two lawmen were on his trail and had seen him on the ledge, but hoped they had given up for the night, even though the moon was shining brightly. He stood in the shadows with his back against the far wall of the cave, about thirty feet from the opening. Holding his revolver in his right hand, Kent hoped that if the lawmen *were* still trailing him, they didn't know he was in the cave. He took a deep, shaky breath. If they spotted his horse nearby and figured out he was in the cave, they'd come in after him for sure. "If they come in here," he said in a faint whisper, "it'll be two against one, but I'll have the advantage. I'm in the shadows, and I'll do my best to shoot 'em both down before they see me!"

Suddenly Fortney heard a deep growl come from the gravelike darkness around the cave's narrow opening. The unexpected sound caused him to jump, and his boots made a shuffling sound on the dirt floor as an icy shudder ran down his spine. Another growl filled the cave. Fortney raised his gun and scooted along the wall, terrified. He stepped near the lit spot created by the moonlight shining through the jagged split in the ceiling.

The instant Timber saw the bad guy his master had told him was there, he sprang for him, lunging for his gun hand. The outlaw was too slow to avoid the snarling wolf. Timber's sharp teeth tore into Fortney's wrist, causing the revolver to fall before he could fire a shot.

Timber attacked the man, gnashing at his face and knocking him down. Panic seized Fortney as he lay on his back, unable to fight off the wild beast, whose teeth and claws ripped at his hands, face, and chest. "Help me-e-e-e! Somebody help me-e-e-e!"

Kent Fortney took a breath to cry out again for help and heard a man's voice shout above the wolf's growling and snapping, "Timber! That's enough! Back off *now!*"

The muscular wolf obediently looked up at the man and stepped back a few feet, licking the outlaw's blood from the edge of his mouth.

The terrified man was relieved to see both lawmen standing over him in the shaft of moonlight.

John leaned down and picked up the outlaw's gun from the dust. "Kent Fortney, I'm chief United States marshal John Brockman, in charge of the Western District. You're under arrest."

Fortney did not reply.

"My deputy and I will do what we can to stop your bleeding. Then we're taking you to the county jail in Denver. From there, you'll be taken back to the state prison in Cañon City. I think you know why."

The outlaw remained silent.

Using water from their canteens and extra bandannas they found in the saddlebags on their borrowed horses, John and Whip washed the blood from Fortney's wounds and managed to get the bleeding under control everywhere except at his wrist and on a couple of deep slashes on his cheeks. They tied a bandanna around the wrist and gave him another to use on his face.

"I'll grab Fortney's horse, Chief." Whip hurried out of the cave with Timber.

While they waited, John tried to talk to the outlaw about his need to know the Lord Jesus Christ as his Saviour, but the outlaw cut him off quickly, saying he did not want to hear it.

When Whip returned, the lawmen hoisted

their prisoner into his saddle. "Fortney, you've got your hands free, one to keep pressing the bandanna against the wounds on your face and the other to hold the reins."

The outlaw nodded solemnly.

"And I warn you," Brockman added, "if you try to escape from us, you'll be in deeper trouble than you are right now. Got it?"

Kent Fortney nodded solemnly. "Yeah."

It was just before dawn when John and Whip arrived at the Langford place with their prisoner. Whip led Timber into the fenced area by the shed. He returned and told the chief he'd go inside to let Annabeth know they had captured the outlaw and were taking him to the jail.

John waited and tried again to talk to Fortney — whose bleeding had stopped — about his need to know Jesus Christ as Saviour, but the outlaw deterred him again. "I don't want to hear it."

Whip came out of the cabin. "Annabeth isn't here. She must be at your place with Breanna."

"You're probably right about that. Let's go."

A half hour later, Chief Brockman and

Deputy Langford rode away from the Denver jail, where outlaw Kent Fortney was now locked up.

At the Brockman ranch, Paul, Ginny, and Meggie were in their rooms asleep. Breanna and Annabeth could not sleep until they knew their husbands were all right. They were at the kitchen table, drinking tea and trying to allay each other's fears.

Annabeth looked across the table at her dear friend. "Breanna, this is a rather strange honeymoon since there is no groom in attendance."

The two friends exchanged grins but were interrupted by the sound of hoofbeats outside the kitchen window. Breanna jumped from her chair and dashed to the window. Annabeth joined her. In the bright moonlight, they saw John and Whip aboard the horses they had borrowed from Barry Sotak's neighbors.

"Oh, thank You, Lord!" Breanna exclaimed as she headed toward the back door. "They look fine!"

"Yes, Lord, thank You!" Annabeth breathed.

The two women dashed out the door onto the porch, just as John and Whip dismounted. Breanna threw herself into John's arms, and Annabeth did the same with Whip.

Annabeth's voice quivered. "Oh, Whip, darling, I'm so thankful you're back safe and sound. I was so afraid!"

Whip held Annabeth close and smiled down into her upturned face, awash with tears of relief. "I'm just fine, my love. God was watching over me and the chief. I — I know this probably brought back terrible memories because you lost your first husband to criminals' violence. I'm sorry this happened so soon after our wedding. Hopefully things will be a little quieter for a while, and you and I can share the joy of just being together." He kissed her tenderly and hugged her.

John and Breanna held each other tightly, smiling as they looked at the newlyweds.

When the emotions of the two couples settled, John told Breanna and Annabeth how they had captured Kent Fortney with Timber's help and that the outlaw was now behind bars.

"Judge Dexter will no doubt give Fortney a much longer sentence because he broke out of the state prison," Breanna said. John agreed. The judge would probably add twenty years to his sentence.

Whip turned to Annabeth. "I sure missed

our 'honeymoon' at dinnertime yesterday."

Breanna smiled. "You two are welcome to come to dinner Tuesday night and make that your honeymoon celebration!"

Whip then turned to his boss. "Chief, tell you what. Annabeth and I will ride these horses home now, and I'll return them to their owners in the morning."

John agreed, and Whip lifted Annabeth into the saddle of the horse the chief had ridden, then swung onto the other horse. The Brockmans stood arm in arm by the back porch and bid the Langfords good night. When they passed from view, the Brockmans went inside.

As John and Breanna prepared to retire for what was left of the night, they talked about their upcoming trip next Saturday to Riverton. Soon, both were fast asleep, held tightly in each other's arms.

Early Saturday morning, June 30, John Brockman and his family arrived at Denver's Union Station and boarded a train headed for Cheyenne, Wyoming. As the train rolled northward, the Brockmans happily discussed the fact that Barry Sotak was recovering from his shoulder wound and that two others of John's deputies were escorting the outlaw to Cañon City, where he would now serve a thirty-four-year sentence. Breanna told the children that their father had estimated that the judge would add twenty years to Fortney's sentence, and he was right.

Meggie's eyes glistened. "Our Papa is *always* right!"

"He sure is," Paul said.

Ginny grinned at her mother. "You've known that for a long time, haven't you, Mama?"

Breanna turned and looked at her husband, whose face had flushed. "I sure have, honey."

When the Brockmans arrived at the Cheyenne station, federal marshal Garth Lane met them. John had wired Marshal Lane to let him know what time they would arrive to catch the train to Riverton.

Lane was happy to see Chief Brockman and his family again. Breanna introduced him to Meggie, and the sweet girl smiled, her dimples on display, and gave him a big hug. After visiting with Marshal Lane for only a few minutes, the Brockmans boarded the train bound for Riverton.

The family sat at the front of the passenger car, the children on the seat facing their parents.

It was a beautiful early summer day, and

the windows of the coach were open a bit, allowing a gentle breeze to enter and keep it cool. The Brockman family was happy to have this time together and looked forward to being with Pastor Philip Landrum and his family.

Meggie had heard the others in the family talk about the previous times Papa had preached at the Riverton Baptist Church. Most of the times, Mama, Paul, and Ginny went with him.

Meggie spoke loud enough to be heard over the rumble of the train's wheels. "You must really like this church to have gone there so many times."

The entire family shared their reasons for liking Pastor Landrum, his wife, Elizabeth, and their daughter, Katy, and the people of the church.

"Katy Landrum mentioned wanting to become a nurse the last time we saw her some six years ago," Breanna said. "She was talking about possibly going to the Cheyenne School of Nursing when she graduated from high school."

When John had been there alone to preach just over four years ago, Katy had just graduated from high school and was still talking about nursing, but he had heard no more since.

"I hope Katy followed through with it," Breanna said. "With her intelligence and personality, she would make an excellent nurse."

Paul chuckled and smiled at his mother, saying that *her* intelligence and personality sure made her an excellent nurse. He then added that being so beautiful made her an even better nurse.

Breanna blushed as John and the girls enthusiastically agreed.

John was looking forward to seeing federal marshal Dub Hawson, who was under his authority as head of the U.S. marshal's office in Riverton. Dub had just been appointed head of the Riverton office when he was there to preach for Pastor Landrum the last time. He had been pleased to learn that Dub and his wife, Marie, were Christians and members of Pastor Landrum's church.

"I am very much looking forward to introducing my beautiful wife, my handsome son, and my two gorgeous daughters to the Hawsons!"

THREE

As the train rolled toward Riverton, the Brockman family sat in silence. The *clickety-clack* of the train wheels on the track and the gentle swaying of the coach lulled nine-year-old Meggie to sleep. Sitting next to her, Ginny noted the bobbing little blond head and closed eyes. She put her arm around Meggie and slowly drew her close so her head was leaning on big sister's soft shoulder.

Meggie was dreaming about her new home on the Brockman ranch, when she suddenly wakened with a start. She bolted upright, her eyes wide. "It's okay, Meggie," Ginny said. "It's just two men arguing."

Several rows ahead of them, two male passengers sitting across the aisle from each other were arguing loudly.

Meggie noted that her mama and papa were twisted around in their seat watching the two angry men. One of them was older

42

with a touch of silver in his hair, and the other was a young man who appeared to be in his midtwenties.

Ginny felt Meggie trembling as she watched the men. Tightening her arm around Meggie and pulling her close, Ginny said, "Honey, don't be frightened. A man just hurried out the door at the front of the coach. I think he's going after the conductor. It will be over soon."

John heard Ginny and turned toward them. "I heard the word *conductor* come out of the man's mouth as he left his seat."

Suddenly both men were out of their seats, swinging their fists at each other. John spun back around, noting that the older man was much smaller than the tall, burly younger man. As the conductor came through the door, followed by the passenger who had gone after him, the younger man's fist struck the older man's jaw, knocking him down hard in the aisle.

The younger man towered over the older man and swung a foot back to kick him. Just then the conductor stepped in front of him. "Back off, mister!"

The younger man glared balefully at the conductor, teeth bared in an angry grimace, and drove a powerful left fist to the conductor's midsection and whipped a cracking right fist to his jaw, dropping him to the floor.

Chief Brockman left his seat like a bolt of lightning and dashed toward the scene.

Meggie snuggled closer to Ginny and closed her eyes tightly, not wanting to see what was about to happen.

Every other eye in the coach was on the tall, broad-shouldered man with the badge on his chest as he walked up to the trouble-maker. A male passenger helped the dizzy conductor to his feet.

The troublemaker raised his meaty fists, ready for the lawman, and swung a hard right. John Brockman dodged the fist and smashed into the man's face with a right cross that knocked him back on his heels, causing him to stagger farther from the older man, who was resting on his elbows on the floor, trying to get his bearings.

John pursued the staggering instigator, who was now staring through a haze but had managed to stabilize himself. The man doubled his fists, ready to battle John. His dark eyes were ugly and his face hard.

He swung at John again. The adept mar-shal ducked the blow and hit the man with a left that made him teeter backward. The muscular marshal followed him along the aisle and hit him on the jaw with a whistling

right that lifted him off his feet and pro-
pelled him to the aisle, flat on his back and
out cold.

By that time Meggie had opened her eyes
and saw her papa knock the big man out.

The passengers who had been watching
from their seats began talking to each other,
marveling at the chief U.S. marshal's
strength and fighting ability.

Two male passengers who had been seated
near the fight helped the older man to his
feet, and John Brockman walked to the
conductor, introduced himself, and asked if
he was all right. A bit wobbly, the conductor said he'd be fine and thanked John for
taking care of the troublemaker.

By this time, Paul was at his father's side
and pointed proudly at his father. "Folks,
this man is my father. Let me tell you
something. *Nobody* can whip my father!"

One elderly man chuckled. "Young man,
are you saying that even younger men can't
whip your father? He's gotta be in his forties."

"He's forty-three, sir," Paul replied, "but
he can handle any younger man who thinks
he can beat him in a fight. Plenty have tried,
and every one of them got himself whipped.
Most of them were knocked out."

The elderly man gasped. "Really?"

"Really, sir."

The conductor turned to John and pointed at the man on the floor. "Chief Brockman, I'm going to lock this man in one of the compartments in the caboose until we arrive at Riverton. Do you want to arrest him for attempted assault?"

"No. I think maybe he learned his lesson."

The conductor grinned. "You're probably right."

"I'll carry him for you." John bent down to pick up the unconscious troublemaker.

"Let's go." The conductor pointed ahead, and John followed him toward the rear of the coach.

Paul returned to his mother and sisters and sat down on the seat with Ginny and Meggie. "I'm so proud of Papa."

"Me too, Paul," Ginny said. "Papa is such a great lawman."

"He sure is!" Meggie snuggled up next to Ginny.

"The greatest!" their mother added.

"Right, Mama, and when I become a lawman, I want to be just like Papa."

Breanna smiled. "I am sure you will be, son."

The girls spoke their agreement, and then all four gazed out the windows and took in the beauty of Wyoming's prairie as the train rolled on.

John returned to his family moments later and told them that the man he'd been forced to knock out was now locked up in the caboose. Since he had paid the fare to Riverton, he would be allowed to go free when they arrived.

Paul thought the man should be put in jail for daring to swing a fist at a lawman, but he heard what his father said and kept quiet.

John sat down beside Breanna. "I sure am looking forward to seeing Dub and his wife again."

"Papa?" Meggie asked. "Is Marshal Hawson called 'chief' because he's head of the U.S. marshal's office in Riverton?"

Paul spoke up quickly and explained that the only men called "chief" were those who headed up the district marshal's offices, like their papa. There were only two other chief United States marshals in the country, since the East Coast didn't have a U.S. marshal's office. One was in Ohio, the other in Missouri. The district centered in Ohio was called the Eastern District, and the one in Missouri was called the Central District. "The third one, which Papa heads up, is called the Western District and goes all the way to the Pacific Ocean."

The head of each of the many U.S. marshals' offices within a district was called a federal marshal, and the men under them were called deputy federal marshals. "The men under Papa's authority in the Denver office are called deputy U.S. marshals."

Meggie's eyes widened. "Wow. Thank you, big brother, for explaining all of that." She looked at her papa in awe, a huge smile spilling across her face. "Wow! I always knew you were special, Papa. I just never knew *how* special!"

"He sure is special, Meggie. Very, very, very special!" Ginny stood and hurried to her father's lap. Meggie followed and settled in on his other knee.

John smiled lovingly at his daughters and hugged both of them, giving each a kiss on the cheek. "Oh, girls, I'm nothing special — just a sinner saved by grace. I love my job, and I try to be good at what I do, but the Lord gives me the strength, courage, and wisdom to do it well. Without Him, I could do nothing."

"I know, Papa," Ginny said. "But you're still mighty special to this country and to us!"

"That's right." Meggie smiled at her papa, her dimples shining. "You sure are . . ."

■ ■ ■ ■

The Brockman family ate lunch together in the dining car, then returned to their seats in the coach. They chatted as the train continued to roll northward.

When the train finally began to slow as it neared Riverton, Paul asked his father what sermon he would preach at the services the next day. John told him, and the boy smiled. "I like both of those sermons. And I remember you preaching them at home a few months ago."

When the Brockman family stepped off the train at Riverton Station, Pastor Philip Landrum, his wife, Elizabeth, and their lovely twenty-one-year-old daughter, Katy, greeted them warmly. Hugs were plentiful as Meggie stood back and observed the reunion. *I'm so lucky to be part of such a loving family,* she thought.

Breanna became aware that Meggie was not in the group. She looked around and saw her still standing close to the train. Breanna motioned to her. "Come here, Meggie dear."

Meggie obeyed.

The rest of the Brockmans and all three Landrums turned their attention to the lovely little blond-haired, blue-eyed girl.

"Pastor Landrum, Mrs. Landrum, Katy," Breanna said, "this is our adopted daughter, Meggie." Breanna briefly told the Landrums about the deaths of Meggie's mother and father, explaining that they had adopted the sweet child soon after her father's death.

All three Landrums greeted Meggie and hugged her, telling her how happy they were to meet her.

John looked at the pastor. "When I responded to your letter asking me to come preach, I didn't tell you about Meggie because we wanted to surprise you. I hope having an extra body won't be a problem at whatever hotel you've booked."

"No problem at all, Chief." Pastor Landrum clapped his hand on John's back. "I made reservations at Riverton's newest and finest hotel, the Western Trails. There's plenty of room for all five of you in the suite I reserved."

John looked down at Meggie and put an arm around her. "Whew! Otherwise you might've had to sleep on the roof of the hotel!"

"Oh no, Papa!" Meggie giggled. "*You* would have had to sleep on the roof!"

"I'd like to tell you all something," Katy said, looking at the Brockman family.

Katy's eyes lit up. "I graduated from the Cheyenne School of Nursing in May!"

"Oh, wonderful!" Breanna exclaimed, hugging her.

John patted Katy on the shoulder.

"I am now employed by Dr. Richard Barnett here in Riverton. I believe both of you remember Dr. Barnett and his wife, Celia, from our church."

"We sure do, Katy," John said.

"Congratulations, sweetie!" Breanna beamed. "I'm so proud of you, and I know you must be a very good nurse."

"That she is!" Elizabeth chimed in. "Dr. Barnett has told Philip and me many times of Katy's great work at his office. She catches on quickly to whatever new things he teaches her. He also says she has an especially kind and loving way with the patients."

Breanna patted Katy's cheek tenderly. "I just knew that's the kind of nurse you would be."

"Thank you, Breanna."

John chuckled. "I knew that too, Katy."

"Ginny and I did too," Paul said.

"And I haven't met you until now, Miss Katy," Meggie said, "but from what my mama has said about you, I know you are a very good nurse!"

Katy smiled broadly at the Brockman family. "Thank you all for your kind words."

John Brockman saw Marshal Dub Hawson and his wife, Marie, walking toward them along the railroad station platform.

John leaned toward his wife as he pointed toward the Hawsons. "Breanna, the Hawsons are here!"

Breanna turned to see the smiling couple. "Oh! So that's them!"

John stepped over and reached out his hand to welcome Dub and Marie. He then guided them toward the group, and they greeted Pastor Landrum, Elizabeth, and Katy. Finally John introduced them to Breanna and the children.

Pastor Landrum spoke up. "Chief Brockman, we need to collect your baggage, and then we'll take you to the hotel so you can leave your belongings and get settled. You'll be joining us for supper at our home this evening, along with the Hawsons."

Dub glanced at his wife with surprise showing on his face. "We are honored to be invited to the parsonage for supper, Pastor."

"We sure are!" said Marie Hawson.

John smiled broadly. "Pastor Landrum, this is wonderful! My wife and two oldest children remember well the excellent meals we've had in your home. It will be a blessing to be with all of you."

"Yes," Breanna agreed. "We will most certainly enjoy the food, plus being with both the Landrums and the Hawsons."

"I took the rest of the day off so Marie and I can spend some time with you. I left the office in the hands of my trusty deputies," said Dub.

"Great!" John's grin stretched from ear to ear. "Well then, let's move out!" He motioned toward the baggage car.

Moments later, the three men placed the Brockman luggage in the Landrum wagon.

The Hawsons followed in their buggy as the Landrums transported the Brockman family to the Western Trails Hotel.

Paul Brockman sat on the driver's seat between the pastor and his father. The women and girls rode together in the rear of the wagon. Elizabeth Landrum told Breanna how beautiful and comfortable the Western Trails Hotel was as Ginny and Meggie listened intently. The Brockman sisters' smiles grew as they listened to the description of the hotel's beauty and comfort. They were eager to stay in a nice hotel that was almost brand-new.

Twenty-five miles south of Riverton, at Lander, Wyoming, four outlaws relaxed on the wooden floor of a small, deserted cabin just outside of town. Two of the men pressed their backs against the south wall of the cabin, facing the other two.

Todd and Stan Zarbo, whose facial features were somewhat alike, looked at their brothers on the other side of the room. At the south wall, Chice and Lee Zarbo, who also slightly resembled each other, stared back. Each of the four brothers had an evil look in his eyes.

Todd, thirty-four years old, was the oldest of the four brothers. Stan was twenty-nine, Chice was thirty-one, and Lee, the youngest, was twenty-seven.

The Zarbo brothers were discussing the news their friend Jake Hepburn had given them when they were in Casper a few days earlier. Jake was employed at the Casper National Bank in Casper, Wyoming.

A large amount of money — approximately twenty-five thousand dollars — was being shipped by stagecoach from Casper National Bank late that afternoon. It was being transported to Riverton, where a very wealthy rancher was planning to pick it up the next day at the Wells Fargo station. It was the rancher's monthly payroll for himself and the numerous men who worked at his three huge cattle ranches in central

Wyoming, the biggest of which was a few miles west of town. The stagecoach would stop for the night in Moneta, Wyoming, and then head for Riverton in the morning.

Todd, the toughest and meanest of the outlaw brothers, adjusted himself on the uncomfortable wooden floor. "Brothers, tomorrow morning we'll stop that stage-coach when it's about ten miles or so from Riverton, and we'll snatch that payroll."

Chice and Lee both laughed greedily as they discussed the money the four brothers would split among them.

Stan chuckled dryly. "With the amount of money in that payroll, we won't mind shar-ing a little with Jake, will we?"

"Of course not," Todd said. "If it wasn't for Jake, we wouldn't know about this money to begin with. Of course, we'll share a little with him. But only a little . . ."

FOUR

That same Saturday at Denver's federal building, Whip Langford came out of John Brockman's personal office, where he had been going through the mail Chief Brockman had assigned him to handle.

Deputy Roland Jensen was on duty at the front desk with Deputy Mike Allen standing there talking to him when Whip walked over. They both greeted Whip, noting the large envelope he was carrying.

"What have you got there, Whip?" Mike asked. "Looks like it might be Wanted posters."

"That's exactly what it is. They arrived in this morning's mail from federal marshal Brent Yarrow in Santa Fe, New Mexico."

"Hmm." Roland scratched his head. "It's been a while since the chief has received any posters from Marshal Yarrow."

Whip nodded. "Well, there are eight of them here. I left the letter from Marshal

Yarrow on the chief's desk. According to the letter, this gang of outlaws has committed numerous crimes in New Mexico Territory but has gone north into Colorado. Marshal Yarrow knew Chief Brockman would want to know about the outlaws coming into Colorado so he could alert the people of Denver by putting up Wanted posters on the board out front."

Mike Allen nodded. "That's good. We should get them up right away."

"You want to help me put 'em up?"

"Be glad to."

Some ten minutes later, the two deputies had posted the eight Wanted posters on the board in front of the U.S. marshal's office. Whip gave a satisfied nod. "Thanks for your help."

"Glad to lend a hand." Mike nodded.

Whip glanced at his watch. "Well, before I do anything else, I've got to get a haircut. See you later."

"Sure enough." Mike headed back toward the office.

About ten minutes later, Whip walked up to Allison's Barbershop, which was distinguished by a red and white barber pole mounted beside the door. He entered through the open door and saw barber Wally Allison just finishing with a customer who was paying for his haircut.

As the customer left, Wally, who was in his late fifties, smiled at the deputy marshal and motioned for him to come over. "Take off your hat, Whip, and have a seat."

Whip removed his hat, hung it on a nearby rack, and walked over to the barber's chair. Wally had cut Whip's hair many times, and they had become friends.

After Whip settled on the barber's chair, Wally covered him with a large white cloth, tied it at the back of his neck, and started trimming his hair.

Only a few minutes had passed when a rough-looking man came through the open door, glanced at Wally and Whip, then peered around the shop, noting that the barber had no other customers at the moment. He whipped a gun from its holster and pointed it at Wally. In a threatening voice he said, "Listen close, mister. I've never robbed a barbershop before, but I figure there's plenty of cash in the register. Hand it over. *Now!*"

Whip's body tensed. The large white cloth draped over Whip covered his badge as well as the holstered gun at his waist. The robber had no idea he was a lawman.

As Wally tentatively moved toward the register, Whip slyly slipped his Colt .45 from the holster beneath the white cloth and cocked it as loudly as possible. "Drop that gun. Right now!"

The robber had not yet cocked his own gun, but when he heard the sound of the hammer on Whip's gun being cocked, he swung on Whip with fire in his eyes as he cocked his weapon, preparing to fire.

Whip had no choice but to shoot first. His gun roared, and the slug plowed through the white barber cloth and into the upper arm of the robber's gun hand.

The man flinched when the slug hit, and he dropped the revolver. It fired when it hit the floor, sending a slug into the thick wood of the nearest wall.

As the robber fell to the floor, clutching his wounded arm, Wally noticed the black-rimmed bullet hole in the cloth as Whip rose from the chair and removed it. The deputy quickly knelt beside the robber and saw that he was almost unconscious.

Grabbing him by his good arm, Whip dragged the man toward the door. "Wally, I'm gonna see if I can find somebody out on the street with a buggy or wagon who can take this guy to the hospital."

"I'll go with you," Wally said as he rushed toward the door. People were gathering on the boardwalk and in the street at the sound of gunshots. Eyes were wide among the growing crowd when they saw the lawman dragging the wounded man.

As Whip hauled the robber onto the boardwalk, he gazed at the crowd of onlookers. "This man just tried to rob Wally Allison. I had to stop him."

Whip noticed a few wagons and buggies stopped on the broad street, their occupants looking on. He noticed the face of one driver he knew well, Mike Sellman, a local farmer who was a member of First Baptist Church. His teenage son was with him.

Whip waved at the farmer. "Hey, Mike! Would you do me a favor?"

In his late thirties and quite muscular, Sellman hopped off the driver's seat and told his son to wait. He hurried to the boardwalk. "Did I hear you right, Whip? This guy tried to rob the barbershop?"

"Yeah, you heard me right. I was in the barber's chair getting a haircut when he came in. I had to shoot him to keep from getting shot. As you can see, he's bleeding and barely conscious. Would you take him to the hospital for me? Wally's got to finish my haircut."

"Of course."

"Great. I'll handcuff him and give you the key so they can take them off at the hospital."

Mike nodded. "Okay. I'll stay in the bed of the wagon with him and have Edgar drive us to the hospital."

"Will you tell Dr. Matthew Carroll what happened and that I'll be there as soon as my haircut is finished?"

"Sure will," Mike said.

Whip removed the handcuffs from his belt, pulled the robber's wrists behind his back, and clamped the cuffs on them. He handed the key to Mike. "Thanks for your help."

"Glad to be of service. Especially since you're my brother in Christ."

Grinning, Whip slapped him playfully on the back. "Thank you, my brother."

Mike picked up the robber and carried him to his wagon, a small crowd still looking on. When the farmer was settled in the wagon bed with the robber, young Edgar put the wagon in motion, and the crowd began to break up.

Quite shaken, Wally looked at Whip with gratitude on his face. "Thank you for stopping that robber, Deputy Langford. I have no doubt he would have shot me if I had refused to give him the money."

"He looked like the kind who would."

"That farmer who's taking the robber to

the hospital . . ."

"Mm-hmm?"

"I noticed . . . well . . . he called you his brother in Christ, and you called him brother as well. I've heard church people talk like that before. What does it mean?"

Whip smiled at Wally's words. This was the opening he had been praying for, to give a gospel witness to Wally Allison. While Wally proceeded with the haircut, Whip told him that there were people on the earth who had become children of God by receiving the Lord Jesus Christ into their hearts. He then quoted the Lord Jesus, who said in John 3:3, "Except a man be born again, he cannot see the kingdom of God."

"I thought all human beings are God's children," Wally said.

"All human beings are God's *creation,* but to be God's child and go to heaven, where the family of God will spend eternity together, a person must be born a *second* time." Whip paused so Wally could take this in. "The first was a physical birth, but to die with only the physical birth, all human beings, who are sinners before a holy God, will spend eternity in a burning hell. However, when they repent of their sins and receive the Lord Jesus, who shed His precious blood on the cross of Calvary, died, and rose again three days later for a world of lost sinners, they are 'born again,' which is a *spiritual* birth into the family of God. This is why they call each other brother and sister."

As he pointed out these truths to the barber, Whip quoted Scripture after Scripture, backing up what he was saying with the Word of God.

When Wally had finished the haircut, he removed the white barber cloth and walked around to face Whip. He was feeling strongly convicted of his need to repent of his sins and receive the Lord Jesus Christ into his heart and be born again.

Whip could see the conviction on Wally's face. He stood and took money from his pocket to pay for the haircut. "Wally, if you want to be born again, you can settle it right now. I strongly suggest that you do so."

Tears welled up in the barber's eyes. "Yes! Oh yes! I want to be born again right now, Whip!"

There, in the middle of the barbershop, Whip had the joy of leading his barber to the Lord. After Wally had called on the Lord Jesus to come into his heart and be his personal Saviour, Whip quoted Scripture, explaining that the first commandment God gives His newborn children is to be baptized. Whip asked Wally to come to First Baptist Church the next morning and present himself to Pastor Bayless for baptism at the close of the morning service. Wally promised he'd be there.

It was a warm Saturday evening in Riverton, and the open windows of the Landrums' large family kitchen allowed a nice breeze in, fluttering the lace curtains as the Landrums and their guests sat down to supper. The kitchen was redolent with savory aromas.

Elizabeth and Katy had prepared a delicious meal of pot roast, mashed potatoes, rich brown gravy, carrots and onions, fresh greens from their garden, home-canned stewed tomatoes, and fluffy yeast rolls.

At Pastor Landrum's request, Dub prayed, thanking the Lord for the food. After the "amen," everyone began passing the food around the table.

"I'm so thankful for the evening breeze during the summer." Elizabeth glanced at the moving curtains. "It really helps cool the house down."

"And a very welcome breeze it is," the pastor added. "Our Lord always knows just what we need and when we need it."

"Amen to that." John Brockman placed a

forkful of food in his mouth. Breanna smiled at her husband.

As the meal progressed, Marie and Breanna commented on the excellent food.

Then Dub spoke up. "Chief Brockman, several weeks ago one of your deputies, Mike Allen, mailed me a copy of Denver's *Rocky Mountain News* that carried a story about an outlaw, Whip Langford, who you caught and arrested and sent to prison."

John nodded. "So you know the whole story then."

Dub recounted to the group that while in prison at Cañon City, Langford saved the warden's life during an attempted prison break and thwarted the criminal. Because of this, Langford was released from prison and ended up being hired by Chief Brockman as a deputy. The newspaper editor had nicknamed Langford the Outlaw Marshal.

"Chief, that was quite a story," Dub said. "Pardon me, but how could you possibly hire an ex-outlaw as one of your deputies?"

"Well, the paper had only *part* of the story, Marshal."

"You mean there's more to it?"

John nodded. "Yes — the *best* part of the story. You see, I had the joy of leading Whip Langford to the Lord shortly after he was released from prison."

Dub's eyes brightened, and a smile spread across his face. "Oh, glory!"

"That's wonderful!" Marie exclaimed.

All three of the Landrums spoke their praise to the Lord. "Was he difficult to deal with?" the pastor asked.

John nodded. "He was when I first started talking with him about salvation after I had arrested him. But I shared a lot of Scripture on the subject of salvation, heaven, and hell. The Holy Spirit drove the Word from Whip's ears into his *heart* and did a powerful work there. When I preached the gospel to him after he got out of prison, he was ready. I mean to tell you, Whipley Langford got *saved*. He's now a loyal, faithful member of our church."

Dub shook his head in wonderment. "Amazing!"

"The reason I hired him," John continued, "was not only because he had become a Christian, but also because of his gun-handling ability and the fighting skills he had developed when he was an outlaw. He's a tremendous Outlaw Marshal. And there's even something greater about Whip — he has also become a tremendous soul-winner."

The Hawsons and the Landrums praised the Lord.

"The Lord certainly is to be praised for

the work He did in Whip's heart and life," Breanna said.

"Amen, Mama!" Paul said.

The girls agreed as well.

"And something else," Ginny said, looking at the Landrums and Hawsons. "The Outlaw Marshal met a Christian widow named Annabeth — who is a nurse and works with my mama — and they fell in love and got married!"

"Yeah," Meggie said. "And Paul, Ginny, and I call them Uncle Whip and Aunt Annabeth. We love them very much."

The Landrums and Hawsons thanked the Brockmans for sharing the story.

The pair of identical scars on John's right cheekbone seemed to light up. "There's something else I'd like to tell you about Whip."

As everyone at the table continued to eat and enjoy the tasty lemonade Elizabeth and Katy had prepared, John continued. He told them about how Whip saved the life of a large timber wolf in the mountains after becoming a deputy and how a short time later the wolf saved Whip's life.

"Whip and the wolf became pals, and Whip named him Timber. Now Timber often travels with Whip when he is pursuing outlaws alone, and he has been a tremendous help in capturing them."

This definitely caught the attention of those around the table, which prompted a conversation about wolves.

When they had nearly finished their meal and the visiting quieted, Elizabeth said, "How about we go out to the front porch to enjoy some chocolate cream pie and get the most of this cool breeze? There's coffee on the stove for the adults, and we've got plenty more lemonade for the young ones."

"Sounds refreshing to me," Breanna said. "Paul, Ginny, Meggie, and I will help with the dessert and drinks, and you three men can go on out and enjoy the cool air."

"Sounds like a good plan to me." John rose from his chair.

"Me too!" Dub chuckled and patted his satisfied stomach.

"Gets my vote." The pastor stood up as well, and the three men trooped through the house and out the front door.

As they settled on the comfortable chairs on the porch, John looked at the pastor. "While we've got a moment before everybody's out here, Pastor Landrum, I need to ask you something."

"What's that?"

"Well," John said, "I feel a bit guilty that the church is spending the money to put us

68

in such a fancy hotel. You didn't have to go to that much expense, my friend."

Pastor Landrum smiled. "A couple of families in the church really think a lot of you and your family, Chief. They both gave extra amounts in the offering last Sunday and told me the extra money was to cover the bill at the Western Trails. I . . . ah . . . wasn't supposed to tell you. They wouldn't want you to know who gave the money."

"Well, I'll leave it to you, but I'd at least like you to thank them for their generosity."

"After you're gone, I'll let them know that I told you about their generosity and that you expressed your thanks."

The Brockman children helped Elizabeth, Katy, Marie, and Breanna carry trays laden with chocolate cream pie, coffee, and lemonade onto the front porch. As everything was passed around, Katy said, "Oh, it *does* feel so much cooler out here!"

John smacked his lips and said around a mouthful of pie, "Yum, yum! This pie is delicious. Sure wish I had room for more than what's on this plate."

Breanna giggled and said teasingly, "John, dear, with what I saw you put away at the supper table, I'm sure what's on that plate is sufficient."

The chief U.S. marshal snickered. "One

69

piece of this delicious pie might be sufficient, sweetheart, but a second piece
would be better."

"Oh, you and your sweet tooth!"

As the group enjoyed their dessert, Dub
looked over at Paul. "What are you planning to do with your life when you grow up,
son?"

Paul's face brightened. "I am going to
become a lawman when I turn twenty-one,
Marshal Hawson. That's less than six years
from now since I'll turn sixteen on October
3."

The marshal smiled. "Oh, really?"

"Yes sir. I just wish the city, county, and
federal laws in the West allowed men to
become lawmen when they're younger, but
as you know, the law says I have to be
twenty-one. I'm positive that the Lord
wants me to follow in my papa's footsteps."

Dub Hawson looked at John. "I imagine
this pleases you a great deal, Chief."

"Sure does." John nodded.

"Papa's been teaching me the fast draw,
Marshal Hawson, so I'll be ready to face
outlaws who attempt to outdraw and outshoot lawmen."

"Sounds like you mean business, Paul."
Pastor Landrum looked intently at the
young man.

"He does, Pastor," John said. "This boy of mine is already a good shot and quite the fast draw with a revolver. He can handle a rifle quite well, but he's really good with a revolver. I'm sure as he gets older and I give him more pointers, he'll be lightning fast on the draw and even more accurate." John gazed proudly at his son. "I am very, very proud that Paul wants to be a lawman."

"Just as Paul wants to be a lawman like Papa," Ginny interjected, "I want to be a nurse like Mama."

"I think that's wonderful, Ginny," Katy said.

Ginny smiled. "I can see why you would, Miss Katy, since you're a nurse too."

Meggie cleared her throat gently and looked around at the group. "Ah . . . could I say something?"

"Go ahead, dear." Elizabeth patted Meggie on the back.

"I haven't told anybody yet 'cause I just felt this in my heart yesterday. I want to be a nurse too, like my mama."

Breanna's face lit up as she turned to Meggie. "Oh, Meggie, this makes me so happy. How wonderful it will be if both of my girls become nurses!" She squeezed the little girl tightly.

John, Paul, and Ginny told Meggie how

pleasantly surprised they were by this news.

It was still daylight when everyone had finished dessert. The parsonage was on the same property as the church building, on Elm Avenue, which ran east to west from one end of Riverton to the other. The parsonage was set back about thirty yards from the road.

The men and Paul helped carry the dishes to the kitchen and went to the parlor.

The women bustled into the kitchen and prepared to wash and dry the dishes and clean up. Ginny and Meggie offered to help.

"Thank you, girls." Elizabeth Landrum gave them each a hug. "But why don't you go back out on the front porch and relax."

Breanna nodded her approval, and the sisters thanked Elizabeth and headed for the front porch.

In the parlor, Paul sat near the large front window and saw Ginny and Meggie sit down on the porch. He mentioned it to the men, who could also see the porch from where they were seated. The girls settled into a couple chairs near the few stairs that led down to the yard.

While the men chatted, Paul glanced out the window periodically, keeping an eye on his sisters.

FIVE

As the sun dropped lower in the sky, a group of teenage boys from nearby ranches were at the west edge of Riverton planning a race through town on their horses.

"Well, guys, as soon as Rick and Harry show up, we'll be able to get this race goin'."

One of the boys leaned forward in his saddle and patted his horse's neck. "I wish those two would hurry up. I wanna test my new horse here, see how fast he can gallop!"

Ginny and Meggie were talking about the upcoming church services the next day as they relaxed on the Landrums' front porch. Suddenly they heard growling and snapping sounds nearby. Looking across the street, they could see two dogs fighting.

"Look at that, Meggie. That big dog is twice as big as the little one!"

"Yeah, he's really big. He'll tear that little

73

dog apart."

As the dogs continued to fight, snarling and snapping at each other, they moved in tight circles. They were soon fighting right in the middle of the street.

Ginny jumped to her feet and gasped. "The little dog is bleeding, and that big bully dog is holding him down and biting his ears!"

Meggie also stood, and both girls watched as the little dog lay helplessly in the dirt street, unable to fight back. He whined in pain.

Suddenly the girls heard a thunderous sound from further down the street. The big dog lifted his head and looked in that direction. He darted away, plunged between two houses, and disappeared.

"Look, Ginny!" Meggie said, pointing in the direction of the noise. "A bunch of riders is galloping this way!"

Ginny's eyes widened and her jaw slacked as she saw a group of about ten horses kicking up dust a couple blocks away, galloping full speed. She looked back at the injured little dog in the middle of the road and turned to her sister. "Meggie, you stay here on the porch. I've got to rescue that poor little dog before he gets trampled to death by those horses." Ginny bounded down the porch steps and ran into the street.

Meggie watched the horses and riders drawing dangerously close, heading straight toward Ginny. The riders did not see Ginny. Something acidic surged up inside Meggie like a giant ocean wave, striking between her stomach and throat, a sharp pain stabbing in her chest. "Ginny-y-y! Ginny-y-y! Stop! Come back before you get trampled too!"

Paul Brockman had been listening intently to the conversation between his father, Marshal Hawson, and Pastor Landrum, at the same time keeping an eye on the girls. When he heard Meggie's shrill scream, he looked out to see Ginny running toward the street. He could now hear the rumbling sound of horses' hooves, though he couldn't see them yet.

Paul jumped from his chair and headed for the front door. "Ginny's in danger!" He swung open the door and dashed outside.

John was first to bolt to the front door behind him, and as he lunged onto the porch where Meggie was standing in terror, he saw Ginny bending over, working to pick up what appeared to be an injured dog. Pastor Landrum and the marshal drew up beside him.

The racing horses and riders were closing

in. The men could do nothing but pray.

When Paul reached Ginny, she had the little dog in her arms. He glanced at the riders bearing down on them and quickly picked up Ginny, who clutched the dog tightly.

Some of the riders caught sight of Paul and Ginny at that instant and tried to swerve and miss them. Paul's only hope of escape was to head for the far side of the street. With every ounce of his energy, he staggered across just in time to avoid two horses that came within inches of them.

John Brockman watched helplessly as the events transpired, losing sight of Paul, Ginny, and the little dog as the bulk of the horses thundered by in a blur, a cloud of dust in their wake.

When the last horse had passed, John bolted across the street. "Paul! Paul! Are you and Ginny all right?"

With the loud rumble of pounding hooves still filling the air, Paul couldn't hear his father's words. Holding his trembling sister and the bleeding little dog, Paul shouted over to his father, uncertain whether John would be able to hear him. "We're okay, Papa! We're okay!" He lowered Ginny to her feet.

Drawing up to Paul and Ginny, the distraught father grabbed them both. "You're all right, Paul?"

Nodding, the teenage boy managed a smile. "Yes, Papa."

John bent down to look Ginny in the eye, the little dog in her arms. "Sweetheart," he said with a tremor in his voice, "you're okay?"

Trembling all over, Ginny replied in a quivering voice, "I . . . I th-think so, Papa."

John hugged her, lifted her and the dog into his arms, and turned to Paul again. "Son, that was a mighty brave thing you did."

Paul gave his father a wobbly grin and tried to sound unaffected by the incident. "God put a barrier around us and kept us safe from harm."

"You risked your own life to save Ginny's, son," said John. "I'm proud of you." He looked toward heaven. "Dear Lord, thank You for protecting Paul and Ginny."

Pastor Landrum and Marshal Hawson came running over to John, Paul, and Ginny with Meggie on their heels.

"Praise God!" the pastor said. "He took care of Paul and Ginny, Chief Brockman."

"Yes, He did." John said, noticing the women just coming out of the parsonage. "Let's go back across the street."

Paul held Meggie's hand, and they walked over to the front of the parsonage. Breanna wrapped one arm around John and Ginny and the other arm around Paul and Meggie, tears streaming down her cheeks. "Are you all right, kids?"

Still a bit shaken, Ginny joyfully bragged about her brother's heroic rescue of herself and the dog. Ginny assured everyone that she was unharmed. While the women praised God, Meggie wanted to hug Ginny, so Paul led her over to where their father was holding Ginny and the little dog. Meggie reached out and hugged Ginny tightly. "I'm so thankful to Jesus you're all right!"

"Me too." Ginny hugged Meggie tightly.

Meggie then kissed her sister's cheek. "Oh, Ginny, if you had been hurt by those horses, I don't know what I would have done. I love you so much. If anything bad ever happened to you, I couldn't stand it."

"You're so sweet, Meggie. I love you too." Then she reached toward Paul, who angled himself so Ginny could kiss his cheek. "Thank you, big brother, for saving my life. You'll always be my special hero."

Paul grinned shyly and hugged her.

Pastor Landrum looked at the dog in Ginny's arms. "I recognize this little fellow. He belongs to the neighbors right over there across the street. Looks like his ears are still bleeding some. I'll take him over there so they can see that he gets the attention he needs."

Ginny kissed the top of the little dog's fuzzy head and handed him to the pastor.

As Pastor Landrum crossed the street with the little dog in his arms, Elizabeth turned to the others. "Let's go back in the house."

The group walked into the parsonage, the adults lauding Paul for his courage and determination to save Ginny from being trampled by the galloping horses.

Marshal Hawson looked around at the others. "Those boys should not have been racing their horses through town."

"That's for sure," John said. "There's a law against such a thing in Denver."

Hawson shrugged. "No written law in this town prohibits what those boys did, so there's nothing I can do about it. Not right now anyway."

Later that evening, when the Brockmans were back in their hotel suite, John gathered them together in a circle. "Let's bow our heads and thank the Lord for His love and grace so plainly shown today."

The family held hands as John led them in prayer, thanking the Lord that Ginny was not injured or killed. He also thanked the Lord for giving Paul the courage to rescue his sister.

When John closed the prayer, Meggie hugged Ginny tightly once again. "I love you so much. I'd be heartbroken if anything bad happened to you." She choked a bit as tears welled in her eyes.

Tears clouded Ginny's eyes as she squeezed Meggie. "Oh, baby sister, I love you so very, very much too."

The next morning, the Brockmans enjoyed a hearty breakfast at the restaurant at the Western Trails. Ginny still looked a little pale and didn't eat much.

Breanna scrutinized Ginny's pallid face from across the table. "Are you not feeling well, dear?"

Ginny managed a slight smile and laid down her fork. "I'm okay, Mama. I just get a little shaken up when I think about what almost happened to me yesterday."

"I know, honey," Breanna said, rising from her chair and walking around the table to where Ginny sat. "You must have been terrified when you saw those horses galloping right at you. I'm sure with time you'll get over it. I am ever so grateful to our loving Lord for using your brother to save you."

She leaned down and hugged her daughter tightly.

John smiled and winked at Ginny, who smiled back.

Breanna lovingly ruffled Paul's hair as she walked back to her seat.

Ginny smiled at Paul. "Thank you for saving me, especially because you could've been trampled yourself."

"You're welcome, little sister. Now eat your breakfast. It's really good, and it'll put some roses back in your cheeks."

Ginny smiled and picked up her fork.

When breakfast was over, the Brockmans returned to their suite and only a few minutes later heard a knock at the door. Paul hurried to the door and found Pastor Landrum standing there with a crooked smile on his face. "Good morning!"

The Brockmans began gathering their Bibles.

"I'd like to take you folks to my church so you can hear one of the world's greatest preachers expatiate the Word of God this morning!"

Meggie giggled as she walked over to the pastor, holding her Bible. "I don't know what ex . . . ah . . . *expatiate* means, Pastor Landrum, but I know you're talking about my papa, and he really *is* one of the world's greatest preachers!"

"Amen, little sister." Paul said.

"Amen and amen!" Breanna chimed in.

John blushed. "Pastor," he said quietly, "I promise I haven't done anything to make my family brag on my preaching like this."

"Oh yes, you have, Chief." The crooked grin came back to the pastor's lips. "You've let them hear you preach. I've heard you too, and I agree with them completely!"

John shook his head, his features still flushing. "Okay, okay. Let's get to church so I can preach to all of you again."

Laughter and giggling sounded from the group as they left the suite and climbed into the Landrum wagon.

As they rode to the church, the pastor told the Brockmans that the children's Sunday school classes were still in the same rooms and that the adults still met in the church auditorium.

When they arrived, Paul, Ginny, and Meggie went to the Sunday school classes for their age groups, and John and Breanna joined Elizabeth and Katy Landrum and the Hawsons in the auditorium, where one of the leading men in the church taught the adults. Pastor Landrum was busy visiting each of the children's classes briefly during the Sunday school hour.

When Sunday school was over and the morning service was about to begin, Paul, Ginny, and Meggie entered the auditorium and quickly made their way to the pew three rows from the front, where their mother was seated with the Hawsons. The children noticed Elizabeth and Katy in the choir and their father sitting next to Pastor Landrum on the platform. The song leader sat on the chief U.S. marshal's other side.

The organist and the pianist began playing the introduction to a well-known hymn as the song leader approached the pulpit and motioned for the congregation to stand. The congregation and the choir sang the hymn with enthusiasm and praise.

When the hymn was finished, the pastor stepped up to the pulpit and welcomed first-time visitors. "While the choir begins a song for us, let's take the opportunity to greet one another — members and visitors alike."

At offering and announcement time, the pastor stepped to the pulpit with chief U.S. marshal John Brockman at his side. He then asked Breanna Brockman and the three young ones to come to the platform. As John stood beside Breanna, with Paul, Ginny, and Meggie at their sides, Pastor Landrum gave a brief history of the Brockman family and their newest addition, little

Meggie. He gave Meggie a special welcome since she'd never been to the church before. She blushed as the congregation warmly applauded.

Pastor Landrum also shared about Paul's gallant rescue of Ginny the evening before. The crowd applauded again, and Paul looked somewhat embarrassed.

Breanna and the children then returned to their seats.

While the offering was taken, the pianist and organist played a beautiful hymn, followed by a rousing gospel song led by the song leader. After that, two ladies from the choir sang a beautiful duet that exalted the Lord Jesus Christ.

When the duet was finished, Pastor Landrum took a moment to share John Brockman's history as the Stranger — when he was the man who traveled the West helping people in trouble, capturing outlaws and turning them over to local lawmen, and preaching in Bible-believing churches. Even though the Stranger was now chief United States marshal of the country's Western District, he still preached in churches quite often. Many in the congregation smiled and nodded as the pastor told the story.

Pastor Landrum then turned to the tall, dark-haired man sitting a few feet behind him. "Chief Brockman, please come and preach what God has laid on your heart."

John rose to his feet, Bible in hand, and stepped up to the podium. "Pastor Landrum, I want to thank you once again for the opportunity to preach in your pulpit. It is always an honor."

The two men shook hands and the pastor returned to his seat.

"Please turn to Matthew, chapter 1." John opened his Bible as the sound of rustling pages filled the auditorium. He explained that when Joseph and Mary were engaged, it became apparent that Mary was expecting a child. Joseph was shocked, but loving Mary as he did, he did everything he could to keep Mary from becoming a public example. In Israel at that time, when a man and a woman were engaged, they were already called husband and wife.

John read Matthew 1:18–21 aloud as the crowd followed along:

Now the birth of Jesus Christ was on this wise: When as his mother Mary was espoused to Joseph, before they came together, she was found with child of the Holy Ghost. Then Joseph her husband, being a just man, and not willing to make her a public example, was minded to put her away privily. But while he thought on these things, behold, the angel of the LORD appeared unto him in a dream, saying, Joseph, thou son of David, fear not to take unto thee Mary thy wife: for that which is conceived in her is of the Holy Ghost. And she shall bring forth a son, and thou shalt call his name JESUS: for he shall save his people from their sins.

John followed this reading with a powerful sermon about how the Lord Jesus Christ had come into the world from heaven by the virgin birth — to be crucified, shed His blood, die on the cross of Calvary, and rise from the dead to provide salvation for a world of lost sinners if they would repent of their sins, put their faith in Him for salvation, and receive Jesus Christ into their hearts as Saviour. He pointed out that when people receive Him into their hearts, they are born again and become His people. As the angel of the Lord had said, "He shall save his people from their sins."

After preaching these truths backed by Scripture so that all could understand, John closed the sermon and gave an invitation for those who wanted to receive Jesus as their Saviour. A good number of adults and young people came forward to ask Jesus into their hearts. Many believers also came to the altar to dedicate themselves more fully to the Lord.

As the new converts were about to be ushered to the baptistry, the auditorium doors swung open, and two bleeding men stumbled inside. Both collapsed in the center aisle.

Several men rushed from their pews to help the injured men. The older of the two had been shot in the left shoulder, and the younger had been shot in his upper right arm and gripped a canvas moneybag in his left hand.

The people looked on as John Brockman and Pastor Landrum hurried down the steps of the platform, rushed to the fallen men, and knelt down beside them.

Pastor Landrum introduced himself and Chief Brockman, explaining John's position with the federal law. Then he asked, "What happened, fellas?"

The older man, who appeared to be in his early fifties, was short of breath. "My young partner, Glenny, and I run a Wells Fargo stagecoach. I'm the driver, and he's my shotgunner. My name's Josh Bridges. A gang of outlaws just tried to rob us. We got ourselves shot up but got away. We went to the doctor's office on Main Street. A sign on the door said he could be found here between ten and noon on Sunday morning, so we came here."

The pastor looked up and saw Dr. Richard Barnett drawing up with Breanna and Katy. "Here's Dr. Barnett right now. The two ladies with him are nurses — Chief Brockman's wife, Breanna, and my daughter, Katy."

The pastor quickly told the doctor who the wounded men were and how they had been wounded. Dr. Barnett assured the men that he and the nurses would take care of them. He told Breanna and Katy to assess the wounds while he found someone to fetch his medical bag from his buggy in the parking lot. He returned a minute later and began looking at the wounds. "I sent Billy Gibson after my medical bag."

Katy nodded. "He's almost nineteen now and very responsible. I'm sure he'll be back in no time."

"It appears that the bullets have passed through both of you, gentlemen. Because they're bleeding so much, I believe the nurses and I can stitch up the wounds immediately and then take you to Riverton Hospital for further care."

The wounded men looked confused. "Dr.

Barnett, we didn't even know Riverton had a hospital, or we would have gone there," Josh said. "All we ever see is what's on Main Street. The sign on your door gave directions to the church, or we wouldn't have known where it was either."

"I understand," Dr. Barnett said. "Anyway, as soon as —"

Billy Gibson ran through the church door with Dr. Barnett's medical bag in hand. "Thank you, Billy." He grabbed the bag from him and opened it. "I've got laudanum powder we'll mix with water for you fellas to drink. It'll ease your pain while we suture you up to get the bleeding stopped."

Dr. Barnett then reached into the bag and took out the bottle of laudanum powder. "Pastor Landrum, could you get us two cups of water?"

"Certainly."

"Okay, about two-thirds full."

"Be right back."

Dr. Barnett took two needles and two rolls of surgery sutures from his medical bag. "Mrs. Brockman is experienced with gunshot wounds. I'll have her stitch up your arm, Glenn, while I stitch up Josh's shoulder. Katy will work at keeping both wounds from bleeding excessively while we work."

"Thank you, Dr. Barnett," Josh said

through a pained smile. "We very much appreciate what you and these dear nurses are doing for us."

"That's for sure," Glenn said. "Thank you."

SIX

"Doctor, I'll go get some water and cloths of some kind to use on the wounds."

The doctor looked up at Katy as he reached into his medical bag. "All we need is the water. I have thick cloth bandages in my bag. If you'll get the water, we're in business."

"I'll be right back."

As Katy rushed away, her father was returning with the two cups of water, the Hawsons at his side.

The people in the auditorium were turned around on their pews with worried looks on their faces.

The pastor quietly introduced the men to Marshal Hawson and his wife. Dr. Barnett and Breanna mixed the laudanum with the water and helped the patients to drink it down. "Please lie as still as you can, gentlemen," Dr. Barnett said. "We'll give the laudanum fifteen minutes to get into your

91

systems before we start stitching up the wounds."

Just then Katy arrived, a bit out of breath. "Here's . . . the water . . . Doctor."

"All right, Katy. I want you and Breanna to soak the cloths, wring them out, and press them tightly against the wounds until the laudanum has taken effect."

Katy knelt between the two wounded men and placed the bowl of water on the floor beside her. Breanna knelt as well, and while Katy worked on Josh, Breanna worked on Glenn, staunching the blood in their wounds.

The pastor took this opportunity to go up to the platform and dismiss the congregation, saying they would baptize new converts at the evening service and asking them to pray for the wounded men.

Soon only the Landrums, the Brockmans, the Hawsons, and Dr. and Mrs. Barnett remained in the auditorium.

After fifteen minutes, the laudanum had begun to take effect. Both men were feeling very sleepy and thankful for the laudanum. Without it, the pain would certainly be much stronger.

"Go ahead and close your eyes," Dr. Barnett said. "Take a little nap now."

Both men closed their eyes, and Breanna

and Katy went to work as their patients sunk further under the effect of the laudanum. In less than an hour, the wounds were sutured, clean bandages covering them.

A few minutes later, the wounded men rolled their heads slowly and blinked as they awakened from the medication.

A low moan escaped Josh's clenched teeth as he tried to move his left arm.

"Mr. Bridges" — Dr. Barnett laid his hand on the driver's right shoulder — "I had to strap your left arm to your chest to keep you from moving it. The bullet tore through some of your shoulder muscle, and there may be some nerve damage. The doctors at the hospital will be able to examine the wound closer, but for now I think it best to keep that shoulder immobile."

His face set against the pain, Josh looked at the doctor with grateful eyes. "Thank you, Dr. Barnett. I appreciate your care."

"One more thing, Josh," said the doctor in a soft voice. "If the nerves are indeed damaged, you might not be able to drive the stagecoach for a long time. Maybe never."

A deep frown pinched Josh's countenance. "That's kind of hard news to hear, Doctor. Bu-but — I was looking for a job when I found this one. Guess if I can't ever drive a stagecoach again, there'll be another job I *can* handle out there somewhere."

"I'm sorry, Josh."

Josh looked him square in the eye. "Don't be sorry, Dr. Barnett. I know you've done your best for me. I'll be just fine."

The doctor grinned. "That's the spirit, my friend. You *will* be just fine!" He paused. "Both of you have lost a lot of blood. The folks at the hospital will take good care of you."

A faint smile showed on Glenn's lips at those words. "I guess we'd better get over there then."

"Dr. Barnett," John said, "I know your buggy is too small to carry these men to the hospital. We can lay them in the back of Pastor Landrum's wagon and transport them."

"That would be great, Chief. My wife and I will follow so I can get these men admitted."

Josh Bridges looked up at John. "Chief Brockman, will you do me a favor?"

"Of course."

"That moneybag Glenn was carrying. There by his side."

"Yes?"

"Would you bring it with you to the hospital?"

94

Josh Bridges and Glenn Sebring were admitted to Riverton Hospital under the supervision of Dr. Barnett and were put in a room together. The ladies and the Brockman children were seated in a waiting area down the hall while the men stood over the patients' beds in the room.

Dr. Barnett recounted the men's medical treatment at the church to one of the hospital physicians. After examining both men thoroughly, the hospital physician assured them and Dr. Barnett that they would be given the best of care. Dr. Barnett told the patients he'd look in on them every day until they were released from the hospital. Then he left to get his wife and take her home.

With Marshal Hawson and Pastor Landrum at his side, Chief Brockman looked down at the patients and said, "Do you men feel like talking?"

"I think we can, Chief," Josh said. "You probably need to know more about the holdup."

"Yes, can you give me more details?"

"Sure." Josh pointed to the moneybag John had carried over from the church.

"That has a large sum of cash inside."

"Uh-huh? Tell me more."

Josh explained that the stagecoach had been carrying the payroll for a well-to-do rancher who owned three large cattle ranches in central Wyoming. Four rough-looking armed men on horseback had blocked their path on the road and forced them to stop the stage about ten miles northeast of Riverton, just a few miles from the spot where the road from Casper turned south. Dismounting, their guns pointed at him and Glenn, the outlaws demanded the moneybag containing the payroll.

John set his lips firmly. "Somehow those outlaws knew your stage had the payroll on board."

Josh nodded, shakily raising his right hand to rub his brow. "They sure did."

Glenn could see that Josh was quite weak. "Chief Brockman," he said quietly, "maybe I should take over and let Josh rest a spell."

"Certainly."

Glenn took a slow, deep breath. "Our stagecoach had only two passengers on this part of the trip, two middle-aged men. When the outlaws demanded the money-bag, both passengers leaned out the windows of the stagecoach with revolvers and told the outlaws to drop their guns."

Landrum and Hawson both looked at John, all three men surprised at the passengers' courage and determination. John raised his eyebrows and was about to comment.

"One of the outlaws swung his gun on the passengers," Glenn said. "Both men fired. Shot him in the chest. But the outlaw's gun went off just as he was hit, and the bullet struck one of the passengers in the head, killing him instantly. The outlaws opened fire on the other passenger immediately, one of them railing at him for shooting his brother. He fell back from the window and dropped dead."

"That's amazing," Pastor Landrum marveled.

"Josh snapped at the reins in the midst of this and shouted at the team to get them moving. The three remaining outlaws fired at us, which resulted in these wounds."

Before Glenn could go on, Josh spoke up. "Glenn was still able to use his gun, so he opened fire on all three just as the team took off and galloped away."

"I didn't hit any of them though." Glenn licked his lips. "Josh managed to drive the stage at full speed to get us here even though he was in a great deal of pain. I expected to see the outlaws come after us, but when I looked, all three were kneeling down beside the fallen one. I — I've been wondering if possibly all four were brothers. There was a slight resemblance among them."

"I wondered too, Glenn," Josh said. "Hadn't considered mentioning it."

Glenn nodded. "Chief Brockman, we never saw those outlaws again. They didn't get any money from holding up the stage. The . . . ah . . . bodies of the two gallant passengers are still in the stagecoach in front of the church."

John thanked the men for all the helpful details. "Do you fellas have any idea who those robbers might be?"

"I have no idea, Chief," Josh said.

Glenn slowly shook his head back and forth on the pillow. "I don't either."

"Tell you what, Chief," Dub said. "They might just be that greedy, bloodthirsty Zarbo gang. You know about them? Gang's made up of the four Zarbo brothers — Todd, Chice, Stan, and Lee."

"I've heard of them, but since they've concentrated their robbing and killing in Idaho and Montana Territories, I haven't had any actual contact with them — just with the federal marshal offices that have reported their crimes to me."

Hawson nodded. "Well, those bloody Zarbos have done some robbing and killing in Wyoming Territory of late too, Chief. You would have been notified shortly by me and the other federal marshals, I guarantee you. In fact, I have some Wanted posters for the Zarbos that have been used in Idaho, Montana, and here in Wyoming."

John's eyes widened. "Photographs?"

"Yes sir."

"That's great. They're better than the artist sketches used on most Wanted posters. Much more accurate."

"Right. Well, when the Zarbo brothers were arrested for lesser crimes in Idaho a few years back, photographs were taken of them, which is why we even have them. It wasn't that long ago, so they likely still look the same as in the photographs.

"Now that the Zarbos are full-scale outlaws, many posters with their photographs have been printed. Like you said, Chief, the photographs are much more accurate. Most of the pictures that go on Wanted boards in this part of the country are sketches, making it harder to recognize the outlaws."

"Only about half of the posters on our Wanted board are photographs."

"Same here." Marshal Hawson turned to the two men in the hospital beds. "I'd like both of you to look at the posters of the Zarbo brothers and tell me if they're the ones who tried to rob the stage. Okay?"

"We'd be glad to do that, Marshal," said Glenn.

"Good. I'll go to my office and get the posters. I'll be back in about a half hour."

Managing a grin, Josh said, "Glenn and I will be right here, I promise."

Dub chuckled. "We're not worried about you two getting up and leaving. See you shortly."

As Marshal Hawson left the hospital room, Pastor Landrum turned to John. "Two of my members are patients here right now. I need to go check on them."

"Sure, Pastor Landrum."

The pastor turned when he reached the doorway. "I'll be back in a little while."

When the pastor had left the room, the chief U.S. marshal turned toward the two wounded Wells Fargo employees. "While we've got a few quiet minutes here, I'd like to talk to both of you about something very important."

Josh and Glenn met his gaze and nodded.

"I want to ask you something. If you had been killed when those outlaws shot you, where would you be right now?"

"You mean, would we be in heaven or

hell?" Josh asked.

"Yes. That's exactly what I mean."

The driver and the shotgunner looked at each other, grinning. "Chief, we would both be looking into the wonderful face of the One who died for us on Calvary's cross," Glenn said. "Our Saviour is in heaven, so that's where we'd be."

"Hallelujah!" Josh said. "We sure would!"

John beamed at the men, and a smile spread from ear to ear. "Sounds to me like you know what you're talking about!"

"We sure do." Josh's voice crackled a bit. "Glenn and I both received the Lord Jesus as our Saviour when a group of people on our stagecoach witnessed to us and led us to Him. We live in Casper, and those people happened to be members of a Christ-exalting, Bible-believing church in Casper. They were traveling back from a revival at a church in Powder River, forty miles from Casper. Part of the harness on the horses broke that day. While we stopped to repair it, the passengers witnessed to us and led us to Jesus. That was a Saturday. When we got home, we told our wives about our salvation and went to church the very next morning. Our wives went with us and walked the aisle at the invitation and came to know Christ as Saviour too."

"We can't be in church every week because of our job," Glenn explained, "but we get to be there every other Sunday. And, of course, we go on Wednesday nights when we're home. Our wives get to go to both the Sunday services and midweek services."

"Well, I'm sure glad to know that you are my brothers in Christ." John grinned. "Marshal Hawson and his wife and Dr. Barnett and his wife are Christians too. They'll be glad to know about you!" He told them that in addition to being chief U.S. marshal of the Western District, he was also a preacher and had preached that morning at Riverton Baptist and would be preaching again that evening.

Both men said they wished they could be there to hear him. As they visited, a nurse came in and asked if the patients needed anything. Both Josh and Glenn told her they were thirsty. The nurse got them some water and helped them one at a time.

John told both men he'd go down to the waiting area and spend a few minutes with the women and children. When John approached the waiting area, his three children left their chairs and dashed to him. They wanted to know how the wounded men were doing. John put one arm around both Ginny and Meggie and the other around

Paul as they walked over to where the ladies were sitting. "I'll tell you all at the same time."

John remained on his feet and told the group where Marshal Hawson and Pastor Landrum had gone and why. Then he told them that he had learned that both injured men were Christians. When they had heard the story, everyone smiled.

"Oh, that's wonderful!" Elizabeth Landrum exclaimed.

"Amen!" said Paul.

John ran his gaze over their faces. "I knew you'd all be glad to hear this. I need to get back to the patients. See you later?"

When John entered the hospital room again, Pastor Landrum was standing over the two men. He looked up at John, tears in his eyes. "Chief, Josh and Glenn just told me that you asked them where they would have gone if they'd been killed and what their answer was. Isn't this terrific?"

"It sure is, Pastor," John replied, smiling broadly.

Marshal Hawson walked in the room just then, carrying a large brown envelope, and addressed the wounded men. "I've got the Wanted posters of the Zarbo gang. I brought two of each so you could look at them at the same time." Dub opened the envelope, pulled out the posters, and handed them to Josh and Glen. "I put them in order of their age. Todd Zarbo, then Chice, Stan, and Lee."

As the men shuffled through the posters, Josh said, "Yep, Marshal. These are the outlaws who tried to steal the payroll."

"Sure are." Glenn pointed at the pictures. "It's them, all right." He lifted the poster with Stan Zarbo on it. "This is the one who was shot by the two passengers. He's probably dead."

Marshal Hawson pointed out Todd Zarbo's photograph. "Though all four brothers are cold-hearted killers, Todd is the meanest of the bunch."

"He looks it," Glenn said.

"Sure does," John said as he leaned over to get a better look.

Hawson looked back and forth at the two men. "Can you tell me the exact spot where the holdup took place? I'll take three of my deputies and see if we can track down the Zarbos and arrest them."

"If you'll get me a piece of paper and a pencil, Marshal," Glenn said, "I can draw a map for you and make it easy to find the spot."

"I'll get some from the nurses' desk down the hall." Dub rushed out of the room and returned with the needed paper and pencil.

With Chief Brockman's help, Glenn sat up in the bed and used the small meal table on wheels to lay the paper on as he drew the map. When he was finished, he handed it to Dub. "Have Josh take a look at this to see if it seems right."

Josh looked at it carefully and nodded. "Glenn has it exactly right. You and your deputies will have no problem finding the spot of the attempted robbery. There will definitely be blood on the ground where Stan Zarbo went down."

Dub took the map back, folded it, and put it in his pocket. "Good. It may take a few days, but we'll do our best to track them down!" He looked at John. "Chief Brockman, would you like to go with us?"

SEVEN

As John heard Marshal Hawson's words, the door of the hospital room opened quietly, and Breanna looked in. John's back was toward the door, but the other men in the room noticed her. Still, they turned their attention to the tall, rugged chief United States marshal as they waited for his answer.

John set his jaw, and the pair of white-ridged scars on his right cheekbone flushed red. His steel gray eyes flashed as he replied, "I sure would like to go after those murderous outlaws, Marshal Hawson."

Breanna and the children stepped into the room, followed by Elizabeth and Katy Landrum and Marie Hawson. Breanna and the children fixed their eyes on John.

"Great!" Marshal Hawson clapped his hands together.

John turned toward his family, and by the looks on their faces, he knew they had heard that he'd like to trail the outlaws. The family was supposed to go home to Denver together the next day.

"Marshal," John said, "even though I'd like to go after the Zarbo gang, I just can't."

The entire Brockman family released a sigh of relief.

Dub frowned. "Oh . . . why can't you go with me and my deputies, Chief?"

"I have an appointment with a very important person in Denver on Wednesday that I can't miss, and we might not catch the Zarbo brothers in time for me to get back by then."

"I see. Well, you know best about that."

Marshal Brockman grinned. "Would you like to know who that important person is?"

"Sure." Hawson shrugged.

"The president of the United States, Grover Cleveland."

Ginny and Meggie looked at each other, giggling under their breath, as Dub's mouth dropped open. Now Breanna and Paul were grinning too.

Dub swallowed hard. "Oh, my. I understand why you can't miss *that* appointment, Chief. How did this come about?"

John patted him on the back. "Well, President Cleveland is coming to Denver for a political convention, and he wrote me about two months ago saying he wanted to meet me while he was there. I've met other presidents since becoming chief U.S. marshal of the Western District, but he and I have not had occasion to meet yet. So I replied saying I'd look forward to meeting him in person."

"I'm envious."

John chuckled. "Sorry about that, friend, but going after the Zarbo gang is a great service to the president, you know."

"That's a good way to look at it, Chief Brockman," Pastor Landrum said.

"I'm glad you agree."

"I believe the rest of us here agree as well," Katy interjected.

"That's for sure," Dub agreed.

"If it wasn't for my appointment with President Cleveland, I'd send my family back to Denver tomorrow as scheduled and go with you after the Zarbo brothers."

"I understand, Chief."

"I want you to let me know how it goes, Marshal."

Hawson nodded. "Of course, sir. You *are* the boss of the entire Western District. I'll send you a telegram when we return to Riverton."

"Thanks. I'd appreciate it."

Hawson looked around at the group. "Since I have the map Glenn drew for me and know which three deputies I want to take along today, I'm going to go to their homes right now and tell them what's up. We'll head out after the Zarbos as soon as possible."

"Good." John gave a firm nod. "And I'll drive the stagecoach to the Wells Fargo station so the officials can see the bodies of the two passengers who were killed and contact their families." He bent down and picked up the canvas moneybag from under Josh Bridges's bed. "I'll take this payroll money to them too."

"Glenn and I appreciate it, Chief Brockman," Josh said.

"It's the least I can do, fellas. What are the names of the two passengers?"

"Mr. Holland and Mr. Smith," said Josh. "We left four other passengers at the Moneta, Wyoming, station, and Mr. Holland and Mr. Smith boarded there. They told us they lived a few miles north of Moneta, in Lysite. They were booked all the way to Jackson."

"I see. And who should I speak with at the station?"

"The manager is David Weber, and his assistant is Burt Cornell. Mr. Weber is in his early sixties, and Mr. Cornell is in his mid-forties. They might both be there."

"Chief," Pastor Landrum said, "we'll take Breanna and the kids to the hotel. We'll wait there with them until you arrive, and then we'll all eat Sunday dinner at the hotel restaurant. Okay?"

"That sounds good to me." John smiled at his family and the Landrums.

"Me too, Papa," said Paul. "I'm hungry!"

"I'll get this errand done as soon as I can and see you all in a little while."

At the Wells Fargo station in Riverton, manager David Weber sat at the telegraph table in the office as his assistant stood leaning over him. The return message from the manager of the Moneta station said that the stagecoach manned by Josh Bridges and Glenn Sebring had left Moneta right on time that morning.

Weber shut off the telegraph machine and sighed as he looked up at his assistant. "Well, Burt, something's wrong for sure. Josh and Glenn are way too late."

"I'll get on my horse and ride toward Moneta, Dave." Burt straightened up. "I'm bound to run into the stagecoach between here and th—"

Both men looked up as they heard pounding hooves and grinding stagecoach wheels.

David Weber jumped to his feet. "They're here!"

The men dashed toward the open front door in time to see an unfamiliar man driving the stage. "Something indeed has happened, Burt."

"Looks like it, sir."

The man driving the stage pulled the four-horse team to a halt and jumped down from the driver's seat. They saw the badge on his chest and the holstered gun on his hip. He was quite tall, exceptionally handsome, looked to be in his early forties. He also had a pair of scars on his right cheekbone. They noticed the gray canvas moneybag in one hand.

As the lawman drew up, he nodded toward the man with some silver in his hair. "You must be David Weber, the manager."

"Yes, Marshal."

John Brockman glanced at the other man. "Are you assistant manager Burt Cornell?"

"I am," Burt nodded.

"I'm chief United States marshal John Brockman from Denver, gentlemen. My family and I came to Riverton yesterday so I could preach at Riverton Baptist this morning. Your stagecoach was robbed this morning by the Zarbo gang about ten miles northeast of Riverton."

Weber swallowed hard. "Chief Brockman, I've heard of you, and I know Burt has too. Are — are Josh and Glenn dead?"

John shook his head. "No. They were wounded, but they're in the Riverton Hospital, and they'll be all right."

"Oh, good."

John held up the moneybag. "You were aware that this payroll money was on the stage, correct?"

"We sure were," Weber replied. "So that rotten Zarbo gang didn't get it?"

"Nope." John handed the moneybag to the manager. "Josh wanted me to be sure you could see that it gets into the proper hands."

"I'll do that," said Weber.

"Only two passengers were on the stage at that point."

"Yes. I don't recall their names, but they were on their way to Jackson."

"A Mr. Holland and Mr. Smith," John reminded them.

"And are they . . . ?" Burt Cornell fumbled for words.

"I'm sorry to say that both men were shot to death during the robbery. Their bodies are inside the stage. I'll give you the details of their deaths after we carry the bodies inside. I know you'll want to contact their families."

"All right." Weber's face was pallid.

"Once I've given you all the information, I'll need a ride back to the hotel."

"I can take you back in the stagecoach, Chief," Burt offered.

The men carried the bodies into the station and placed them in a room passengers often slept in when coaches stopped for the night.

They went to the office, and John gave them every detail of the robbery and the wounds Josh and Glenn had received.

"I'm so glad Josh and Glenn weren't killed," David said. He also had information on the rancher to whom the payroll belonged and would see that it was delivered on the next stage coming through.

"Good," said John.

"Chief Brockman, Burt and I have heard many good things about you. You have quite a reputation for being tough on outlaws and for carrying out your job as chief U.S. marshal of the Western District in an excellent way. It's a real pleasure to meet you."

"It sure is, sir," Burt said emphatically. "And thank you for bringing the coach back. I'll take you to Riverton whenever you're ready."

John rose to his feet. "Well, I've got to get back right away so I can have Sunday dinner and get ready for tonight's church service."

"Of course, Chief," Weber said. "Burt and I will go visit Josh and Glenn at the hospital this afternoon as well."

"I'll go by the hospital after I let Chief Brockman off, boss," Burt said. "I won't stay long so I can get back here to take care of things while you go visit."

"Sounds like a deal." Weber shook hands with Marshal Brockman and watched from the door as his assistant and the lawman climbed up onto the driver's seat and Burt put the horses into motion.

That evening, John Brockman preached the sermon he had been planning, and it honored, glorified, and lifted up the Lord Jesus Christ, showing from the Scripture that He is the only way to heaven and that Christians should endeavor to serve Him with all their hearts.

Pastor Landrum baptized those who had been saved in the morning service as well as two from the evening service.

When the service was over, those who attended passed by the Brockmans at the front door of the church, greeting them and the Landrums. Many told the chief and his family what a blessing they had been to them.

Monday morning, July 2, dawned under a clear blue sky with plenty of sunshine and a few white clouds riding the high breezes. The Brockmans enjoyed a delicious breakfast in the restaurant at the Western Trails — bacon and eggs, golden fried potatoes, and fluffy biscuits.

As everyone at the table was finishing up, John and Breanna lingered over their steaming cups of coffee. After John took his last sip, he set the cup in its saucer, pulled out his pocket watch, then looked at Breanna and the children. "Well, family, we'd best go back to our suite, fetch our bags, and check out. Pastor Landrum will be here soon. We can wait for him out front."

"Okay, Papa." Paul pushed back his chair as he stood up. "You and I can carry the suitcases down the stairs. There aren't too many."

"You're right, son." John turned to Breanna. "Honey, you and the girls go on outside, and we'll join you shortly."

John stood, and Breanna and the girls quickly followed suit. John left money on the table to cover the meal even though

Pastor Landrum had told him that the church would pay for their meals. He ushered Breanna and the girls out of the restaurant to the lobby. Paul went ahead and opened the wide double doors, allowing his mother and sisters to step out into the warm sunlight.

As father and son headed across the lobby toward the winding staircase, Breanna shepherded her two girls onto an empty bench against the wall of the hotel. The overhang on the porch afforded them some shade.

Meggie fanned her face with her hand. "Whew! It's getting hot already."

"Yes," Breanna agreed. "I think we're in for an uncomfortably hot ride on both trains today, girls."

A gust of hot wind blew dust along the street.

"I remember the wind blowing quite a bit when we were here those other times." Ginny brushed at the dust gathering on her dress. "Does it blow here a lot, Mama?"

"That's what I've been told."

"Well, if that's the way it is here," Meggie said, "I'll be glad to get back home."

"Yes, dear." Breanna smiled warmly. "I think we'll all be glad to get home. The church services were very good, but the rest of our time here brought some very nerve-racking events, didn't it?"

Both girls nodded silently.

The three watched John and Paul exit the hotel through the wide double doors, carrying the bags, as the Landrums pulled up in their wagon.

"Hey, good timing, Chief!" the pastor said with a smile. He quickly hopped down from the driver's seat and walked around the rear of the wagon. "I'll help Elizabeth onto one of the rear seats so she and Breanna can sit together on the way to the railroad station. Then I'll help Breanna and your girls in too."

"Thank you, Pastor," John replied with a smile. "While you're doing that, we'll get our luggage loaded in the rear."

The wagon was soon loaded up and pulling away from the hotel. Paul and John joined Pastor Landrum on the driver's seat.

Some fifteen minutes later, the wagon drew up in front of Riverton's railroad station. While the three men carried the luggage inside, Elizabeth told the Brockmans that Katy had said to tell them good-bye for her. She was disappointed that she had to be to work earlier than expected and wouldn't be able to see them off.

When railroad employees had loaded the luggage into the baggage car, the Brockmans were ready to board their coach. Good-byes were said, along with some handshaking and hugs.

The Brockmans arrived in Cheyenne early that afternoon. Moments later they boarded the train bound for Denver.

The train rolled south out of Cheyenne. John and Breanna were seated about midway along the coach, and Paul, Ginny, and Meggie were in the seat behind them.

Breanna noticed a silver-haired couple across the aisle looking past her at John and talking in low voices. She was about to tell John when both of them left their seat and stepped across the aisle. The man looked intently at John. "You're John Stranger, aren't you?"

It took John a few seconds to recognize the couple. Then with a smile he said, "I don't go by that name anymore, but I *am* John Stranger. I remember you! You're Hector and Sarah Williams."

"We sure are." Hector grinned. "I see you're wearing a badge now. Chief U.S. marshal, eh?"

"Yes sir. My office is in Denver. My real name is Brockman, so now I'm chief U.S. marshal John Brockman."

"Well, some twenty years ago, John Stranger, you gave Sarah and me a generous amount of money when our house burned down. As I remember, you happened to be passing through Cheyenne when you saw Sarah and me standing outside our burning house, clinging to each other and weeping."

"I remember it clearly," John said.

Sarah's eyes filled with tears. "You led us to the Lord that day, John Stranger — er — Chief Brockman. After you gave us the money to build a new house."

"Yes! What a blessing!"

"Well, the *real* blessing is ours, John Stranger." Hector's eyes twinkled at his wife and back to John. "We want you to know that after you led us to Jesus, we were able to lead some of our family members and neighbors to Him. And we're still faithful in church and in serving the Lord."

John's eyes lit up. "Wonderful. I'm glad to hear it!" John introduced Breanna and their children to the Williamses.

Hector reached into his trousers pocket and held up the silver medallion that John had given them. "I have carried this medallion for all these years."

Paul, Ginny, and Meggie knew about the medallions their papa had given to people he had helped when he traveled the West as the Stranger. They were about the size of a silver dollar and had words engraved that told something about himself.

"I've always loved this medallion — centered with a five-point star in capital letters around the edge: 'The Stranger That Shall Come from a Far Land.' Then in small letters is the Scripture reference: Deuteronomy 29:22."

"And when I asked you what that Scripture verse had to do with it," Sarah said, "you told me that the verse refers to 'the stranger that shall come from a far land.' "

"We still live in the house you paid to have built for us," Hector added. "We're on our way to Denver right now to catch a train to Albuquerque, New Mexico, where we are going to visit some relatives."

"Well, it's wonderful to see you again," John said.

Breanna smiled up at the couple. "I'm so glad I got to meet you folks."

"Us too," Paul and the girls said from the next seat.

Hector and Sarah smiled warmly, telling Breanna and the children that they were glad to meet them too. "We'll say our goodbyes when we get off the train in Denver. Come, Sarah dear. Let's let these sweet people enjoy the ride as a family." With that, the couple went back to their seat across the aisle.

EIGHT

When the train arrived at Denver's Union Station early that evening, the Brockmans and the Williamses stepped out of their coach together. John and Hector gave a railroad employee the numbered stubs for their bags, and chatted for a few minutes until the employee returned with their luggage. The employee told Hector he'd put their luggage on the train to Albuquerque.

The Brockmans and the Williamses hugged, and Hector gazed at the entire Brockman family. "If we don't see each other again here on earth, we *will* meet in heaven."

John, Breanna, and the children spoke their agreement.

When the Williamses walked away to board the train to Albuquerque, John told his family to sit on one of the benches in front of the station while he went down the street to get their mare and buggy, which he had left at a nearby stable.

John returned a few minutes later driving the buggy. While Breanna and the girls climbed in, John and Paul placed the luggage in the rear compartment.

Breanna nestled in at John's side on the driver's seat as the buggy pulled away from the railroad station. John glanced down at her. "Honey, instead of stopping at my office to ask the deputies if anything significant happened while I was gone, I'll let you and the children off at home and just drive down the road to the Langford cabin. Whip can tell me if anything happened I should know about."

"Okay." Breanna smiled. "Since we haven't had supper yet, the girls and I will prepare a snack while you're at the Langford place."

Paul spoke from the seat behind his parents. "While Mama and the girls fix a snack, I'll do the chores at the barn and the corral."

A short time later, John pulled the buggy up to the Brockmans' ranch in the country. "Okay, sweet family, I'll be back in a little while."

As Breanna and the children climbed down from the buggy, Paul pointed to a yellow envelope stuck in the screen door on the front porch. "Looks like we've got something from Western Union, Papa. I'll get it for you."

Breanna and the girls waited beside the buggy as Paul dashed to the front porch, took the envelope from the door, and hurried back. "It's addressed to chief U.S. marshal John Brockman, Papa. That's *you*, isn't it?"

John chuckled as he opened the envelope. "Last time I checked, I was still chief U.S. marshal, son."

"It's from Marshal Hawson. He sent it from Lander, Wyoming."

Breanna and the children waited eagerly for John to read the telegram.

When he had finished, John looked at his family then back at the telegram. "Marshal Hawson says he and his three deputies found the spot where the stagecoach was stopped by the Zarbo gang. There was a great deal of blood on the ground." He sighed. "Sounds like one of the deputies noted a pile of rocks nearby and wondered if Stan Zarbo had been buried under the rocks if the brothers didn't have a shovel to dig a grave. When they removed the rocks, they indeed found Stan Zarbo's body.

"Marshal Hawson and his deputies piled the rocks back and left it as they found it.

The telegram goes on to say that they are trailing the other three Zarbos. There was no sign of Stan's horse. He says the outlaws are riding south in Wyoming and that he and his deputies are getting closer. He closes by saying he will keep me posted."

As John looked back at his family, he noticed a strange look on Paul's face. "Paul, what's bothering you?"

The fifteen-year-old boy frowned. "Papa, I can't understand why the Zarbo brothers wouldn't take their dead brother's body with them and have it buried in a cemetery."

"Well, son, Todd, Chice, and Lee Zarbo are probably headed somewhere to pull off another robbery and didn't feel they had time to give their brother a proper burial. So they did what they could to get Stan buried in a hurry."

Paul shook his head. "I can't understand putting Stan under a pile of rocks. Somebody was bound to come along and notice the way the rocks were piled and examine them. If whoever found the body under the rocks could figure out who the dead man was, wouldn't that draw attention to the other brothers?"

"It very well could do that. But it wouldn't make any difference since the other three brothers would be long gone by then."

Paul shrugged his shoulders. "I'll be able to figure these kind of things out when I've been a lawman for a while."

"I assure you, son, that is true!"

"Paul, you are very intelligent." Ginny patted her brother's arm. "I know you'll be a real good lawman someday."

"Yeah!" Meggie chimed in. "You'll be almost as good as Papa!"

Paul laughed. "Well, Meggie, if I can be *almost* as good as the great Chief United States Marshal John 'the Stranger' Brockman, that'll be good enough for me!"

The rest of the family laughed too. "Son, I'll help you unload the luggage and put it on the front porch. Then you can carry it inside to Mama's and the girls' bedrooms."

"Sure, Papa." Paul headed for the rear of the buggy.

John followed him, and Breanna and the girls watched as father and son carried the luggage onto the front porch and sat it down. John climbed back onto the driver's seat to head for the Langford cabin so he could talk to Whip.

Adjusting himself on the seat, John picked up the reins and said, "I'll be back for that delicious snack!"

"You'd better hurry back then!" Breanna said, laughing. "The girls and I will have it ready in about a half hour!"

"I'll be back in time. I promise." He put the mare in motion and drove away.

Breanna turned to the girls. "Okay, young ladies, let's get to the kitchen and prepare the food while your big brother hauls the luggage in."

Paul watched his mother and sisters enter the house, then picked up his first load of luggage. He had to make three trips to get it all inside, most of it belonging to his mother and sisters. After his third trip, leaving the luggage in each bedroom, Paul made his way down the hall toward the rear of the house. In the kitchen, his two sisters were setting the table while their mother worked at the cupboard. "You girls sure took a lot of stuff to Riverton for one short weekend!" he exclaimed.

"That's just the way girls are," Meggie quipped, her irresistible dimples showing.

"Yeah." Paul ruffled Meggie's hair playfully. "That's because you never have to carry 'em!"

Breanna turned from her work at the cupboard. "Paul, I think you'd better take care of your chores, don't you?"

The lanky fifteen-year-old grinned. "Guess so, Mama. We slaves always have more work to do." With that he hurried out the back door of the kitchen as his mother and sisters laughed and shooed at him.

Twenty-seven minutes after his departure, John Brockman entered the kitchen from the hallway just as Paul stepped in through the back door.

Paul neared the cupboard to wash his hands at the small water pump, and John said, "Well, Whip wasn't home, but Annabeth was."

"Where was Uncle Whip?" Meggie asked.

"Your aunt Annabeth told me that Uncle Whip is presently trailing a killer with Timber at his side."

"Is this some killer who's on the Wanted list?" Breanna asked.

"Nobody knows who he is." John frowned thoughtfully. "Annabeth said that about four o'clock this afternoon, the man shot and killed George Woodworth on Broadway."

"George Woodworth!" Breanna gasped. "He was one of the wealthiest men in town."

"Yes. From what Annabeth said, the killer apparently knew who George was and attempted to steal his wallet at gunpoint right there on the Broadway boardwalk. According to witnesses, George resisted, and the man shot him. The man snatched the wallet, jumped on his horse, and galloped westward out of town."

Breanna's hand went to her mouth. "Oh, how awful!"

"Annabeth said Whip happened to be a block away when the man shot George. Hearing the shot, Whip ran to the spot and found a group of people gathered around George, who was already dead. County deputy Don Reiger also heard the shot and came running.

"When the witnesses described the killer to the two lawmen — how he was dressed, what his horse looked like, and what road he took out of town — Whip asked Deputy Reiger if he planned to go after the killer. Deputy Reiger already had an assignment from Sheriff Carter and couldn't go after him.

"Whip left to follow the killer immediately since I wasn't here to ask if he should. He ran to the federal building, jumped on his horse, and galloped for home. He told Annabeth what had happened and that he was taking Timber with him to track the killer, who no doubt was headed for the mountains."

John paused and wiped a hand over his face. "I wish Whip had taken another deputy with him . . . county or federal. He only takes Timber when he goes alone."

"They're some kind of a team, all right," Breanna said. "I sure hope Whip stays safe. Well, our snack — such as it is — is ready."

"Go ahead and sit down, everybody." John moved toward the sink. "I've got to wash my hands."

John sat down with his family after washing and reached his hands out. "Let's pray."

Head bowed, John thanked the Lord for the food, then asked Him to protect Whip as he trailed the ruthless robber. He closed the prayer in Jesus' precious name and said "amen." The rest of the family echoed the "amen."

Staring at the spread on the table, Paul rubbed his hands in anticipation. "Wow, Mama. You called this a snack, but it sure looks like a full-fledged meal to me. And it looks mighty good too. I'm starved!"

It was relatively quiet at the table as the Brockman family ate, each one lost in his or her own thoughts.

After a while, Meggie broke the silence. "I sure am glad to be home. It's cooler here than it was in Wyoming — at least where we were — and that pesky wind isn't blowing."

They all laughed, and the tension of their Wyoming trip eased away.

■ ■ ■ ■

That evening, Deputy Whip Langford was trailing the killer high in the Rocky Mountains with his muscular timber wolf. Timber had demonstrated many times that he loved being Whip's partner.

Whip had taken the road west that witnesses had seen the outlaw take. He stopped several times to ask people along the way what they had seen, and a number had seen the man Whip described. There was no question that he was following the right man.

As he had been trained, Timber veered off the road into the woods or some other unseen spot when his master made a casual stop. He would then rejoin Whip when he was once again riding hard on the trail.

As darkness fell, Whip suddenly caught sight of the horse and rider up ahead. Unaware of Whip's presence, the rider did not look back. The Outlaw Marshal spurred his gelding to a faster gallop, winding his way toward the spot where he had caught sight of the man who had murdered George Woodworth.

Whip periodically lost sight of the killer, who was definitely gaining an advantage as he spurred his horse to pick up the pace. Whip knew the outlaw's horse was indeed larger and faster than his, but he kept his horse riding as hard as possible in the dusky light.

Unknown to Whip and Timber, a large black bear was moving through the forest toward the spot on the winding mountain road the killer had just galloped past. The bear was following a young wolf that was unaware of the predator's presence.

The massive bear's attention was on the spot where it had last seen the small wolf pup it had chosen for its evening meal. The bear was unaware that a human on horseback was thundering along the road with a large wolf.

Some two hundred yards higher than the lawman, the killer noticed that darkness was now enveloping the mountains. He had no idea he was being followed. A pale light glowed around him — the light of the rising moon, and he could make out a number of twinkling stars above. He decided to pull off the road into a grove of towering pine trees, where he could build a fire, cook a meal, and get a good night's sleep.

Hauling up some twenty yards from the road, he dismounted and began gathering twigs and small limbs to build a fire.

As Whip and Timber drew near the black bear, they suddenly heard a growl. By the dim moonlight, Whip and Timber were able to see a bear as it lunged for a wolf pup. The bear dropped a paw on the little pup, which was followed by a yelp.

Like a bullet, Timber bolted toward the huge bear and the pup, which was like family to Timber. The full-grown wolf ran at full speed, growling viciously.

Whip knew it would do no good to call Timber back. He slid from the saddle and pulled his .44 Winchester from its leather saddle scabbard and cocked it as he ran toward the violent scene.

When the bear saw the large gray wolf drawing near, it let go of the pup, rose high on its hind legs, lifting its four hundred fifty pounds to its full seven-foot height, and gave off a fearsome roar that filled the woods.

Showing no fear of the huge bear, Timber lunged between the swinging paws and clamped his sharp teeth on the bear's big nose.

Now within thirty feet, Whip skidded to a halt and raised the Winchester just as the bear's huge right paw slammed down on

Timber, knocking him to the ground. Timber gasped for air and shook his head as he staggered to his feet. The look in the bear's wild eyes hardened to granite as it roared at the man before him and prepared to attack. Whip took careful aim with the Winchester and fired. The slug plowed between the bear's eyes, throwing its head back from the impact. It let out a pitiful moan, staggered backward a few steps, and fell flat on its back.

Cocking the rifle again, Whip moved up close to the fallen beast and studied it in the moonlight. Twice he put a foot on the bear's head and gave it a hard shove. The bear did not move. Whip was sure the slug had penetrated the bear's brain, killing it instantly, which was the very reason he had shot it between the eyes.

Whip turned around and saw Timber standing face to face with the wolf pup, licking the pup's face. "You'd make a good papa, Timber." Whip grinned. "Well, boy, you and I have a killer to catch. Kiss your little friend good-bye. We've got to go."

Higher up the mountain, the man who had robbed and murdered George Woodworth was beside the fire, pouring his first cup of coffee when he heard a rifle shot from down the mountain to the east. Figuring someone camping must have had to shoot some night creature, he sipped his coffee and went back to eating his meal.

Whip Langford was riding up the steep road in pursuit of the killer, Timber trotting alongside him. The deputy suddenly smelled smoke and then spotted a small fire some twenty yards from the road in a grove of towering pine trees. A lone man sat beside the campfire.

Drawing rein, Whip looked down at Timber, who was also watching the man beside the fire. Timber growled as Whip quietly dismounted. "It's him, all right, boy. We're going after him. You stay close to me, and only attack if I give the signal."

Timber's low whine acknowledged that he understood.

Whip stealthily led his horse into the woods and tied the reins to one of the tall pines. He drew his Colt .45 and quietly moved toward the killer, whose back was toward him.

When Whip and Timber were about thirty feet from the man, Whip pointed his gun at him and said in a loud, gruff voice, "You're under arrest for the murder of George Woodworth in Denver this afternoon! I'm a deputy United States marshal, and I've got my gun aimed directly on you! Raise your hands above your head, and turn around!"

While his master spoke, Timber moved silently through the shadows toward the man, crouching, ready to attack, but out of the man's line of sight.

The killer dropped his food and threw himself on the ground beside the fire, rolled, and drew his weapon.

"Drop that gun! Right now!" Whip shouted.

This was Timber's signal to attack. Just as the killer was about to chance a shot at the lawman, the big gray wolf flung himself from the darkness, clamped his powerful jaws on the wrist of the man's gun hand, and with a wild growl shook his head, causing the gun to fall to the ground.

The killer screamed above the wolf's growl, "Please, deputy! Shoot the wolf before he tears my hand off!"

"The wolf is my partner, mister! I will *not* shoot him. Settle down immediately, and I'll tell him to back away from you."

The killer panicked, twisting his body and kicking at Timber, who let go of his wrist and leaped at his face, snarling and snapping. "I surrender, deputy! I surrender! Plee-ease! Call him off me!"

"Timber! That's enough! Back off!"

Timber obediently backed away a few steps, regarding the man with eyes of fire and continuing to growl fiercely at him.

The killer's eyes were filled with terror. He felt as though tiny ants were running across his scalp. His heart was pounding, and his body felt cold. His face was a mask of pain. Blood dripped from his cheeks, nose, and right wrist as he breathed hard, rolled to his knees, and looked up at the lawman. "Please, deputy!" he cried. "Get the wolf completely away from me!"

"My wolf won't attack you again if you do as you are told." Whip's tone meant business. "Now get up and put your hands behind your back. Don't even think about trying to grab your gun."

The killer responded obediently, and after he scrambled to his feet, he stood unsteadily, licking his bloody lips. He then put his hands behind his back. While Whip handcuffed him, the killer glanced fearfully at the big gray wolf, which watched his every move from just a few steps away.

"Now you stand real still while I search you, mister." Whip holstered his weapon. "I'm going to find out who you are."

NINE

The killer's bleeding face pinched with cold trepidation, and he gritted his teeth as Deputy Langford searched his pockets and soon found a wallet in a front pocket of his trousers, an unusual spot. Whip opened the wallet and searched through it. He could see by the light of the fire that it was filled with fifty- and one-hundred-dollar bills. He then found two types of identification belonging to George Woodworth.

Whip looked the man in the eye. "Just as I was told. After you shot and killed George Woodworth, you snatched his wallet and rode out of Denver in a hurry."

The look in the killer's eyes told Whip that he was obviously abashed. He did not reply.

Whip wore his own wallet in his right rear trouser pocket, so he placed Woodworth's wallet in his left one. He reached into the killer's rear pocket and removed the wallet found there. Noting different cards and

137

papers inside, he found the name Ross Dover on all of them.

"So your name is Ross Dover. There's even a card in here with your photograph on it, so I know this is yours and not a stolen wallet."

Ross Dover ran his tongue over his bleeding lower lip but remained silent.

Whip then found two cards and a slip of paper with Dover's name, each with the same Denver address. He raised his eyebrows. "So that's how you knew that George Woodworth was one of Denver's wealthiest men. You used to live there, right?"

Dover, who appeared to be in his late thirties, knew he might as well come clean. "Yeah. I used to."

"None of the witnesses on the street knew who you were. It must've been a while."

Dover gritted his teeth and nodded.

As Timber stood close by, ready to leap if necessary, Whip looked Dover in the eye. "Ross Dover, I am deputy U.S. marshal Whipley Langford. You are under arrest for the murder and robbery of George Woodworth."

Dover's lips pulled into a thin line. He knew it would do no good to deny that he had shot and killed the wealthy man.

"Okay, let's get you on your horse. We're

heading back to Denver right now. Before I help you mount your horse, I'll use that bandanna you're wearing to stop the bleeding on your nose and cheeks."

Removing the bandanna from the handcuffed man's neck, Whip soaked it in water, wrung it out a little, and tied it around Dover's face, covering his nose and cheeks where Timber had torn the flesh. Whip then gripped his prisoner and hoisted him up onto the saddle as Timber stood close by observing.

Dover set cold eyes on the deputy U.S. marshal. "Just how am I gonna ride this horse with my hands cuffed behind me? How am I gonna hold the reins?"

"You won't need to." Whip's face was stern. "I'll hold them from my saddle."

A sour look twisted Dover's features as Whip walked toward his horse and swung into the saddle. Dover cast a malignant glance down at the big gray wolf. Timber met the harsh glance with his piercing eyes and low growl.

"Dover, I'd advise you to be friendly to Timber. Believe me, you don't want him thinking any worse of you than he does right now."

The man did not comment.

Whip guided his horse up close to Dover's

and took hold of the reins. "When we get to Denver, I'm going to put you in the county jail. You'll stand trial before Judge Dexter and a jury of people who knew and respected George Woodworth but who are mature and will fairly access the facts. The people who witnessed your heinous crime will be there to give testimony."

Ross Dover gave the lawman a frosty look but said nothing.

Picking their way down the steep mountain roads in the bright moonlight, Timber trotted alongside his master's horse, and both men rode in silence. When they drew up to the Langford home about one thirty in the morning, Whip looped Dover's reins over a fence post at Timber's yard, then dismounted and opened the gate. He petted his trusty partner and told him what a good job he had done.

Whip then closed the gate and mounted his horse again. He had decided not to go into the cabin and disturb Annabeth's sleep. He would be back home a little later, and when his precious wife awakened, he would tell her that George Woodworth's killer was now in jail.

A half hour later, the deputies in charge at the county jail in Denver were astonished to see Deputy Langford enter the office with the handcuffed killer. They congratulated Whip on his successful capture. Whip showed them the papers from Ross Dover's wallet that proved his identity. Dover was immediately registered as in the custody of county sheriff Walt Carter and locked up in a cell.

Whip returned to his horse in the moonlight just outside the jail, mounted up, and headed for home, thanking the Lord for keeping him from harm and for helping him to capture the killer. "Dear Lord, thank You also for my sweet new bride, whom I will soon hold in my arms."

When Whip arrived home, he put his gelding in the small corral to the rear of the cabin, unsaddled him, removed his bridle, patted him affectionately, and headed for the cabin. As he walked the short distance in the moonlight, he pulled out his pocket watch. It was five minutes past three o'clock. Rather than disturb Annabeth, he decided to sleep what was left of the night on the couch in the parlor.

Whip was unaware that Annabeth had awakened a few minutes before and was praying for his safe return.

When Whip quietly stepped up on the front porch, his eye caught sight of a lantern burning in the parlor. Before he could unlock the front door, it swung open, and there stood his lovely new bride, clad in her brightly colored robe. Her long dark hair lay beautifully on her shoulders.

Annabeth opened her arms with a smile. They embraced, kissing each other lovingly. Annabeth eased back in his arms. "Did you catch the killer, darling?"

"Yes, praise the Lord, Timber and I caught him! His name is Ross Dover, and he is now behind bars at the jail."

"Wonderful!"

Whip frowned. "Honey, have you been up all night?"

She shook her head and told him she had awakened only a few minutes before and was praying for him when she heard hoofbeats outside the house. She had dashed to the bedroom window and saw him riding toward the corral. So she put on her robe and lit the lantern in the parlor.

Whip smiled, folded her in his arms, and kissed her again. "I'm so glad to be home with you."

Annabeth looked up into his eyes. "You must be hungry. In my heart, I knew you'd be home tonight, so I saved you some supper."

"Well, I am quite hungry, but I just figured I'd take care of my hunger at breakfast."

Heading for the kitchen, Annabeth looked back at him. "No, we're going to take care of it right now."

Whip hurried up beside her and wrapped an arm around her waist. "I'll light one of the kitchen lanterns so you can see what you're doing."

"You're so kind, Deputy U.S. Marshal Whipley Langford."

He chuckled. "No, it's not me who's so kind, Mrs. Deputy Marshal Whipley Langford. It's *you!* Thanks for saving me some supper."

The sliver of moonlight shining through the kitchen window gave off enough light for Whip to find the lantern on the table. While he lit it, Annabeth stoked up the fire in the cookstove and put the coffeepot on.

Whip sat down at his place at the table and watched Annabeth's graceful moves as she puttered between the stove and the cupboard, preparing his food. She placed it on the table before him and sat down. "After you pray over the food, I'll get myself a cup of coffee, and you can tell me how you and Timber caught the killer."

They bowed their heads, and Whip thanked God for the food and for giving him victory in his pursuit of Ross Dover.

As he devoured his meal, Whip told the

lovely brunette the story of capturing Ross Dover with Timber's help. When she heard the details of Timber's part in the capture, Annabeth sat up straighter. "Timber should be made a deputy U.S. marshal and given a badge to wear."

Whip laughed. "Believe me, sweet stuff, I sure wish it was possible."

Annabeth then told her husband about Chief Brockman's visit earlier in the evening and that she had told him what she knew about her husband being on the trail of the man who killed George Woodworth.

Whip nodded his approval. "The chief will get any other information he needs from the deputies when he arrives in the morning. And I'll tell him myself how I captured Ross Dover."

Annabeth slid her chair back and stepped close to her husband. He held a coffee cup in his right hand, so she took hold of his left hand and kissed it, then held it to her cheek. Her voice was soft. "I'm so very thankful that once again the Lord has placed His protecting arms around you in your dangerous work as a lawman." She looked deep into his eyes.

"I love you so much. I knew you were praying for me. I could literally feel those prayers."

Annabeth whispered softly close to his neck, "And I will always be praying for you." With that, she placed a tender kiss on his lips.

The next morning, after a small breakfast, Whip kissed his bride, stepped off the porch, and mounted up. He would be a little more tired than usual as he rode to Denver today.

When Whip entered the marshal's office, he paused to quickly tell the deputy at the front desk about capturing George Woodworth's killer, then went immediately to the chief's office and knocked on the door.

The familiar voice from inside called out, "Yes? Who is it?"

"It's Whip, Chief."

"Well, come in!"

As Whip stepped into the office and closed the door behind him, Chief Brockman rose to his feet behind his desk. "Congratulations, Whip! You caught that lowdown killer and put him behind bars!"

"You already know?" Whip frowned. "How did you find out?"

"I needed to stop at Sheriff Carter's office to leave some information, and the deputies told me you had caught George's killer and brought him to the jail in the wee hours of the morning. They also told me his name."

"Yes sir."

"Come and sit down so we can talk."

Whip settled onto one of the two wooden chairs in front of the chief's desk.

"I'd like to hear the details and if Timber had a part in it."

Whip grinned. "He sure did." He told John the entire story of Ross Dover's capture.

When he finished, John smiled and shook his head. "Again, congratulations on a job well done! And the next time I see Timber, I'll congratulate him too!"

"He'll appreciate it, sir."

"Since Dover used to live here, I know a few things about him."

"I thought you might."

"He does have a criminal record and has been in Leavenworth Prison in Kansas for about four years. As far as I know, he's never killed anyone before."

Whip nodded. "Was Dover's sentence at Leavenworth for four years, or did he escape?"

"I don't know," John said. "But I plan to telegraph the warden and find out. Either way, since there were witnesses to the shooting, they'll no doubt testify in court that they saw Dover shoot and kill George

Woodworth. I guarantee you, Judge Dexter will sentence him to be hanged."

Whip nodded solemnly. "I'm sure he will."

The chief rose to his feet. "Well, I'd better go send that telegram."

Whip stood up as well. "Let me know what you find out, okay?"

"Sure will."

"Well, Chief, I'll begin my duties for the day. See you later."

"Sure will. And once again, congratulations on a job well done."

Whip thanked the chief and left the office.

A few minutes later, Chief Brockman stepped out of his office. As he walked past the deputy on duty at the front desk, he said, "I'll be back shortly. I'm going to the Western Union office to send a telegram."

"All right, sir."

A tall, slender, square-jawed man stood on the boardwalk a few doors up the street and had watched the chief U.S. marshal exit the federal building. He smiled to himself, patting the gun in the holster slung low on his right hip. He followed, noting that people on the boardwalk greeted Brockman in a friendly manner as he hurried down the boardwalk four blocks to the Western Union office.

When Brockman reached the telegraph

building and went inside, the mean-eyed man stopped and leaned against the wall for a moment. Rubbing his chin, he told himself that Brockman would likely head back to his office at the federal building when he had finished his business at the Western Union office. He headed back in the direction of the federal building, looking over his shoulder periodically to see if Brockman was coming.

When the man was a full block from the telegraph office, he stopped and looked back. Still no sign of Brockman. He leaned against the front of a clothing store on the corner and waited. Quite a few townspeople bustled about on the street.

The man wanted as many people as possible to see him challenge Brockman to a fast draw. He knew the crowd would stand there to watch when they realized a quick-draw gunfight was about to take place. He grinned to himself. A few women might hurry away to avoid being near the spot where bullets would fly — especially those who might have children with them — but most would stand right there and watch. It was part of the well-known code of the West. He kept watching for Brockman, a sly grin breaking on his face occasionally.

In the Western Union office, Chief Brockman had the teller send a wire to the warden of Leavenworth Prison, asking if Ross Dover had escaped or been released.

The telegrapher told the chief he'd deliver the return telegram to him when it came. John thanked him and returned to the boardwalk.

When John was about a block from the Western Union office, he suddenly caught sight of a tall man stepping in front of him, blocking his way. The man's hand hovered over his low-slung holster as John stopped eight or nine feet from him and looked into his grave and emotionless eyes.

People on the street seemed to know what was about to happen and began gathering around the scene. Only a few women moved away, half of them holding their children by the hand or carrying infants.

"I know who you really are." The man sneered. "That badge doesn't fool me. You're the guy they call the Stranger. Go for your gun!"

Eyes wide, the people in the crowd took a few steps back.

John recognized his challenger, whose face he had seen in newspapers many times. A number of people in the crowd appeared to recognize him also. A quick-draw gunfight was definitely coming. The man who was challenging the Stranger was well-known quick-draw gunfighter Kurt "Killer" Condon.

While the crowd stood breathless, waiting for what was about to happen, John Brockman said, "I know who you are, Condon. A hotshot gunfighter. Listen to me now. Many gunfighters like yourself have challenged me thinking they could outdraw the Stranger and make a name for themselves. The only time I've drawn against these fools and aimed just to wound them was when there was no crowd around. I learned quickly that even if I put a bullet in an arm or a shoulder, if they were exceptionally fast they might have the gun out of its holster and cocked before my bullet hit. The impact of my bullet could cause their gun to go off and hit a bystander. I will not take that chance. Now just —"

"Cut the silly talk, Stranger!" Condon cut in. "Go for your gun!"

"Just listen to me!" John snapped. "I've lost count of the foolish men trying to make a name for themselves by challenging me to a quick draw. Their bodies now lie in graves all over the West. Mr. Kurt 'Killer' Condon, I'm telling you to forget it and walk away while you still can. I don't want to be forced to kill you."

Condon's eyes were filled with fire. "You're overrated, Stranger!"

Some of Brockman's deputies had arrived at the scene by this time, as well as county sheriff Walt Carter and some of his deputies. They heard what the chief U.S. marshal said and were hoping Condon would walk away.

The crowd gasped as Condon went for his gun. It was barely out of its holster when John's Colt .45 roared, and the would-be gun-fighting champion took a slug in the center of his heart and fell down dead. In the strange brevity of swift violence, the battle was over.

While people in the crowd talked about Chief Brockman's fair warning to Killer Condon, the other lawmen commended Brockman for trying to keep from having to kill him.

John shook his head in anguish. "I wish I could've just wounded him, but I simply couldn't take the chance. If Condon's gun had gone off and hit someone in the crowd, an innocent life could have been taken."

"You had no choice in the matter, Chief," Sheriff Carter said. All of the other lawmen in the group agreed.

Sheriff Carter asked some of the townsmen to carry the gunfighter's body to the nearest mortuary, then told one of his deputies to go to the chief editor of the *Rocky Mountain News* and give him the story so an accurate article could be printed.

The Western Union telegrapher approached Chief Brockman a moment later and handed him a telegram from the warden at Leavenworth. John thanked him and turned to his deputies. "Let's head back to the office, men. There's no more to be done here."

TEN

As Chief Brockman and his deputies walked back to the federal building, John filled them in. "I assume you fellas know about Whip catching George Woodworth's killer."

"Yes sir," said one of the deputies. "We heard he's in the county jail when we came on duty this morning. We also know he used to live here in Denver."

John nodded and unfolded the telegram. "I sent a telegram to the warden at Leavenworth asking if Dover had escaped or been released. Let's see what he says."

The deputies remained silent as they walked along the boardwalk with their boss.

A minute later, Chief Brockman lowered the telegram. "Okay, here's the story. Ross Dover served a four-year sentence at Leavenworth for a robbery he committed in Emporia, Kansas. He was released two weeks ago."

"Of course, now he's up on a murder

charge," said one of the deputies.

John nodded. "Right, and with plenty of witnesses." He paused. "I need to handle a small matter at the office. Then I'll go see Judge Dexter and tell him everything."

A few minutes later, the lawmen entered the federal building. Chief Brockman took care of his matter, then headed for the judge's office.

The judge's secretary ushered Chief Brockman into Judge Dexter's private office. The judge greeted John warmly.

"I need to talk to you about something important, Judge."

Dexter nodded as he looked across his desk. "Okay, but first I want to tell you that Deputy Sheriff Bob Norris was here just a few minutes ago and told me about your having to take out that gunfighter, Kurt 'Killer' Condon."

John nodded solemnly. "Yes sir."

The judge smiled. "I want to commend you for the way you tried to keep Condon from drawing against you. I appreciate your concern for the people in the crowd."

"Thank you for understanding, Judge Dexter. I'm actually here to inform you of something else."

"And what is that?"

"I'm sure that you're aware that George

Woodworth was robbed and killed yesterday afternoon."

The judge nodded. "Yes, and some of the county deputies told me your deputy Whip Langford pursued and caught the killer."

John eased back in the chair. "Well, I guess you know nearly everything I was going to tell you about Dover. He just finished a four-year term for robbery in the Leavenworth Prison in Kansas and was released two weeks ago."

"I wasn't aware of that." The judge looked at his calendar. "I'll set Dover's trial for Friday morning. That'll give me time to collect a jury. And it will give Sheriff Carter time to gather the witnesses. Dover will no doubt be convicted by the jury and be sentenced to hang."

"According to federal and state law, that's the way it has to be. When potential murderers see the result of taking somebody's life, it just might prevent them from murdering as well."

"Capital punishment was established in this world a long time ago for two basic reasons." Judge Dexter folded his hands on his desk. "Number one, to punish the murderer for his wicked deed. Number two, as you just said, to frighten potential murderers with the consequences of committing murder."

John rose to his feet. "Right. Well, Judge, I'd better get back to my office."

Dexter stood and John extended his right hand over the desk. The judge gripped it tightly. "Chief, I'm glad it was you who was the victor in the quick draw."

Just past nine thirty that morning, Breanna Brockman and Annabeth Langford finished assisting a Mile High Hospital surgeon with an appendectomy on a teenage girl. After washing their hands in the washroom, they stepped out into the hall.

Standing there waiting for them was Darrell Fisher, an orderly. He was a Christian young man and a member of First Baptist Church.

"Is there something we can do for you, Darrell?" Breanna asked.

"No, Mrs. Brockman, but I need to tell you something."

Breanna's brow furrowed. "Yes?"

"Dr. Carroll sent me downtown on an errand a couple of hours ago, and on my way back I joined a crowd of people on the street watching a famous gunfighter, Kurt 'Killer' Condon, challenging your husband to a quick draw. He was saying he knew Chief Brockman was the Stranger."

"Oh no!" Annabeth gasped, taking hold of Breanna's arm.

Before Breanna could speak, Darrell said, "Chief Brockman is all right, ma'am. Condon is dead. I just came to tell you. I felt you should know."

Breanna sighed with relief, not even realizing she had been holding her breath. She wrapped her shaking arms around herself as a chill ran through her body.

Annabeth let go of Breanna's arm and slid an arm around her waist. "Oh, thank God," she said in a half whisper. "Thank God!"

"Thank you for letting me know, Darrell." Breanna's voice was just above a whisper. "I guess I'll never completely get over my fear of these gunfighters who find out that John is the Stranger and know of his reputation. So often some gunfighter decides he's fast enough to outdraw and kill my husband and knows such a thing would make him a big name. It's hard enough because John wears a badge, but this makes it extra hard."

Annabeth squeezed Breanna's waist. "I think you handle it quite well, sweetie."

"I still have a deep fear inside me, Annabeth. I don't think I'll ever get over this fear as long as John's facing killers — of any kind. I'm grateful the Lord is so patient with me. As the Scripture says, 'Like as a father pitieth his children, so the LORD pitieth them that fear him. For he knoweth our frame; he remembereth that we are dust.' I know He has a plan for each of us who know Jesus as our Saviour, and I rely on His will, but I'm still human enough to have fears and worries when it comes to my dear husband and what he faces. I know the Lord understands."

"Yes, He does, Breanna," Annabeth said. "It is much the same for me with Whip."

Both women turned their attention to Darrell. He told the ladies how Brockman had warned Condon that if he drew, Brockman would have to kill him so that Condon's gun wouldn't have the chance to go off and hit someone in the crowd. Despite the chief's warning, Condon went for his gun, and Chief Brockman was forced to kill him.

Breanna sighed. "My husband is always bothered when he has to take a man's life, even though he had no choice."

"Pastor Bayless preached on that very thing a few months ago," Darrell said. "Remember?"

Both women nodded, and the three of them discussed the pastor's sermon, in which he made it clear that Christian soldiers who fight enemies in war or Christian lawmen who are forced to battle outlaws often must kill — to protect their own lives as well as others' lives.

The pastor showed from 1 Samuel 17 how Goliath, an enemy of Israel, threatened to kill David when he was just a youth, and David was forced to put Goliath down with a slingshot and cut off Goliath's head with his own sword. The pastor had then taken the congregation to Psalm 144:1, where David, as an adult, said that God had taught his hands to war and his fingers to fight. Pastor Bayless concluded that when Christian lawmen in the congregation had to kill outlaws in the course of duty, to protect innocent citizens or themselves, they were doing no wrong.

"Ladies," Darrell said, "after Chief Brockman shot Condon, some other lawmen in the crowd — county and federal — commended the chief for trying to avoid killing the gunslinger. The man gave him no choice in the matter."

Breanna closed her eyes and said aloud, "Dear Lord, thank You that John is all right."

"Amen and amen, ma'am." Darrell shifted his weight. "Well, I need to get back to Dr. Carroll's office."

"Thank you, Darrell, for coming to tell me and Annabeth about the incident."

"Yes, Darrell," Annabeth said, "thank you. Like my dear friend here, I'm so glad to learn that her husband is all right."

Late that afternoon, Dr. Matthew Carroll, who was chief administrator of Mile High Hospital but also actively practiced medicine, was closing up a very serious wound in a rancher's right arm. One of the man's bulls had plunged the tip of his left horn into the rancher's arm where it joined the shoulder.

Dr. Carroll's sister-in-law, Breanna Brockman, and Annabeth Langford assisted with the surgery. As the doctor and nurses washed up after the surgery, Dr. Carroll looked at them. "Breanna . . . Annabeth, I love having you two at my side when I'm doing surgery. In my mind, you're in the same class as Florence Nightingale when it comes to nursing."

Drying her hands on a towel, Breanna smiled. "That's quite a compliment, dear brother-in-law."

"It sure is, Doctor," Annabeth said. "Florence Nightingale became a legend in my mind when she organized that unit of thirty-eight nurses during the Crimean War and saved so many lives. I'm honored that you would put me in the same class as her."

"Me too," Breanna said. "And Miss Nightingale is doing an excellent job training nurses in that nursing school she established in London in 1860."

Dr. Carroll smiled as he finished drying his hands. "She's terrific, all right, but so are both of you — in your dedication and hard work." He looked at Breanna. "And even after learning about your husband's shootout today, you were able to keep your mind fastened on helping me repair that rancher's arm. I'm proud of you, Breanna."

Tears welled up in Breanna's sky blue eyes. "I would have been different if John had been killed."

"Of course, dear, but still, another nurse whose husband had been through a quick-draw shootout with a deadly killer — even though her husband came out the victor — probably wouldn't be able to so calmly do her job like you just did."

"That's right, Doctor," Annabeth said. "Breanna is one marvelous nurse."

Breanna placed the towel she was holding in the nearby laundry box and smiled. "Well, Annabeth, it's time for you and me to head for home."

A few minutes later, the nurses climbed into the Brockman buggy, which Breanna always drove to work, and headed for the federal building. Breanna wanted to tell her husband how glad she was that he was all right. Annabeth wanted to express her feelings about the incident to John also.

When the two women arrived at the chief U.S. marshal's office, they approached Deputy Jensen, who was on duty at the front desk.

Jensen looked up and smiled. "Hello, Mrs. Brockman. Hello, Mrs. Langford."

Breanna smiled in return. "We need to see my husband if he isn't too busy, Roland."

"Well, Chief Brockman isn't here right now, ma'am. He had some places to go in town but didn't say where."

"Oh."

Deputy Jensen's face went serious. "Ah . . . Mrs. Brockman, do you know about the chief facing that gunfighter this morning?"

"Yes. An eyewitness told Annabeth and me the whole story. I wanted to tell my husband how glad I am he came out the victor. Annabeth wanted to tell him the same thing."

"I can understand that, ma'am," Jensen said, "but I guess it'll have to wait until he comes back to the office."

"Roland, is Whip back yet?" Annabeth was aware that her husband was to make a trip that morning to deliver a subpoena to a farmer on the plains east of Denver. The subpoena summoned the farmer to appear in court on Wednesday as a witness at a trial involving a neighboring farmer who had assaulted another local man.

"He's not back yet, Mrs. Langford, but —"

"Annabeth!" At that instant, Whip stepped into the office. He strode quickly to Annabeth's side and hugged her. "You get more beautiful every time I see you."

Annabeth blushed. "Are you just getting back from delivering that subpoena?"

"Yes." He turned to Breanna. "Just before I left town, I heard about the chief taking out Killer Condon. Breanna, what a gallant man you are married to!"

"I know, Whip. I know. Annabeth and I just got off of work and came here so we could tell John how glad we are that he was the victor. But he's not here. Roland said he's somewhere in town, but he doesn't know where. So I guess I'll go on home and tell Paul, Ginny, and Meggie about it."

"Well, I'm about to head for home myself," Whip said. "You go on now, and I'll take Annabeth home on my horse."

Breanna nodded. "All right."

Annabeth wrapped her arms around Breanna. "Praise the Lord your husband is all right."

"Yes." Breanna gave her dear friend a kiss on the cheek.

Whip led Annabeth to an office at the rear of the building, saying he had to leave some papers for another deputy.

Breanna drove away from the hospital in her buggy and headed home. She was eager to tell her children that their father had had to face Kurt "Killer" Condon that morning and that he was the victor.

As she guided her mare out of town, Breanna was thankful for the quiet ride home. She praised the Lord over and over for His protection of her beloved husband. Then a brief thought of self-reproach entered her mind. *Breanna, as long as you and John have been married, you'd think you'd be beyond this fear. But it seems that every shooting incident brings forth new fears to conquer.*

She drove on, praising the Lord for keeping His mighty hand on her husband. She brought the buggy to a halt at the front porch of the ranch house, and as soon as her feet touched the ground, she saw the front door of the house open and Paul emerge. "Hi, Mama. I'll put the horse and buggy away for you."

Breanna gave him a smile. "Thank you,

son. I very much appreciate it."

Paul noted what he thought was a grim look on his mother's face. "Mama, you look a little peaked. Are you all right?"

"Oh, honey, I'm fine. But you'll understand when I tell you what happened today. Where are the girls?"

"In the kitchen, getting things ready for supper."

"Okay. Go ahead and put the horse and buggy away. Then come into the kitchen, and I'll tell all three of you."

Paul took hold of the reins and began to lead the mare toward the barn and corral, a perplexed look on his face. Breanna mounted the porch steps and entered the house.

When John Brockman rode his horse up to the ranch, his family was gathered on the front porch waiting for him. As he dismounted, the whole family raced over to him.

"Whoa, now!" John said, eyes wide. "What's this all about?"

With tears in their eyes, the whole family embraced him and began talking at once, telling him how glad they were that he was still alive.

John smiled widely at his loved ones.

"Hold on. One at a time, please. I think my big experience this morning preceded me home." He looked at his son. "Paul, would you please put Blackie in the corral and remove his saddle and bridle?"

"Sure, Papa."

"Thanks. I'll give you all a firsthand description of the shootout while we eat supper. I'm a hungry man. I haven't eaten anything since breakfast."

There was a twinkle in Breanna's eyes as she said, "Okay, girls, while your brother takes care of the horse and your father gets washed up, let's finish getting supper ready."

Breanna mounted the porch steps, and John and the girls trooped toward the kitchen behind her. Delicious aromas filled John's senses as he stepped into the kitchen.

A few minutes later, while the Brockman family ate supper together, Breanna and the children learned every detail of the fast-draw shootout John had faced.

When the meal was over, Paul looked at his family. "If it's all right, I'd like to lead in prayer and thank the Lord for protecting our papa."

All agreed, bowed their heads, and closed their eyes.

Early the next morning, President Grover

Cleveland and some of his aides arrived at Denver's Union Station from Washington, D.C. The political convention was scheduled to begin at one o'clock that afternoon in Denver's town hall.

At ten o'clock that morning, the president was alone in his hotel suite going over the notes he had prepared for the speech he'd be giving at the convention. He heard a knock on the door.

"Yes, Andrew?"

The key turned in the lock, and one of the two aides guarding the door stepped in. "Chief United States Marshal John Brockman is here to see you, Mr. President."

The president laid aside the notes and rose to his feet. "Please show him in."

John Brockman stepped into the suite, and the aide closed the door behind them. The president was amazed at how tall and broad-shouldered the dark-haired chief was. He admired the man's uniform and badge and the way he wore the gun on his hip.

John had seen photographs of the president, of course, and found that he indeed was heavyset and balding and looked every bit his fifty-one years.

The two men shook hands, and Cleveland motioned for Brockman to sit in an over-stuffed armchair as he eased into an identi-

167

cal chair facing him.

They spent almost an hour together, during which President Cleveland commended John for the fine job he was doing as chief U.S. marshal of the Western District. John thanked the president for his kind words and commended him for the good job he had done the previous three years as the twenty-second president of the United States.

They chatted about things happening in the West of late. Before long, both men stood, and John shook hands with the president again and left the suite.

ELEVEN

As John Brockman passed through the hotel lobby, the desk clerk said, "Well, Chief Brockman, did you enjoy your visit with President Cleveland?"

"Sure did, Wally."

"Good! I knew you would."

John kept walking toward the hotel's front doors. "Well, you were right."

Stepping out the right side of the double doors into the sunshine, John descended the few stairs onto the boardwalk, intending to head for the hospital. Breanna had asked him to come by after his meeting with the president and tell her how it went.

He had taken only a few steps when he saw a silver-haired man sitting next to a silver-haired woman on a bench in front of the hospital. The couple rose and headed straight toward him, looking him in the eye.

The man smiled as they drew close.

"Chief Brockman, may I speak to you for a moment?"

John stopped. "Have we met before, sir?"

The man looked up at John, who towered over him. "My name is Frank Wyrick. We've never met."

Taking his wife's hand, Frank said, "Chief Brockman, this is my wife, Lela."

John touched the edge of his wide-brimmed hat and smiled at her. "It is my pleasure to meet you, Mrs. Wyrick."

"And it is my pleasure to meet *you*, Chief Brockman."

"We're from North Platte, Nebraska, Chief Brockman," Frank said. "We have been visiting Lela's sister and her husband in Colorado Springs." He paused briefly. "I've heard much of your work as head of the United States marshal's office here in Denver. I . . . ah . . . I also know that you were once known as the Stranger and that you were faster than lightning in a quick draw — and that you *still* are. Lela and I have seen your photograph on the front page of the *North Platte Daily News* a few times."

"I see."

Frank's eyes brightened. "And we learned something else years ago."

"What's that?"

"That the Stranger was a born-again man."

John's eyes twinkled as he smiled. "You've got that right, my friend. You must know what *born again* means."

"Lela and I both do, Chief. We received the Lord Jesus Christ into our hearts as our Saviour, trusting Him and Him alone to save us, wash our sins away in His precious blood, and to take us to heaven when it is our time to leave this world."

"I sure am glad. When were the two of you saved?"

"Way back when we were courting." Lela's eyes shone. "We were invited by a man Frank had met on his job a few days earlier to attend a revival meeting at a lively church. We walked the aisle after hearing the sermon and were led to the Lord."

"Great!"

"We were baptized that night and became members of that church, and then we were married there." Frank looked lovingly at his wife. "God gave us three children as the years passed, and all three were saved when they were young."

"Wonderful!" John said.

"Let's come back to the present now," Frank said. "Lela and I arrived here by stagecoach about an hour ago. The Wells

Fargo manager and one of his men told us about how you took out Kurt Condon when he challenged you yesterday."

John nodded. "I see."

"Lela and I had some time before we need to board the coach for North Platte, so we asked the Wells Fargo men where we could find you. They told us how to find the federal building, so we went there to meet you. A deputy told us you were visiting President Cleveland and where the hotel was. When we arrived at the hotel and explained to the desk clerk that we were looking for you, we decided to wait outside on a bench so we could meet you when you came out."

"Well, I'm glad I got to meet both of you," John said, smiling.

Lela touched her husband's arm. "Tell him, honey."

"I was just getting ready, sweetie."

"Tell me what?"

Frank took a deep breath and let it out slowly. "Chief Brockman, our oldest son, Brad, was town marshal of North Platte for several years and, somewhat like you, was known for his speed on the draw."

John snapped his fingers. "Of course! Wyrick. Marshal Brad Wyrick. I heard about his fast draw but have never had the pleasure of meeting him."

Frank blinked. "Well, I'm glad you've heard of Brad, Chief. Just over a year ago, Condon came to North Platte and challenged Brad to draw against him."

Lela's face fell ashen.

"Oh?" John said.

"Brad tried to talk Condon out of it," Frank continued, "but the gunslinger wanted to gain respect for his fast draw by taking out a marshal well known for his own fast draw. Condon forced it, and Brad had no choice but to go for his gun. Condon was faster, however, and killed our son on the spot."

"I'm so sorry," John said softly.

Lela wept quietly.

With tears in his eyes, Frank touched the chief's arm. "Lela and I wanted to meet the man who took out the wicked gunslinger who killed our son."

John nodded silently.

"But praise the Lord," said Frank. "Brad is now in heaven with the Lord, and one day Lela and I will be with him there."

John smiled. "Amen. I will have the privilege of meeting Brad up there."

"Well, Lela," Frank said to his wife as she dabbed at her eyes with a hanky, "we've got to catch our ride now."

John shook hands with both of them, saying how glad he was to get to meet them, and added that they would get better acquainted in heaven. The Wyricks agreed and hurried away.

When Chief Brockman arrived at Mile High Hospital, many people greeted him and commended him for ridding the world of the blood-hungry gunfighter.

John soon found Breanna and Annabeth together, having just assisted with a serious kidney surgery on an elderly man. They walked down the hall to a small unoccupied office and sat down together.

"All right." Breanna clapped her hands together. "Tell us about your visit with President Cleveland!"

"Yes!" Annabeth chimed in. "We're so excited to hear about it."

John told them about the president's suite and how warmly he had welcomed John for the visit. He had barely begun talking when Dr. Carroll and his wife, Dottie — Breanna's sister — entered the office.

"John," Dr. Carroll said, "Breanna told us about your private appointment with President Cleveland this morning. We want to hear all about it."

John chuckled. "All right. Sit down." He

happily started over so Dr. Carroll and Dottie could hear the whole story.

By the looks on his audience's faces, John could tell they were proud to hear how the president of the United States felt about John's work as chief United States marshal of the Western District.

"Oh, darling," Breanna said, "I'm so thrilled that President Cleveland feels this way about you!"

The others chimed in quickly, putting the same feelings into their own words.

John's face flushed, and he nervously rubbed the back of his neck.

Dr. Carroll saw it. "John, you don't need to be embarrassed that the president likes your work so well. You're the best chief federal marshal in this country. The truth is the truth."

John knew he could argue the point, but no one would listen to him, so with his face still flushed, he smiled, letting his eyes finally rest on Breanna.

She smiled back. "Darling, Matthew is right. The truth is the truth."

"Amen!" Dottie said.

"*Double* amen!" Annabeth said.

John flushed a deeper red but remained silent.

■ ■ ■ ■

At the Brockman home on Thursday evening, Paul talked about the fact that his father was going to give him some further instruction on the fast draw right after supper was over.

Breanna looked at her husband. "John, you've bragged about how good Paul is at the fast draw. What's to teach him now?"

"Just some more basics on the speed, honey," John replied. "His accuracy is nearly perfect. When we set up a target, he doesn't miss the tiny spot marked for his bullet. But there's still some speed to instill in him."

Ginny giggled. "Paul, one thing is for sure. Not you or anyone else will ever be as fast on the draw as Papa is."

"I know that, little sis, but I still want to learn to draw my gun as fast as I possibly can." He chuckled, looked at his father, then back at Ginny. "My teacher is the fastest quick-draw artist on the planet. So there's plenty more he can teach me."

Ginny glanced at her father. "I'm so very proud of Papa's speed with his gun. You're right. He is the fastest on the draw of any man in this world."

"Can't argue with that," said Breanna.

176

"That's for sure." Meggie grinned widely at her papa.

Soon supper was over, and John and Paul strapped their gun belts on, ready to head out the back door together.

John looked at Ginny and Meggie. "Girls, I have a suggestion. Since your mama has been working extra long hours at the hospital this past week or so, how about you clean up the kitchen and do the dishes? Just let your mother go to the parlor and relax."

"Okay, Papa," Ginny said. "Meggie and I will do that if you can convince Mama to let us."

John looked at his lovely, though obviously weary wife. "Okay, sweetheart?"

Breanna smiled at him. "Well, since you'll remind me about what the Bible says about a wife being in subjection to her husband, I'll do as you say."

"Thank you," John said. "All right, Paul, let's go polish up your fast draw."

As Breanna headed down the hall toward the parlor and the girls began clearing the table and preparing to wash the dishes, a trickle of fear slithered down Breanna's spine. She was exceptionally proud of her husband and his fast-draw ability, knowing he used it only when there was no other way to resolve an impossible situation.

But Paul was another matter. He was already so confident with a gun, and because his father had taught him the fast draw, he was sure of his ability to follow in his father's footsteps. In her heart, Breanna knew that John would continue to teach their son well and take every precaution with him. But as Paul's mother, her deep-seated wish and hope was that Paul would change his mind about his life's work and become a doctor or take on a career that was not dangerous. *Lord,* she said in her heart, *Thy will be done in Paul's life.*

Later that evening, John entered the parlor alone, while the children were in their rooms. Breanna was reading her Bible. "So you got some rest, right?"

She smiled at him. "Yes, thanks to my husband and my daughters. And what about Paul and the fast draw?"

There was a pleased look on John's face. "Oh, honey, he's a natural. He really took to the new things I showed him this evening. He's faster than ever. And, of course, just as accurate as before."

Covering her feelings as she closed her Bible and stood up, Breanna said, "Well, like father, like son."

John grinned as she slipped into his waiting arms. "Breanna, sweetheart, our boy is going to be a tremendous lawman."

Quelling the fear in her heart, the lovely blonde whispered, "As I said, 'Like father, like son.' " In her heart she thought, *How secure I always feel with John's arms around me, and how much more secure with God's arms around me.* A deep peace flooded her heart.

On Friday morning, July 6, Ross Dover went on trial at the county courthouse for the murder of George Woodworth. Seated next to Ross was his appointed public defender. Clyde Harrison had already made it clear to Dover that he did not have a chance of being found innocent.

The courtroom was almost full of spectators, who looked on with deep interest, feeling sure they knew the outcome. Deputy U.S. marshal Whipley Langford was there sitting beside chief U.S. marshal John Brockman. Seated close to them were Sheriff Walt Carter and two of his deputies. Judge Ralph Dexter, of course, was presiding.

As the trial progressed, a dozen Denver citizens — men and women — took the stand and testified under oath as having seen Ross Dover shoot and kill George

Woodworth on the street and steal his wallet before galloping away.

Whip, who had captured and arrested the killer, gave testimony under oath before the judge, the jury, and all the observers in the courtroom. He told of finding George Woodworth's wallet in Dover's pocket when he captured him.

The jury was sent to a room to make their decision. They returned within five minutes.

When the jury was seated once again, Judge Dexter set his eyes on the jury spokesman. "Mr. Demming, has the jury reached a verdict?"

The middle-aged man stood. "We have, your honor. The jury is in one hundred percent agreement. We find the defendant, Ross Dover, guilty of murder as charged."

The judge looked at Ross Dover. "Will the defendant please rise?"

A shaky Ross Dover stood to his feet, as did the public defender.

Judge Dexter fixed his stern gaze on the defendant. "Ross Dover, because of your guilt in this heinous crime, I hereby sentence you to be hanged by the neck until dead at six o'clock next Monday morning, July 9."

The judge banged his gavel on the desk before him. "Court dismissed."

As people rose from their seats, the defender leaned over to a stone-faced Ross Dover. "Like I told you, Ross, you didn't have a chance."

Ross Dover's face was sickly pallid. Terror bubbled up like acid in his chest as he drew the tip of a shaky finger along his upper lip, pondering his fate. He could not utter a word.

The next morning, Saturday, July 7, Chief Brockman was at his desk when he heard a tap on his office door. "Chief, it's Whip. May I come in?"

"Of course."

Whip opened the door and stepped into the office holding a folded newspaper. Closing the door behind him, Whip held up the folded newspaper. "Have you seen today's edition of the *Rocky Mountain News*, Chief?"

"No, I haven't."

Whip sat down on one of the wooden chairs in front of the desk. "The front page story is about Ross Dover's murder of George Woodworth, his trial, and his upcoming execution."

"I figured it would make the front page."

"Well, you figured correctly. Denver's appointed hangman is deputy sheriff Willard Stokes, and he'll be assisted by deputy sheriff Travis Yelick. Yelick usually assists

Stokes with hangings, right?"

"Yes. In fact, for the past four years Yelick has always assisted."

"I see. Looks like it'll happen at Denver's gallows, in the 400 block of Curtis Street, downtown."

"Mm-hmm. That's so everybody who reads the paper and wants to be there will know exactly where and when it is taking place."

Whip nodded and adjusted himself on the chair. He looked Brockman in the eye. "Chief, I — I have something I want to tell you."

John leaned forward a little. "What's that?"

"Well, I — I could hardly sleep last night. I had Ross Dover on my mind, and by sunrise I felt strongly that I should go to the jail today and try to lead him to the Lord."

"You know what? I had the same thing on *my* mind. I was going to go over there after I finish this paperwork. But Whip, since you've become an excellent soul-winner and since you were the one who captured him, I'd like you to go and try to lead him to Jesus."

"All right, sir. Will you pray for the power of the Holy Spirit on me?"

"Let's pray right now."

They bowed their heads, closed their eyes, and John led in prayer, asking the Holy Spirit to fill Whip with His power as he tried to lead Ross Dover to the Lord.

When the chief closed the prayer in Jesus' name, Whip thumbed tears from his eyes. "Thank you, Chief. I'll go to the jail right now."

"I'll be praying for you, Whip."

Whip entered the county jail, Bible in hand, and one of the deputies guided him to Sheriff Carter's office. "Sheriff, I'd like to spend some time with Ross Dover if it's all right with you."

The sheriff glanced at the Bible in Whip's hand. "Well, Dover might not want to talk to you, but I'll take you to his cell and we'll find out."

When the sheriff and Whip arrived at Dover's cell, they found him sitting on the cot, his head hung low. Dover heard footsteps at his cell door and looked up. When he saw who was there with the sheriff, he swallowed hard.

"Ross, Deputy Langford has asked to spend some time with you."

Dover was angry with the man who had captured and arrested him, but when he saw the Bible in Whip's hand, he said, "That's all right with me, Sheriff."

A bit surprised, Sheriff Carter took the key ring off his belt. "I'll take the two of you to one of the rooms where attorneys meet with their clients so you can have some privacy."

The sheriff released Dover from his cell and led the two men to one of the small rooms. When they had entered and sat down at a table, the sheriff told Whip to ring the bell by the door when they were through, and one of the guards would take the prisoner back to his cell.

Whip laid his Bible on the table, then looked at the man who had less than two days to live. In a very compassionate tone, he said, "Ross, I want to talk to you about where you're going to go when you die Monday morning."

Whip's words set loose a thin quivering of dread in Ross Dover, and his blood chilled in his veins. He rubbed a nervous hand over his face. "All right. I'll listen."

TWELVE

Whip Langford silently asked the Lord for His power. "Ross, we only get one chance on this earth. When you are hanged on Monday, that's it. And when human beings die, they go to one of two places — heaven or hell. There's no third option. I want to show you from God's Word how to end up in heaven on Monday."

Ross's face paled. He licked his lips and swallowed hard.

Noting Ross's obvious fear, Whip asked, "Have you ever read the Bible, Ross? Or ever heard it preached?"

The condemned man swallowed hard again. "I haven't read it, but when I was in my teens, I had some neighbors who took me to church a few times. That preacher preached a lot about hell, and it always put me on edge."

"Oh? How come?"

"Well . . . uh . . . because the thought of

dying and going to hell — which that preacher showed from the Bible is real, literal fire — scared me."

Whip nodded. "You're aware, then, that you are a guilty sinner before God, right?"

"Yeah. That preacher gave God's definition of sin in one of his sermons. He pointed out that the Bible is God's law and that sin is the transgression of the law. He also shared a verse about how all human beings are sinners."

Whip opened his Bible to the passage he wanted, moved to Ross's side, and laid the Bible in front of him. "Here's the first verse you referred to. First John 3:4. Read it to me."

Ross looked at the page and took a short breath. " 'Whosoever committeth sin transgresseth also the law: for sin is the transgression of the law.' "

Whip flipped farther back in his Bible. "And here's the second verse you referred to. Romans 3:23. Read it."

" 'For all have sinned, and come short of the glory of God.' "

"Who is 'all,' Ross?"

"Well, uh . . . *everybody.*"

"So all humans are guilty sinners before a holy God."

"Yes."

"That includes me, and that includes you."

"Yes sir."

Whip moved back to the other side of the table, picked up the chair he had been sitting on, and carried it to where Ross was sitting. He placed the chair next to him, and sat down. "Ross, I want to tell you about this sinner you're looking at. Then we'll talk about *you*, okay?"

"Okay."

"Ross, I used to be an outlaw."

Ross Dover's eyes widened. "Really?"

"Yes. Let me tell you my story."

Whip Langford then gave Ross Dover his own testimony of having been an outlaw, though he never murdered anyone, and how chief U.S. marshal John Brockman led him to the Lord and what peace he had about where he would spend eternity.

Whip saw that he had Ross's undivided attention. "Now, Ross, you did murder George Woodworth, and murder is one of the worst sins a human being can commit. But God won't allow *any* sin into heaven. We saw that all humans are guilty sinners before a holy God, didn't we?"

"Yes."

"God hates *all* sin, Ross. But, praise God, *all* sins can be forgiven." Whip saw a slight look of relief in Ross's eyes. "Now, let me ask you something, Ross."

"Yes sir?"

Whip then asked Ross if he believed that Jesus Christ was all that the Bible claimed Him to be, and as he touched on His virgin birth, His deity, His death on the cross of Calvary, His burial, and His resurrection, Ross said he had heard a lot about all of these things and had no reason to disbelieve any of them.

"Ross, let me ask you . . . Where are you going to go when they hang you Monday?"

Fear leaped into Ross's eyes. His answer came in a tremulous voice. "To — to hell."

"As it stands right now, you're right," Whip said. "But you don't have to go there. I told you a few minutes ago that Chief Brockman led me to the Lord. And since then I've had peace about where I'll spend eternity. I'm not going to burn forever in hell like I would have if I hadn't made the Lord Jesus my Saviour. You certainly don't have to go to hell, Ross. God's only begotten Son shed His blood and died on the cross to provide a way for all sinners to be saved, forgiven of their sins, and go to heaven when they die. The choice is theirs . . . and the choice is *yours*."

Ross frowned. "You make it sound so

simple."

"God's plan of salvation for sinners is simple, Ross. It's the religious crowd that makes it seem complicated. They add religious deeds and so-called good works to getting saved, and in so doing blind people to the truth. Salvation is only in the Lord Jesus Christ, nothing added."

Whip picked up his Bible again and flipped pages for a few seconds. Then laid it on the table in front of Ross. "We're in Romans 6 now. Read verse 23 to me."

Ross took a deep breath. " 'For the wages of sin is death; but the gift of God is eternal life through Jesus Christ our Lord.' "

"Now think about it, Ross. If you get what you earned by sinning against God and His Word, it would be death, right?"

"Yes."

"That's more than physical death, Ross. In the book of Revelation, we learn that hell in its final and everlasting state is called the lake of fire. Repeatedly in Revelation, the lake of fire is called the second death. So if you die without being saved, the wages you receive for a lifetime of sin is to burn forever in the lake of fire. Understand?"

"I'm beginning to."

"Good. Now look at that verse again. Death is mentioned, but so is life — *eternal* life. That means forever with God in heaven, doesn't it?"

Ross nodded. "It *has* to."

"All right. Now notice the word *gift.* Eternal life — spending forever with God in heaven — can't be earned by good works and religious deeds. It is a gift. If you earn something, it's a *wage,* right?"

"Uh-huh."

"But if you receive it as a gift, is it earned?"

"No."

"Correct. It is by *grace.*" Whip quickly flipped pages forward in his Bible. "This is the book of Ephesians. Look here in chapter 2, and read me verses 8 and 9."

" 'For by grace are ye saved through faith; and that not of yourselves: it is the gift of God: Not of works, lest any man should boast.' "

"Do you see it, Ross?" Whip asked. "Salvation, forgiveness of your sins, and a place in heaven forever do not come from human works or religious deeds, but by God's grace, which is a gift. The word *grace* here means 'God's unmerited mercy.' Understand?"

"Yes sir. Like never before."

"Remember what it said in Romans 6:23? 'The gift of God is eternal life through . . .'

Can you finish it for me?"

"Yes. It says, 'The gift of God is eternal life *through Jesus Christ our Lord.'* "

"Right. Then salvation — eternal life — does not come through anything we can accomplish for ourselves or some religious leaders can accomplish for us. It comes *only* from the Lord Jesus Christ *Himself.* We must obtain salvation through Him and Him alone. It was Jesus who shed His sinless blood on the cross, gave His life for us, and came back from the dead so He would be alive to save every sinner who came to Him for salvation."

A faint smile crossed Ross's lips.

Whip turned back to Romans 3. Pointing to verse 24, he said, "Now, look at the verse just after the one we read earlier."

" 'Being justified freely by his grace through the redemption that is in Christ Jesus . . .' "

"To be justified, Ross, is to be able to stand before God just as if you had never sinned. Redemption is the same thing as salvation. And notice that we are justified freely. We cannot earn it. It is by *grace.* Redemption for a lost, hell-bound sinner is *where,* Ross?"

"In Christ Jesus."

"Then to miss hell and go to heaven, you

must be where redemption is, Ross. In Christ Jesus. Let me show you."

Whip turned to 2 Corinthians 5:17 and read: " 'If any man be *in Christ,* he is a new creature.' " He explained, "Jesus said in John 3 that a person must be born again to go to heaven. That is because when we are born physically, we are born sinners by nature and sinners by choice. We have to be born *again . . .* this time spiritually, which makes us each a new creature, a child of God."

Whip went on to show Ross John 1:12. "The Bible says of the Lord Jesus Christ, 'But as many as received him, to them gave he power to become the sons of God.' And Ephesians 3:17 says we must receive Him into our hearts — not the muscle that pumps the blood in our bodies, but the *center of the soul,* which is the heart of every human being."

Whip then turned to 1 Corinthians 15:17. "Read this verse aloud, Ross."

" 'And if Christ be not raised, your faith is vain; ye are yet in your sins.' "

Whip looked him in the eye. "If there were no risen Saviour, Ross, where would every person be?"

"In their sins."

"Right. But there *is* a risen Saviour, isn't there?"

"Yes."

"But if you are not *'in Christ,'* Ross, as 2 Corinthians 5:17 says, according to 1 Corinthians 15:17, where are you?"

Ross's features were pale. "I — I'm in my sins."

"Right. Do you realize there are only two ways to die? In Christ or in your sins."

Ross wiped a shaky hand over his forehead. "I — I realize it now, sir."

"Do you want to be saved so you can die in Christ and not in your sins?"

Tears welled up in Ross Dover's eyes. "Yes, I do."

Whip flipped to Romans 10, placed the Bible in front of Ross again, and said, "Read me verses 9 through 13."

Ross's heart was pounding against his rib cage. " 'That if thou shalt confess with thy mouth the Lord Jesus, and shalt believe in thine heart that God hath raised him from the dead, thou shalt be saved. For with the heart man believeth unto righteousness; and with the mouth confession is made unto salvation. For the scripture saith, Whosoever believeth on him shall not be ashamed. For there is no difference between the Jew and the Greek: for the same Lord over all is rich

193

unto all that call upon him. For whosoever shall call upon the name of the Lord shall be saved.' "

Whip paused momentarily. "Notice the use of the word *heart.* Verse 9 says you must believe in your *heart.* Verse 10 says it is with the *heart* that a person believes unto righteousness. A person can believe about Jesus in his mind, Ross, but that doesn't save him. As I said, the heart is the very center of the soul. You must receive Jesus into your heart as your own personal Saviour. You do that by repenting of your sin and doing what it says here in Romans 10:13 — *call* upon Him."

Whip cleared his throat and continued. "Scripture makes it plain that the death, burial, and resurrection of the Lord Jesus is the gospel. In Mark 1:15, Jesus said, 'Repent ye, and believe the gospel.' Repentance is to acknowledge to the Lord that you are a guilty, hell-deserving sinner but that you are turning from your sin and unbelief unto Jesus and asking Him to come into your heart and be your Saviour."

Tears were now streaming down Ross Dover's cheeks. "Deputy Langford," he said with a trembling voice, "I *do* believe the gospel, and I *am* ready to call on the Lord Jesus in repentance and ask Him to come into my heart, forgive me of all my sins, and save me *right now!*"

Whip closed his Bible and put his arm around Ross's shoulders. "Let's bow our heads, and you do exactly as you just said."

When Ross had finished his prayer for salvation, Whip kept his arm around the man, and with his own tears flowing, he asked the Lord to give Ross a full measure of peace when he faced the gallows Monday morning.

Wiping tears from his cheeks, Ross said, "Deputy Langford, thank you for coming and showing me how to be saved. It's only natural that I want to live, but I know for sure that when I die on Monday, I will go to heaven to be with my Saviour."

Wiping his own tears away, Whip stood to his feet. "And one day I'll meet you in heaven, Ross."

Whip went to the door and rang the bell to call the guard on duty. The guard escorted Ross to his cell with Whip at his side. Just before Ross entered the cell, Whip gave him a brotherly embrace and told him he'd be there on Monday morning. He asked the guard to supply Ross with one of the Bibles from the jail's library. Whip encouraged Ross to read certain books of Scripture before he left.

When Whip arrived back at Chief Brockman's office and told him that his prayers
had been answered, both men rejoiced. Ross
Dover had repented of his sin and received
the Lord Jesus as his Saviour.

John praised the Lord at the good news,
wiping tears from his eyes, and suggested
that they go tell Pastor Bayless about it.

A tear ran down Pastor Bayless's cheek
when he heard the story. He promised he'd
go to the jail right then and encourage Ross
before Monday arrived. Both Whip and
John thanked him.

As the two men left the pastor's office,
John told Whip that Breanna was not working at the hospital that day. He was going to
ride home right then and tell her and the
children about Ross's salvation. Whip said
he would head for the hospital and tell
Annabeth the good news.

Whip asked at the nurses' desk where
Annabeth was and was told she was helping
one of the surgeons with a minor surgery
on a teenage boy but would be finished in
just a few minutes. Whip waited outside the
operating room as his lovely wife came out.

Annabeth smiled at him, batting her
eyelashes. "Well, hello, darling. What brings
you here?"

"Some wonderful news . . ."

"Did — did Ross Dover get saved?"

Whip folded her into his arms. "He sure did, honey! He sure did!"

Clinging to him as people passed by them, Annabeth wept tears of joy. When her weeping subsided, Whip said, "I'll tell you the details at home this evening, but I just had to come and let you know that your prayers had been answered."

When John arrived at the Brockman ranch, he sat Breanna, Paul, Ginny, and Meggie down on the front porch. Then with a big smile, he told them about Whip leading Ross Dover to Jesus at the jail that morning. There was much rejoicing at this good news.

John rubbed his forehead. "From what Whip told me when we were on our way to Pastor Bayless's office, Ross seems to have real peace now about what is coming Monday."

"Only the God of heaven could give him that kind of peace."

Little Meggie suddenly began to cry. Sadness was written all over her face as the tears spilled down her cheeks. Breanna started to get up to go to Meggie, but John was ahead of her. He lifted the weeping girl in his arms. "Meggie, what are you crying about?

Why are you so sad?"

She eased back in his arms, looked him in the eye through her film of tears, and said, "Papa, I don't understand why Mr. Dover has to hang and die. Now that he is saved and God has forgiven him of all his sins, even the murder of Mr. Woodworth, why does he have to be hanged? Can't everyone forgive him and let him live?"

Meggie looked pleadingly at her stepfather, her blue eyes flooded with tears. "I — I just can't believe that man has to die."

"Oh, honey," John said, "if only it were that simple. You see, Ross Dover broke one of the laws of the land by murdering Mr. Woodworth, and it's because of the established law that he must die. Yes, God has forgiven him, and we as Christians have forgiven him, but there is always a price to pay for our actions. The consequences must be paid. Society looks at Mr. Dover as a murderer, one who wickedly took another man's life, and the consequence for that is death. He knew that when he committed the murder. Taking another person's life is indeed a great injustice."

Kissing Meggie's teary cheek, John looked deep into her sad eyes. "The precious truth here is that because Ross Dover took Jesus into his heart as his Saviour, the God of heaven has forgiven him for the murder and all his other sins. By Jesus' precious blood, Mr. Dover's sins have been washed away forever. But the laws of man must still be upheld."

John took a clean white handkerchief from his hip pocket and used it to wipe Meggie's tear-stained face. "Do you understand better, little pumpkin?"

Taking a moment to process what her papa had told her, Meggie looked at him, her eyes still somewhat troubled. "I understand better, Papa, but it still makes me sad."

John kissed Meggie's cheek again. "Well, my sweet, many things in this life we humans don't fully understand, and that sometimes causes us to be sad. But always remember that God — and God alone — knows what's best for *all* of His born-again children. And just think, honey, Mr. Dover will be in heaven instantly when he dies at the end of that rope. There is no place that can match heaven. He will be with the Lord Jesus, where all is peace and goodness."

Meggie sniffed and blinked at the remainder of her tears. "You're right, Papa. I sure don't understand all of this, but I know Jesus loves all His children, and Mr. Dover will be very happy when he is with Jesus."

Meggie wrapped her arms around her papa's neck and gave him a tight hug. "I love you, Papa."

John kissed her cheek again. "I love you too, Meggie girl."

"We *all* do, Meggie," said Breanna.

THIRTEEN

On Sunday, July 8, in the morning service at First Baptist, Pastor Bayless asked Whip to come to the platform.

Whip left his seat beside Annabeth, not sure what was happening. He mounted the platform and stepped up beside the pastor.

The pastor put an arm around Whip's shoulder and then spoke to the congregation, telling them about Whip leading murderer Ross Dover to the Lord. There were many "amens" from both men and women in the crowd.

Pastor Bayless then told the crowd how well he himself had been received when he visited Ross Dover Saturday afternoon and of the peace the newborn child of God had in the face of dying on the gallows on Monday morning.

There was much rejoicing among the crowd, and when the service was over, several people told Whip how much they appreciated the burden he had for the soul of the murderer.

As the Langfords and the Brockmans walked toward the wagon they had shared to drive to church, Annabeth turned to Breanna. "May I ask you something, Breanna?"

The lovely blonde nodded and smiled. "Of course."

A slight frown touched Annabeth's brow. "Are . . . are you going to attend the hanging in the morning? I know that women here in the West do."

Breanna's words seemed to cascade over one another. "Annabeth, I don't usually attend hangings, but I'm going to be there because I want to say a few words of encouragement to Ross before he dies."

"I had thought of doing the same thing if the officers would allow me to speak to him before they hang him."

"That's great, sweetheart," Whip said joyfully. "I know you'll be a blessing to Ross. And so will Breanna."

John agreed.

Paul flashed questioning eyes at his father.

Knowing what his son was about to ask, John said, "No, Paul. You can't attend the hanging. You know that Sheriff Carter has strict rules about teenagers and children attending hangings. Only adults are allowed to do so."

"I only wanted to say something encouraging to him since he is going to die as a Christian, Papa."

"I appreciate that, son, but Sheriff Carter will not bend on this rule."

Meggie looked at Ginny. "I'm sure glad for the rule. I don't want to go to that hanging."

"Me neither."

As they reached the Brockman wagon, John said, "You ladies can take the buggy to town as usual in the morning since you'll need to go on to work afterward. Whip and I will ride our horses to town as usual so we can get on over to the office."

Just before six o'clock the next morning, a small crowd gathered on the front side of the gallows on Curtis Street in downtown Denver as the sun's early light spread over the city. Among them were John and Breanna Brockman, Whip and Annabeth Langford, and Pastor and Mrs. Bayless. About a dozen other men and women of First Baptist Church joined them. In addition were some eighty people from Denver and the surrounding area.

People in the crowd were talking quietly about the hanging that would take place in a matter of minutes when a wagon pulled up and stopped about thirty yards from the front side of the gallows. Sheriff Walt Carter rode alongside the wagon on his horse. On the driver's seat, prisoner Ross Dover sat between the two official hangmen, deputy sheriff Willard Stokes and deputy sheriff Travis Yelick.

The tailgate was down, exposing the black coffin in the bed of the wagon.

The crowd watched as the two hangmen hopped off the driver's seat and helped Ross Dover down, his hands shackled behind his back.

Chief Brockman told the others in his group to wait there and hurried across the yard to the sheriff. "My wife and Deputy Langford's wife would both like to say a few words to your prisoner."

"Of course, Chief. But they'll need to make it brief."

"Will do," Brockman assured him as he made a half turn and motioned for Breanna, Annabeth, and Whip.

The two hangmen held their prisoner firmly by the arms and looked on with the sheriff as Chief Brockman said quietly, "I think you know who I am, Ross."

Dover nodded. "Yes, Chief Brockman. I believe you know that I used to live here in

Denver a few years ago."

"Yes."

"Well, sir, I knew very well who you were, though we never actually met personally. And . . . I, uh, know from Deputy Langford what you did for him to see a powerful change in his life."

John smiled kindly as Breanna stepped up beside him, and Whip and Annabeth moved up on his other side. "Yes, Ross. And because of that same powerful change in your own life, which Whip brought to you from the same source, my wife, Breanna, and Whip's wife, Annabeth, would like to say a few words to you."

Ross looked at the ladies as they stepped closer to him.

Breanna and Annabeth introduced themselves and told Ross how glad they were he had listened to Whip and had opened his heart to the Lord Jesus Christ.

Ross managed a smile. "Ladies, I'm glad I listened to Whip too."

"Mr. Dover," Breanna said, "Sheriff Carter said we needed to make this little talk brief, so let me tell you something that God's Word says about your dying today."

Ross's features paled. "Yes ma'am."

"In 2 Corinthians 5:8, we are told that when those of us who have made Jesus our

205

Saviour leave this body on earth, we are then absent from the body but present with the Lord. So when we die, we are instantly in heaven with Jesus." She swallowed hard. "When — when you drop to the end of that rope in a few minutes, Mr. Dover, you will instantly leave this world and be in the presence of your Saviour in heaven. I know Whip has already given you many Scriptures about dying and going to heaven, but I just wanted to give you this one in case he hadn't."

"Not that one, Breanna," Whip said. "Thank you."

Ross's eyes filled with tears. "Th-thank you, Mrs. Brockman. Thank you very much. And thank you, Mrs. Langford, for caring enough to come and talk to me. God bless you."

Sheriff Carter looked at John. "All right, Chief, we need to get him to the gallows now."

John nodded, and they followed the sheriff and the two hangmen as they ushered Ross Dover toward the gallows.

When the hangmen and the sheriff reached the gallows, John and his group joined the crowd. Sheriff Carter halted at the bottom of the steps and watched as Deputies Stokes and Yelick led Ross Dover up to the platform some fifteen feet above the ground. They stood Dover on the trap-door, directly beneath the hangmen's rope that dangled in the breeze directly above his head.

Stokes reached up toward the noose, but before he grasped it, Ross interrupted him. "Deputy Stokes, may I speak to the crowd for a moment before you put the noose on me?"

Stokes looked down at the sheriff, and Carter nodded his consent. "Yes, you may, but only briefly."

His hands still cuffed behind his back, Ross fixed his gaze on the crowd and spoke so all could hear. "All of you know that I am a criminal and that not only did I rob and steal, but I murdered and robbed George Woodworth."

Ross stared at Whip Langford. "Folks, it was deputy U.S. marshal Whip Langford who trailed me and, with the help of his pet wolf, Timber, captured me and put me in jail. But Deputy Langford also did something else. He came to me at the jail this past Saturday morning with his Bible and led me to Jesus Christ. He showed me clearly from the Bible that salvation from hell and the wrath of God is *only* in the Lord Jesus Christ and His finished work at Calvary — nothing added. Seeing that truth, I called on the Lord Jesus in repentance of my sins and received Him into my heart as my own personal Saviour. When I die here today, I am going to heaven."

The Christians in the crowd smiled and nodded.

Ross looked toward the wagon, and tears filled his eyes. "The coffin in the bed of that wagon is for me. Because the Lord Jesus is my Saviour, when my body is placed in that coffin, my soul will be in heaven."

The Christians gave open praise to the Lord at that statement.

Sheriff Carter then commanded the two hangmen to carry out their duty. Deputy Stokes dropped the noose over Ross's head and cinched it tight on his neck. Seconds later, Yelick stood a few feet from the trapdoor and pulled the lever that opened the trapdoor and dropped Ross Dover to his death.

Moments later, when Ross's body hung dead and the crowd began to disperse, some of them quite emotional, John put his arm around Whip's shoulders and said, "Well, Whip, Ross is in heaven with Jesus now — even though he was a murderer — because he repented of his sins and received Jesus his Saviour. *You,* my friend, showed him how to be saved."

Whip wiped his tears. "What a precious privilege, Chief. Even though he was a murderer, he got saved!"

"Amen!" John said. "Remember 1 John 1:7, where the Word says that for all people who have received God's Son as their Saviour, 'the blood of Jesus Christ his Son cleanseth us from *all* sin.' That includes the sin of murder and, praise God, Ross is in heaven right now!"

Annabeth and Breanna, as well as Pastor Bayless and Mary, heard what John had said and they rejoiced together in that powerful scriptural truth.

The chief expressed his appreciation to Pastor Bayless for visiting Ross at the jail. Then he told Breanna and Annabeth that he hoped they would have a good day at the hospital. "Whip, I'll see you later, at the office." John mounted his horse and rode off.

Whip watched Breanna and his wife drive away in the Brockman buggy, then looked toward the wagon and saw Deputies Stokes and Yelick lifting the black coffin into the wagon's bed. They had already taken Ross Dover's body from the rope and placed it in the coffin.

Whip quickly made his way to the wagon, just as both deputies were hopping down.

Whip asked them who would bury the body.

Stokes told him that the mortician who had sold them the coffin had dug the grave at Denver's cemetery. As the county hangmen, it was their job to take the coffin to the cemetery and bury it.

Burying executed criminals in Denver had been Yelick's job for almost ten years. The past four years, he'd had Stokes's assistance. It was this way in towns all over the West. Since the law hanged criminals, it fell on the appointed county hangmen to take care of the burials.

Whip hadn't been aware of this and thanked them for explaining it and for their care in this matter.

As John Brockman rode back from the gallows along the busy downtown street, he passed the Wells Fargo office just as a stagecoach pulled to a halt.

From inside the coach, a man called out, "Chief Brockman, I need to talk to you!"

Recognizing the voice, John pulled rein. It was Marvin Grange, the owner of Rocky Mountain Gun and Ammunition Shop.

Grange, a man in his late forties, stepped out of the coach, and John guided his horse toward him. "What do you need to talk to me about, Marv?"

Grange stepped up beside Blackie while the other passengers and the crew alighted from the coach and went about their own business. He looked up at the lawman. "Chief, there's something you need to know. I left Denver a week ago Monday for Fort Collins. I know all about your having to shoot down Kurt Condon on Tuesday. The story was in both of Fort Collins's papers on Thursday. When I boarded the stagecoach this morning to come home, only one other man was aboard, Hugh Stedman."

John frowned. "You mean Hugh Stedman, the big-name gunfighter?"

"Yes sir. And as we rode south out of Fort Collins, Stedman admitted that he had been planning to go to Denver and challenge the Stranger, now chief U.S. marshal John Brockman, to a quick-draw shootout. He said he was sure he could outdraw Brockman and make a bigger name for himself. Then he told me that he had read in the *Fort Collins Daily News* of last Tuesday's quick draw between you and Kurt 'Killer' Condon."

John's features were stolid.

Marvin Grange chuckled. "At that point, Chief, Stedman said he had never challenged Condon because of his exceptional speed and accuracy. Since John 'the Stranger' Brockman had taken him out so handily, he said he'd never challenge you now. I told him he would be a fool to challenge the Stranger. We were pulling into the town of Longmont right about then. As Stedman got off the stage, he looked at me and said he'd never be that kind of fool."

"Good," John said levelly. "One less gunfighter for me to battle." Then he smiled warmly. "Thanks, Marv, for letting me know about this. I'd better move along to my office."

Marvin Grange smiled back and watched the chief U.S. marshal ride away.

When John arrived at his office, Deputy Dickson, who was on desk duty, handed him a large brown envelope that had come a few minutes earlier by special delivery. It was from the federal marshal's office in Riverton.

John hurried to his private office, closed the door, and sat down at his desk. He hoped it contained good news concerning Marshal Hawson and the pursuit of the despicable Zarbo gang.

Once John opened the envelope with his large letter opener, he found several Wanted posters on each of the three Zarbo brothers, along with a separate white envelope. The letter was on Marshal Hawson's stationery but was written by one of Hawson's deputies, Ken Jackson.

John hastily read Deputy Jackson's letter. During Marshal Hawson's pursuit of the Zarbo brothers, the outlaws had discovered that the four lawmen were pursuing them and had ambushed them near Laramie. They shot all four lawmen.

When they quickly examined the men, the outlaws thought all four were dead, having only checked to see if they were breathing. They jumped on their horses and rode south toward the Colorado border.

As it turned out, Marshal Hawson was still alive, three bullets in his body, but had kept his eyes closed and held his breath when the Zarbos looked him over. Shortly after the outlaws rode away, Marshal Hawson saw a farmer and his two teenage sons coming along the road in a wagon and was able to move enough and call out to gain their attention. They put him and the three dead deputies in the bed of the wagon and rushed the wounded marshal to the hospital in Laramie.

Deputy Jackson went on to say in the letter that Marshal Hawson was now home in Riverton and recovering under his doctor's care. He had asked Jackson to write this letter and to send the Wanted posters to Chief Brockman so they could be posted in Denver, since the Zarbos were headed that direction.

Marshal Hawson said that if the three Zarbos showed up in Colorado and Chief Brockman could lead in their capture, they should be hanged immediately. Not only did Hawson witness Todd, Chice, and Lee Zarbo kill his deputies in cold blood as well as trying to kill *him,* but all four Zarbos had already been sentenced to be hanged in Montana last year for numerous murders but had escaped.

John picked up the posters again. All three said, Wanted: Dead or Alive, and the posters also clearly stated that all three men were convicted thieves and murderers. John nodded and told himself that the courts would back any lawmen who hanged Todd, Chice, and Lee Zarbo immediately upon capture.

He bowed his head and prayed right then, asking the Lord to see to it that the Zarbos were caught soon so they did not murder anyone else.

John opened his eyes and studied the faces of the three outlaws. They were probably coming to Colorado, since things were pretty hot for them in Wyoming. It was no doubt the same in Montana and Idaho too.

Rising from his desk, John picked up one of each of the posters, took a small hammer from a desk drawer, and hurried out his office door. He walked to the big board of Wanted posters on the front of the building and removed three other posters from the center of the board so he could tack the Zarbo posters in the very center, where they would be prominently seen.

While he pounded the tacks in place, Deputy Jensen came down the boardwalk and noted what the chief was doing. He focused on the three new posters. "Hey, Chief, how did you get those posters of the Zarbo brothers?"

"One of Marshal Hawson's deputies in Riverton sent them. Let me finish getting them tacked on, and I'll explain it to you."

A couple minutes later, with the three new posters in place, John told Deputy Jensen about the letter he had received advising him of what had happened with Marshal Hawson and his deputies and saying that the Zarbos were headed for the Colorado border.

"I saw you had to take a few posters off the wall to make space for the Zarbos. It's a good thing all the head law officers in the western states and territories don't send every poster of every outlaw to one another, or we'd have to cover the entire building just to post them all."

The chief grinned. "I agree, Roland. Of course, such posters are sent to other states and territories when particular outlaws are believed to be heading in a certain direction."

"Yes sir."

"I wish it were possible to have posters on all wanted outlaws in the West because many times they go to other states and territories unbeknownst to the head lawmen. Such a thing, however, is impossible."

Deputy Jensen sighed. "You're right, Chief."

"Until it is, we'll be grateful for crack marshals like Hawson who think to keep us in the loop."

FOURTEEN

In Fort Collins, some sixty miles north of Denver and less than thirty miles south of the Colorado-Wyoming border, Todd, Chice, and Lee Zarbo were sitting on a bench on College Avenue's boardwalk across from First National Bank.

The Zarbo brothers had been talking about robbing the bank. Todd, who was sitting between Chice and Lee, opened a copy of the *Fort Collins Daily News* they had found on the bench when they sat down. One page gave some details on the history of Fort Collins. Todd read the brief article to his brothers.

In 1864, a military outpost had been established there and named Fort Collins for its commander, Lieutenant William O. Collins of Fort Laramie, Wyoming. The outpost was abandoned in 1872, but the civilian settlement around the fort was already growing at the time, and a good-size town was now there, so the town kept the name Fort Collins.

Chice commented on the tremendous growth of the civilian settlement around the fort in just sixteen years while Todd flipped through the paper. Suddenly he stopped and began reading an article.

"What are you reading now?" Lee asked.

"Let me finish it, and I'll tell you."

A minute later Todd shook his head. "Boys, you're not gonna believe this article. See that bank across the street we were talking about robbing? Well, this article is about the bank president, Horace Richards, and his wife, Ellen. They're celebrating their forty-seventh wedding anniversary today. All their children and grandchildren have come to Fort Collins for the day, it says, to join in the celebration. The article has a photograph of the Richardses' house, on Whitcomb Street, number 322."

Chice frowned at Todd. "So what's so exciting about that?"

Todd chuckled. "I have an idea. Instead of just walking into the bank and robbing it at gunpoint, as we've done many times before — and would instantly have the law on our trail — we should kidnap the president's wife. We know where the house is. We'd do it while her husband was at work and leave him a note telling him we're holding his wife captive and we'll kill her unless he leaves a package with fifty thousand dollars at a designated place."

Chice chuckled. "I like your idea, Todd."

"Me too." Lee grinned evilly. "Tell us more."

"Sure. The note for Mr. Richards will also say that only one of us will pick up the money and the others will stay with his wife until we have it. And that nobody had better be watching or following the person picking up the money. If our instructions aren't followed perfectly, the president's wife will die. If he does what we say, Mrs. Richards will be set free unharmed."

Lee punched a fist in the air. "Yeah! That's good, Todd."

"And think of this, guys," Chice said. "Since we've never committed crimes in Colorado or even *been* in Colorado, none of the county or federal law offices have our faces on Wanted posters. We won't have to worry about someone around here recognizing us and advising lawmen of our presence. If the bank president follows our instructions, we'll set his wife free and take the money and run." Chice frowned at his brothers. "We *will*, won't we?"

"Yeah." Todd nodded. "We'll keep our

word to him."

"It's only right that we do." Lee leaned forward with his hands on his knees. "By the time Mrs. Richards could describe us to lawmen, we'll be long gone and no one will know where to look for us." His eyebrows arched as he smiled. "And we'll have that fifty thousand dollars."

"We sure will." Chice said.

"Yep," agreed Todd. "I figure the best way to kidnap the bank president's wife is to have Lee clad in a dress like a woman, like he did at that party in Helena last year — wearing the wig and makeup. He could knock on her door, hold Mrs. Richards at gunpoint, and take her away from the house. Lee could walk close and keep the gun hidden. Anyone who saw them on the street would think that the unfamiliar woman was one of Mrs. Richards's friends from out of town. Lee will leave the note to her husband at the house."

Chice laughed loudly. "This will work, Todd. It will work."

"I've got a *good* idea, huh?"

Lee joined in their laughter. "For years you guys have kidded me about my high-pitched voice. This is one time that'll come in mighty handy!"

"Indeed it will," Todd said. "You can really

put it to good use this time!"

Chice laughed. "Yeah, fifty thousand dollars of good use."

"Since I'm gonna be the star of this caper," Lee said, "I oughta get a little extra money."

"We'll see about that," Todd said.

Chice stood up and poked Lee in the ribs with his finger. "I well remember that party in Helena, when you showed up in a dress, wearing makeup and a wig of long hair. You fooled everybody! You had shaved clean so no stubble showed beneath the makeup, and you made your voice so soft and feminine while expertly using mannerisms that were totally feminine."

"Tell you what, Chice, I'll even do it better this time. I'll make a quick ride to Cheyenne and go to the women's clothing store. I'll buy everything I need and tell the person who waits on me that I'm buying it for my wife. If I did it here in Fort Collins, someone might figure it out if Mrs. Richards lives to tell the story."

"I'm exceedingly happy with the plan," Todd said.

"Me too." Chice playfully poked Lee in the ribs again.

"We need to find a place outside of town where we can hold the bank president's wife hostage, somewhere close to whatever spot we choose for the money to be left."

"I know a good spot where we can have Mr. Richards leave the money for us." Chice leaned in close. "Remember the bridge over the Cache la Poudre River we crossed to come into town?"

Todd and Lee both nodded.

"That'd be excellent," Todd said. "We could tell Richards to put the moneybag at a certain spot underneath the floorboards of the bridge. Then we can make camp close by in the area just north of the riverbank, where it's thick with trees and bushes. From there we can't be seen, but we can position ourselves so *we* can watch the bridge and anybody who crosses or approaches it."

"Good idea," Chice said.

Lee stood up. "Let's mount our horses, ride to the bridge right now, and pick the spot for our camp."

Todd tore the article out of the newspaper along with the photograph of the bank president's house, folded it up, and placed it in his shirt pocket.

The Zarbo brothers made their way a short distance to the hitching post where their horses were tied. They mounted up and headed north out of Fort Collins.

When they reached the bridge they had

discussed, they looked the area over. They found a choice spot in the nearby woods to make camp. From there they could see the bridge but not be seen by anyone on the road or on the bridge. They set up their campsite.

Then Lee told his brothers he'd be back as soon as possible and galloped toward Cheyenne.

Todd and Chice left their horses tied in the woods where they couldn't be seen and hurried to the bridge. They soon found a perfect spot beneath the heavy wooden floor at the east edge, where the moneybag could be placed safely out of sight and be in no danger of falling into the river.

When they returned to the campsite, Todd took paper and pencil out of his saddlebag, and he and Chice sat down against trees and began to write the letter to bank president Horace Richards. Todd made sure the banker would clearly understand that if he did not cooperate fully, Mrs. Richards would be killed.

The two men rode into town and walked their horses slowly down Whitcomb Street until they came to the house marked 322, the house pictured in the newspaper.

As they rode slowly past the house, Todd glanced at his brother. "Well, Chice, now we can tell Lee exactly where the house is located."

As they headed back in the direction of the campsite, riding side by side, Todd furrowed his brow. "I've been thinking. Lee should have a horse and buggy to transport Mrs. Richards from her house to the campsite."

"I hadn't thought about how he would get her to the campsite, but you're right. Lee will need a horse and buggy to do it. It'll look like a normal situation with two women riding together."

"Right. Let's look around town and find a stable where horses and buggies are rented out. There must be two or three such stables in a town this size."

Guiding their horses onto the town's main thoroughfare, Todd and Chice soon found just such a stable. While Todd waited a half block from the stable with their horses, Chice went into the stable and rented a horse and a low-built buggy, paying a two-day fee. When he met up with Todd, they decided to go to a store to buy food to take to their camp. With the food loaded in the buggy, they headed back to the campsite, Todd leading Chice's horse while Chice drove the buggy.

Late that afternoon, Todd and Chice

watered their horses at the river, and as they were leading them back to the campsite, they caught sight of Lee riding toward them from the north. He had a large cloth bag tied behind his saddle.

Lee put his horse to a trot and soon drew up to his brothers. "If I'm thinking right, you just watered your horses at the river."

"You're thinking right," Chice said.

"I'll go water mine right now," Lee said. "Then I'll come to the campsite and show you what I bought in Cheyenne."

Fifteen minutes later, Lee rode his horse onto the campsite. His brothers had taken the bridles and saddles from their horses, tied their steeds to trees in the nearby woods, and were now sitting on the ground, leaning against a couple of trees. Lee dismounted and set the large cloth bag on the ground. He removed the saddle and bridle from his own horse and led him to where the other horses were tied.

When Lee returned to where his brothers were sitting, Todd asked, "You gonna show us what's in the bag?"

Lee picked up the bag. "Sure am."

The first object he took from the bag was a pink and white gingham dress with long sleeves. He held it up against his body and chuckled. "Figured long sleeves would hide

225

my masculine arms, just like the one I wore in Helena."

Chice laughed. "You sure don't want those big biceps showing!"

Todd laughed as well. "The bustle inside the dress will look cute on you. It'll really add to your femininity."

Lee ignored their comments and laughter. "You will note that the dress goes all the way to my ankles as well. It will almost cover the lace-up woman's shoes I bought." Placing the dress over his shoulder, he bent down and pulled out the two white lace-up shoes. "See?"

"Oh, beautiful," Chice drawled.

Lee then showed them the long blond wig, sunbonnet, makeup powder, rouge, and lipstick he had purchased, as well as white gloves to disguise his hands.

Chice was grinning from ear to ear. "Lee, you certainly know how to prepare to look like a woman."

"Well, boys, it's my part in getting that fifty thousand dollars for us."

Todd stood. "Now it's time for you to see what we rented for you."

Lee put the items he had purchased back in the bag. His brothers led him past their horses, deeper into the woods, where they had stashed the horse and buggy. Todd explained why he felt Lee would need the buggy, and Lee agreed that it would make it a lot easier.

The Zarbo brothers returned to the campsite, and Todd let Lee read the message he had written for him to leave in the Richards' house for the bank president to find.

"So you found a good place under the bridge for Richards to leave the moneybag?"

"Sure did," replied Todd. "Everything is all set."

"Good. I'm ready!" Lee rubbed his hands together.

On Tuesday morning, the Zarbo brothers rose from their sleeping bags a short time after sunrise.

While Todd and Chice were preparing breakfast, Lee shaved behind a nearby tree, then used a hand mirror he carried in one of his saddlebags to put on the makeup. He slid into the pink and white dress, donned the blond wig, topped the wig with the sunbonnet, and put on the women's shoes.

When he walked over to the campfire for breakfast, his brothers looked at him wide-eyed. "Wow, Todd. He looks more like a woman this time than he did at the party in Helena."

"For sure," said Todd and commented on

how well Lee had applied the rouge and lipstick.

The sunbonnet really helped him look like a woman, especially the way he had it fixed on the blond wig.

Todd snickered. "Since you're blond, Lee, it helps it all go together perfectly."

Lee dipped his right hand into the fluffy pocket on the side of the dress and pulled out a short-barreled .38-caliber revolver he had bought in Cheyenne. "This will come in handy when I kidnap Ellen Richards. I'll be able to press it against her side without anyone seeing it. But she'll *feel* it, I guarantee you!"

"Good thinking, Lee." Todd leaned down toward the pan over the fire. "Well, breakfast is ready. Let's eat!"

During breakfast, as the Zarbo brothers sat on the ground around the cook fire, with Lee perched on his bedroll to keep the dress clean, Todd and Chice told Lee exactly how to find the Richards house. They would be waiting right there at the campsite for him to show up with his captive.

Todd added, "Lee, when Chice and I were in town, we drove right past the bank and noticed a sign on the front door that said the bank opens at nine o'clock. I figure the president is likely there earlier than nine.

So, if you arrive at the Richards house by nine o'clock, Mr. Richards should be long gone."

Lee sipped hot coffee from a cup. He swallowed. "Makes sense. That's what I'll do."

The Zarbo brothers finished their breakfast. Then, while Todd and Chice began washing the dishes, Lee went into the woods and soon reappeared, leading the rented horse by the reins with the rented buggy trailing behind.

"Well, fellas," Lee said, placing the reins at the front of the buggy, "guess I'd better get going so I can knock on Mrs. Richards's door by nine o'clock." He reached down and slipped the .38 into his dress pocket, pulled on the white gloves, and hopped up onto the buggy seat.

"Oops!" he admonished himself. "I'll have to remember to walk like a lady and climb into the buggy like a lady. No more hopping."

Todd and Chice laughed. Then Todd looked at his pocket watch. "It's twenty-five minutes to nine, Lee. Better get going."

Lee took the reins in hand, looked at his brothers, and in his female voice said, "Be back with the hostage in a little while."

"See you then, missy." Todd waved delicately.

As Lee drove toward town, he practiced his female voice some more and felt quite confident. He drove up in front of the bank president's house at precisely nine o'clock. Being careful to move like a woman, he stepped down from the driver's seat, checked for his gun, and walked toward the front porch.

When he reached the porch, he moved carefully up the steps, approached the door, and gave it a few light taps.

Lee heard footsteps, and the door opened.

Lee smiled in a friendly manner, using the feminine voice he had invented. "Mrs. Richards, my name is Lee Ann Smith. May I talk to you for a minute?"

Ellen Richards appeared totally relaxed at his presence because she believed he was a woman. She smiled and pulled the door open wider. "Of course. Please come in."

As Mrs. Richards closed the door behind him, she asked, "Have we met before, Miss Smith?"

Lee quickly pulled the .38-caliber revolver from the dress pocket, cocked it, and pointed it between her eyes.

Ellen gasped. "Wha-a-a-what is it you want, young woman?"

Maintaining the feminine voice and mannerisms, Lee held the muzzle of the gun steady, still pointed between her eyes, and said quietly, "You are being kidnapped, Mrs. Richards, but if you do just as I say, you will not be harmed." He pulled the folded paper from the dress pocket. "I have a message here for your husband. If both you and he do as directed, I promise, you will not be harmed."

The terrified banker's wife had turned pale, and she watched as Lee unfolded the note and laid it on the large hall table. "Your husband ought to find the message in this conspicuous place, wouldn't you say?"

Ellen nodded shakily. "Y-yes."

"Good. Now you are going with me. This gun will be pressed against your side, and if you cry out to get somebody's attention, I'll kill you. Understand?"

Ellen Richards was breathing hard now. "Y-yes. I — I won't do that, Miss Smith. I promise."

"Good. I have a buggy out on the street. We're going for a ride."

Lee escorted the silver-haired woman out onto the front porch, pulled the door shut, and guided her along the stone walkway to the buggy. He held the gun on her as she climbed up onto the driver's seat, then climbed in beside her, holding the gun with his right hand against her side, and drove the buggy down the street.

Frozen with fear, Ellen Richards sat silently next to her abductor.

When the buggy turned onto Fort Collins's main street, Ellen looked furtively from side to side. She nodded to friends and acquaintances and tried to smile.

"Don't get cute, honey," the abductor said in a tight feminine voice. "No tricks. You can acknowledge people you know with a smile, so they won't suspect that you're in danger, but if you make one false move, you'll be dead, and your husband will be killed too. Understand?"

"Yes, I understand," Ellen replied, her voice quivering as she looked at the person who had blatantly kidnapped her.

"What are you staring at?" Lee snapped. "Keep your eyes straight ahead."

"Yes ma'am." In her mind, Ellen kept a clear image of what her abductor looked like and committed every facial detail to memory.

FIFTEEN

On Thursday, July 12, at Denver's Mile High Hospital, Breanna and Annabeth were finishing a day's work together in the surgical unit.

As they prepared to leave for home, Breanna said, "I'm sure looking forward to having you and Whip for supper at our house this evening."

Annabeth took a towel from the rack. "Whip and I are looking forward to it too, Breanna. We just love your family so much."

Taking another towel from the rack, Breanna began drying her hands as well. "And we love you and Whip so much. That's why Paul, Ginny, and Meggie call you Aunt Annabeth and Uncle Whip. They love you." Breanna chuckled. "John and I love you too even though we don't call you aunt and uncle."

Annabeth laughed. "That goes *two* ways, honey, but we sure do love you and John!"

A few minutes later, Breanna and Annabeth walked out of the hospital together, made their way to the employee lot, and climbed into the Brockman buggy.

As the buggy rolled onto the street, Annabeth looked at the small flower gardens growing in front of buildings. "Those flowers sure are pretty, aren't they, Breanna?"

As Breanna held the reins, guiding the mare along the street, she took a deep breath of the flower-scented air. "They sure are. After a long day, it's good to be out in the fresh air again. Those flowers not only *look* beautiful but they *smell* lovely too!"

"They sure do. The antiseptic odors at the hospital seem to get clogged up in my nose sometimes, and I'm always glad to leave them behind."

"I know just what you mean. I love my job at Mile High Hospital, and there's always something exciting and fulfilling about each day and each case, but I'm ever so glad to get back home to *my* house and family."

"I know exactly how you feel." Annabeth closed her eyes and enjoyed the ride and the aroma of summer flowers filling the warm air.

Soon they were out of town, enjoying the scent of newly mown alfalfa as they passed fields where farmers were putting up hay.

When they arrived at the Brockman ranch and entered the house, they hurried to the kitchen and found Ginny and Meggie already working on supper.

"Smells good, girls!" Breanna said. "Fried chicken and mashed potatoes with gravy, as planned."

"That's right, Mama," Ginny said. "We just thought we'd get an early start so supper will be ready when Papa and Uncle Whip get here."

Breanna and Annabeth joined in to help get supper completely ready. They saw Paul come in the back door a few moments later with Whip by his side.

"Uncle Whip saw me heading for the house from the barn when he rode up," Paul said, "so I motioned for him to come in with me."

Breanna was about to ask about her husband, but Whip beat her to it. "Chief Brockman said to tell you he'll probably be a little late for supper but for us to go ahead. He received a lengthy telegram when it was time for us to leave. It looked important, so he told me to go on. He also had some important paperwork to finish."

"Well, we'll just slow it down a bit," Breanna said. "Maybe John will get here before we start."

"Good." Whip looked at his wife and smiled. He turned back to Breanna. "Since you're going to slow it down a bit, Breanna, could I steal Annabeth and give her a kiss or two since I haven't seen her all day?"

Ginny and Meggie giggled at Uncle Whip as their mother said, "Sure you can. You two go out on the back porch and have a little time together."

Smiling broadly, Whip took Annabeth by the hand. "Let's go, sweetheart."

A moment later, when the Langfords were alone on the back porch, Whip took hold of Annabeth's shoulders, squeezing them tightly. Annabeth lifted her head and stared at him, softness in her eyes and around her mouth. Whip looked into her eyes, and they said a lot of things to each other without speaking a word.

"Sweetheart," Whip said, "we've been married barely twenty days, but I love you a thousand times more than I did the day you became my wife." He folded her in his arms, lowered his head, and captured her lips with his.

When their lips finally parted, Annabeth took a deep breath, looked up into her husband's eyes, and said softly, "Darling, I love you a *million* times more than I did the day you became my husband."

"But *my* love for you just grew a *billion* times more as you were speaking."

He kissed her again and then Annabeth said, "My love is even greater now, but I'll have to tell you how much later." She winked at him. "We need to get back to the kitchen."

Whip kissed her again. "All right. Let's get back to the kitchen."

When the Langfords entered the room, Breanna and her children smiled at them. "Well, Uncle Whip," Paul said, "did you get your kiss or two?"

"Yes, I did." Whip grinned.

"Good," Paul said. "Uncle Whip? I need to remind you of something."

Whip's eyebrows arched. "What's that?"

"You promised me that when I felt I was ready, you would let me draw against you with our guns unloaded to see if I can outdraw you."

The ex-outlaw and gunfighter known as the Outlaw Marshal looked at the maturing young man. "We can go outside and draw against each other right now since supper's not quite ready."

No one had heard John step inside the open kitchen door. "Oh, boy!" he said. "I've got to see this!"

Everyone turned to look at John, and Breanna rushed to him with open arms. While he folded her into his own arms, he said, "Sweetheart, is there time enough before supper for these two famous gunfighters to square off?"

Breanna nodded. "Of course."

"Paul," Whip said, "let's empty our guns right now."

Both Whip and Paul pulled their guns from the holsters and began to pull the cartridges from the cylinders. Breanna looked at her son, who was now nearly six inches taller than she was, and saw the same expression and confidence in his eyes that she had seen in her husband's eyes so many times.

The same fear Breanna had felt every time she knew John was squaring off with gunfighters snaked its way down her spine. Shaking off the fear, knowing that Paul would be in no danger squaring off with Whip, Breanna put a smile on her lips. "Okay, fellas, let's go outside and put you to the test. Supper can wait a few minutes."

"Can Meggie and I go out and watch?" Ginny looked at her parents.

"Of course you can," their father said.

Annabeth laughed. "Well, I'm going too!"

While the others headed out the back

door, John put an arm around Breanna and spoke in a low voice only she could hear. "I saw the fear that crossed your face when you thought about Paul's desire to be fast and accurate with a gun, honey. I know it scares you. But since Paul wants to become a lawman, he must become an expert with the gun. He must know exactly how and when to draw it, and he must be prepared to do so at all times."

Breanna looked up at John's cherished face. "I know it, darling, but in my heart, there is still a fear when *you* are out facing bad guys. I can't help it. You and Paul are both so dear to me. John, I — I do place you in God's care every day in my prayers, and I know He can protect you, but I'm only human. I know the Lord understands and accepts that."

John smiled down at her. "Yes, He does, and so do I."

When John and Breanna reached the spot where the rest of the group was looking on as Paul and Whip squared off, the deputy looked at his boss and said, "Chief, you want to count to three for Paul and me so we'll know when to go for our guns?"

John shook his head. "When you fellas are facing cold-blooded gunfighters, nobody's going to count for you. Just go for your guns."

Whip nodded. With his right hand hovering over the gun in his holster, he said, "Go ahead, Paul."

Paul shook his head. "*You* go ahead, Uncle Whip."

As Whip's right hand darted downward, Paul's right hand moved with amazing speed, and he had his gun cocked and aimed at Whip's chest before Whip's gun was out of the holster. "Bang!" Paul said, laughing.

Whip's hand froze on his gun, and he stood in absolute shock. "Wow. Paul, you *are* fast! Wow."

Ginny giggled. "Uncle Whip, you must be getting old!"

"Yeah!" Meggie said. "And Paul, you really are fast."

Paul holstered his gun and walked over to the Outlaw Marshal. "Thanks for letting me draw against you, Uncle Whip."

"Well, thanks for challenging me, Paul. You just showed me that I've got to get faster." He looked over at Ginny. "Guess I'd better resign my job as one of your papa's deputy marshals and go live in a nursing home!"

"Oh no, you don't, Whip!" John said. "I'm older than you, and I guarantee you, Paul can't outdraw me!"

"I'm sure of that, Papa. But I'm gonna keep practicing. The main thing is that I will become lightning fast like *you* by the time I turn twenty-one and become a lawman."

Later, at the supper table, while everyone was eating, Breanna leaned toward her husband. "John, darling, Whip told us that you received a very important telegram just before he left the office to come here and that you needed to stay and read it. Can you tell us who the telegram was from and what it was about?"

John swallowed and nodded. "Sure. It was from Sheriff Frank O'Brien in Fort Collins. He felt I should know about the kidnapping of Ellen Richards, the wife of the president of First National Bank there, on Tuesday morning."

"Oh no!" Breanna gasped. "Why was she taken hostage?"

John took a sip of coffee. "Apparently a woman took Mrs. Richards from her house at gunpoint on Tuesday morning, shortly after her husband went to work at the bank."

"A *woman*?" Paul asked.

"Yes. She left a note at the house for Mr. Richards to find when he arrived home from work that evening."

John had the rapt attention of everyone at the table. He went on to tell them the contents of the message — that Mrs. Richards was in the hands of a gang of robbers and that the bank president was to put a moneybag containing fifty thousand dollars in a certain spot on the bridge that spans the Cache la Poudre River just north of Fort Collins. One member of the gang would pick up the money at the designated spot, and the rest of the gang would wait with the wife until they had the money. If anyone was seen watching or following the pickup man, Mrs. Richards would be killed. If it happened as directed, Mrs. Richards would be set free unharmed.

The family held their breath as they waited to hear the outcome. John went on to explain that on Tuesday evening as commanded, the bank president left the money at the designated location. Mrs. Richards was found shortly afterward at the north edge of Fort Collins, free and unharmed.

A pale-faced Annabeth heaved a great sigh. "Oh, how horrible for poor Mrs. Richards! She must have been frightened out of her mind."

"And to think that it was a woman who abducted Mrs. Richards." Breanna shook her head. "She was a bold one to do a wicked thing like that. I guess it takes all kinds, doesn't it? A woman isn't even safe in her own home. Maybe this incident will teach all of us women to be more careful and more alert."

"That's good thinking, sweetheart. And I can tell you as a lawman that it makes a lot of sense. I don't want any of my family to live in fear, but just be a little more cautious, wherever you are. Even regarding *women*. And I know Whip feels the same, Annabeth."

Whip looked at Annabeth and nodded.

John went on. "We lawmen do our utmost to protect our families, but the Bible tells us there is a lot of evil in this world. That's why Whip and I pray daily for our families and ask the Lord to take care of you."

Breanna sighed. "I'm just so glad that neither Mrs. Richards or her husband were harmed. Strange as it seems, those outlaws kept their word."

"Yes," Whip said. "That in itself was a miracle."

"And what a relief it must have been for Mr. Richards to have his wife return to him unharmed."

"That's for sure," Annabeth agreed. "And what a relief for *Mrs.* Richards too!"

"Frank O'Brien told me that Horace Richards didn't tell him about the incident until he had put the money under the bridge and his wife had been freed and was safely back home with him."

"I can't blame Mr. Richards for that," Whip said.

"For sure," John replied.

Whip's brow furrowed. "Chief, do you have any idea who this woman and her outlaw partners might be?"

"I have no idea, but since I've been advised by Wyoming lawmen that the Zarbo brothers are heading south toward Colorado, I wonder if the woman might be working with them. I'll wire Sheriff O'Brien in the morning and tell him that the gang who abducted Mrs. Richards just might be the Zarbos."

"Wow, Papa," Paul said. "If it *was* the Zarbos, it's really amazing they didn't kill Mrs. Richards once they had the money."

"You're right about *that,* Paul." Whip gave a firm nod.

"Those Zarbos are vile, wicked, and bloodthirsty," John said. "I'm sure when Mr. Richards realizes it could have been the Zarbos, he'll understand how very fortunate he is to have his dear wife alive and unharmed."

The next morning, as Chief Brockman was at the Western Union office sending his telegram to Sheriff O'Brien in Fort Collins, the three Zarbo brothers were riding southward toward Longmont, where they planned to stop and eat breakfast if the town had a café or restaurant.

They were chuckling over the success of their plan to cheat First National Bank of Fort Collins out of fifty thousand dollars.

As they rode along the dusty road, Todd cleared his throat. "Boys, I've been thinking. Since we were so successful in Fort Collins, maybe we need to come up with a plan to hit one of Denver's big banks for *a hundred thousand!*"

Chice laughed. "Sure. Why not?"

"And I want you to disguise yourself as a woman again, Lee," Todd said, "and to abduct the wife of this bank's president or one of the other bank officers' wives."

"I'll do it, Todd."

"I figured you would." Todd shook his head, then looked over at his brothers. "And I just thought of something. I wonder if that stable owner ever found the horse and buggy since we unhitched the horse near the Poudre River and turned it loose."

Chice and Lee laughed with their older brother.

Soon they rode into Longmont and checked out the town's main thoroughfare. After a few minutes, Lee pointed about a block away. "Lookee there, fellas! Harry's Café."

Todd and Chice focused on the sign. "I see it," Todd said. "And I'm hungry. Let's get up there."

Putting their horses to a trot, they made their way up the street, noting people on the boardwalks on both sides and a few riders and buggies with horses on the street.

As they drew near the café, Chice pointed across the street. "Hey, guys, look over there."

Todd and Lee quickly noted the Longmont City Bank on their left. Smiling broadly, Chice said, "Maybe after we eat breakfast, that bank will be open. Should we, uh —"

"No," Todd cut in under his breath. "If we hold up that bank, we'll have whatever law is in this town on our heels. We're going to Denver to get a hundred thousand dollars out of one of the big banks."

Chice and Lee exchanged glances and shrugged at each other.

Chice said, "We'll do as big brother says."
Todd smiled to himself.

The Zarbo brothers dismounted at Harry's Café and tied their horses at the hitch rail, noting the number of horses tied up. It took a moment to find an empty table, but Lee spotted one at the back of the place, and the three brothers made their way to it.

They enjoyed a breakfast of oatmeal, pancakes, and bacon. They talked in low voices about the hundred thousand dollars they were going to take from one of Denver's banks. When they had finished, they left the café and continued southward toward Denver.

Five miles out of Longmont, the Zarbo brothers stopped to water their horses at a small brook. All three men dismounted, led their horses to the bank of the brook, and stood with the animals as they loudly slurped water. The horses' thirst was finally quenched, and the Zarbo brothers mounted up. Suddenly a rattlesnake struck at Chice's horse.

The horse jumped, throwing the unsuspecting Chice from the saddle. He hit the ground hard, and his face twisted in pain. The snake coiled again, preparing to strike him.

Todd and Lee whipped out their guns,

took careful aim, and fired. Both bullets ripped through the rattler, killing it instantly.

Todd and Lee knelt down beside their brother, whose face showed extreme pain.

"It — it's my left shoulder," Chice said through clenched teeth. "I landed pretty hard."

Todd examined him quickly but carefully. Despite the pain, Chice managed to move his left shoulder and arm quite a bit. "Since you can move your shoulder and arm, there probably aren't any broken bones, but your shoulder is quite bruised." Todd looked around them. "We'll make camp amid some of those trees on the other side of the brook and wait a couple days for you to get better. Then we'll go on to Denver and force the hundred thousand dollars out of one of the banks as planned."

"Guess I'll have to give my arm and shoulder a little time to heal up."

Lee looked at Todd. "Tell you what. I'll ride on into Denver right now and check out the banks so I can pick the one I believe we'll want to rob. I'll find a way to get information about the bank president's wife or the wife of another bank officer."

Todd nodded. "All right, Lee. Go ahead. I trust your judgment. Chice and I will be right here when you return."

SIXTEEN

That Friday morning, July 13, as Lee Zarbo was galloping toward Denver, John Brockman left his office and walked toward the closest gun shop. Mile High Gun Shop was owned by Brockman's long-time friend Kyle Lamson.

When John stepped inside the shop, Kyle was placing some new revolvers in a glass display cabinet. He looked up and smiled. "Howdy, John. How're things in the federal law business?"

"Rough, as usual." John extended his hand. "Lots going on."

John gave Kyle a few things to think about as he told him about some of the criminal activities going on in the West. Lamson brought up some of the things he had read in the newspapers about the Zarbo brothers.

They chatted about the Zarbos for a few minutes. Then John said, "Well, Kyle, I'd better get what I came in here for and keep moving. Friday is payday, so I've got to deposit my paycheck and get back to my office after this."

Kyle smiled. "What can I do for you, John?"

"I need a few boxes of .45-caliber cartridges. Paul and I are running a bit low."

"So you're still instructing Paul on how to shoot his revolver more accurately?"

"Yep. We spend time together quite often, doing target practice by shooting at sticks, boards, and broken tree limbs. That boy of mine is becoming a better shot all the time."

"Good! Glad to hear it. How many boxes you need?"

"I'll take a dozen."

After paying, John told Kyle he'd see him later and left the gun shop, carrying the large cardboard box containing the dozen smaller boxes of cartridges, and headed for Denver's First National Bank.

When John entered the bank and had made his deposit, several people came up and wanted to chat with him. A few bank employees also got in on the conversation.

Meanwhile, Lee Zarbo rode through downtown Denver, purposely passing all four of Denver's banks once he had learned their locations. When he had looked over the four banks, Lee decided that First National Bank was the largest and no doubt handled the most money. It definitely seemed to be the one he and his brothers should extort money from, so Lee rode back toward it to check it out in more detail.

By now, John Brockman had finished chatting and said he needed to get back to his office. He stepped out of the bank onto the boardwalk. Lee Zarbo had arrived at that part of the street and was standing near the hitching post in front of First National Bank, giving the bank another good looking over when John stepped out the door.

Lee smiled to himself and murmured, "Yes sir! Todd and Chice will definitely agree that this is the one we should squeeze for a hundred thousand dollars!"

At the same moment, John's eyes settled on the young man standing in the dusty street. His mind flashed to the Wanted posters of the Zarbo brothers. This young man was *Lee Zarbo!*

A few people were walking in both directions along the boardwalk, and some folks were on the street as well. Walking casually so as not to stand out to Zarbo, John moved toward one of the benches in front of the bank and set his cardboard box of cartridges on it.

Zarbo had seen the tall man carrying the cardboard box but hadn't seen his badge.

John did not let on that he recognized the outlaw until he was within less than twenty feet.

Lee Zarbo's attention was still on the big bank building when the chief U.S. marshal drew his gun, cocked the hammer, and pointed it at the outlaw. "Lee Zarbo, you are under arrest!"

People looked on with interest as a stunned Zarbo froze in place, his eyes wide as he looked at the lawman who had him at gunpoint. Lee had seen the chief U.S. marshal's photographs in newspapers and recognized him immediately.

"Ease your gun out of its holster, and drop it on the ground."

Biting his lower lip, Lee obeyed.

The people who were gathered around looked on as Brockman cuffed Lee's hands behind his back, then picked up his gun and stuffed it under his own belt. John asked one of the men he knew to pick up his cardboard box and go with him to the county jail. Another man volunteered to lead the outlaw's horse.

John led the way as they walked toward the county jail with Lee Zarbo at his side.

"Lee, where are your brothers?" John said.

Silence.

"I asked you where your brothers are!"

Silence.

"It will go a lot better for you if you answer my question."

Silence.

Less than twenty minutes after leaving First National Bank, the group arrived at the county jail. Lee's horse was tied to the hitching post out front, and the man carrying the cartridges handed the box to Chief Brockman. John thanked the two men for their help.

John ushered the outlaw inside the jail and found Sheriff Carter at the front desk, talking to the deputy on duty. It took the sheriff only a few seconds to recognize Lee Zarbo from the Wanted posters on the front of the federal building.

"Hey, Chief, that's one of the Zarbo brothers!"

"Sure is. *Lee* Zarbo, to be exact."

"How and where did you catch him? What about his brothers?"

"Let's take him to a cell," Brockman said, "and I'll tell you. Then we'll see about his brothers."

Once Lee Zarbo was behind bars and alone in a cell, he sat down on one of the cots. Eventually the two lawmen came and stood looking at him through the bars.

"Okay, Lee," John said, "Sheriff Carter now knows how and where I caught you. What he and I want to know now is where your brothers are."

Lee looked up at the marshal with a heated scowl. "I remained mum on the way over here, and I'm gonna *stay* mum. I'm telling you nothing about my brothers." He ran angry eyes between the two men and hissed angrily. "I'll never tell either of you where Todd and Chice are!"

Sheriff Carter scowled at Lee. "Well, let me tell you something, Zarbo. You are going to hang for the murders you have committed even if we never catch your brothers! You are wanted — dead or alive. And I guarantee you, our Judge Dexter knows all about you, and when you face him, your neck will be in a noose! When Judge Dexter knows we've got you behind bars, he will set an official time to hang you for your crimes."

Lee glanced up through the bars but said nothing. He quickly looked down at the floor and spit on it. He kept his head down and continued to stare silently.

The two lawmen left the cellblock. "How about you and I go to Judge Dexter's office and talk to him right now?" John asked.

"Let's go."

Fifteen minutes later, John and Sheriff Carter entered the judge's office.

Standing behind his desk, Judge Dexter motioned for his two friends to sit down. Then he sat in his desk chair. "What can I do for you gentlemen?"

The sheriff looked over at John. "Chief Brockman has something very important to tell you, Judge. I wanted to come along."

The judge eyed the cardboard box in Brockman's hands. "Are you here to tell me about the contents of that box?"

"No sir. This box contains bullets I had purchased to take home with me this evening. I still haven't had the chance to take them back to my office. I'm here to tell you that I ran into one of the Zarbo brothers in front of First National Bank. I arrested him, and now he's locked up."

Judge Dexter's eyes lit up. "Which one is it?"

"The youngest one — Lee."

"Okay. Have you found out where the other two are?"

"Nope. Lee refuses to give out that information."

The judge chuckled and looked at his desk calendar. "Well, Lee Zarbo is going to hang. Let's see . . . this is Friday, July 13. I want to give that killer a few days to think about his death at the end of a hangman's rope. Lee Zarbo will hang a week from tomorrow, Saturday, July 21, at six o'clock that morning. As you men know, I have full authority to do this."

"Yes sir." The sheriff nodded. "We certainly do."

"Every one of the Zarbo brothers has been proven guilty of murder in four territories of the West," John said. "My hope is that the fear of death will loosen his lips.

The judge rose to his feet. "Since it's my job in the courtroom to sentence a guilty man, I may as well go to the county jail and tell Mr. Lee Zarbo that I'm sentencing him to hang a week from tomorrow."

By this time, both the sheriff and the chief U.S. marshal were standing.

"I'll go with you since my office is at the jail," the sheriff said.

"And I'll head back to my office." John nodded at the two men.

As the judge and the sheriff headed down the street, John hurried to the federal building. When he entered the outer office, the chief found three of his deputies in conversation with Deputy Sotak. They were Mike Allen, Roland Jensen, and Whip Langford.

The chief told the four men about capturing and jailing Lee Zarbo and about how the judge had set next Saturday as Lee's day to be hanged. The deputies were glad to hear this.

John turned to Deputy Langford. "I need to talk to you about a few things in my office."

"Let's go."

At the hospital, Breanna and Annabeth were assisting Dr. Jacob Handon, one of the surgeons, with a stomach operation on an elderly woman. One of Breanna's tasks was to administer ether to the patient to keep her unconscious throughout the surgery.

While the surgery was in progress, Breanna, Annabeth, and Dr. Handon heard a loud male voice crying out in agony from a room down the hall where broken bones were dealt with.

Dr. Handon paused with the scalpel and looked toward the hall, then at his assisting nurses. "That patient sounds like quite a big man, doesn't he?"

"He sure does," Annabeth said.

During the next half hour, as Dr. Jacob Handon proceeded to work on the elderly woman, he and his nurses continued to hear the big man cry out in pain.

When the surgery was done, Breanna and

Annabeth went down the hall to the surgical washroom. The big man was still crying out, and they could hear him even more clearly since the washroom was closer to his room.

The loudest cry yet suddenly rang out from the man down the hall.

Breanna shook her head. "I wonder what they're doing to him to bring on so much pain."

"I wonder too. I don't know about you, but those long, plaintive cries are rather unnerving."

"They sure are . . ."

Annabeth began drying her hands. "I'm sure whatever doctor is working on the man is doing all he can to keep from hurting him, but I feel so sorry for that man."

"I'm sure he's in good hands," Breanna responded as the continued wail of the patient penetrated her ears. She looked at the clock on the wall. "Annabeth, we're due to help Dr. Harrington with a serious surgery just two rooms down in forty minutes."

Annabeth nodded.

"Tell you what," Breanna said. "I need to go downstairs to Dr. Carroll's office for a few minutes. I'll meet you back up here before it's time to start the surgery."

Annabeth patted Breanna's cheek. "Okay, sweetie, see you there."

Breanna left the washroom and hurried down the hall. As she passed the closed door where the wails had been coming from, the injured man let out a bloodcurdling cry that caused Breanna to jump, and her hand went to her mouth to stifle her own scream. Stopping momentarily, she looked at the closed door. "Lord, I don't know what is happening in there, but I pray for that man who is in such pain. Give the doctor wisdom, and help him to ease that poor man's agony."

She proceeded down the hall to the stairs near the front of the building. She moved swiftly toward the chief administrator's office. When she reached the outer office, she stepped through the open door and asked Dr. Carroll's secretary if he was in so she could talk to him. When she entered, her brother-in-law smiled and greeted her warmly.

While they were talking about a family matter, they suddenly heard the patient on the second floor howling in agony.

"Annabeth and I were just helping Dr. Handon finish a surgery, and we could hear that man crying a few doors down. He sure sounds like a big man and like he's in a great deal of pain. Do you know who he is?"

"Yes, he *is* a big man, Breanna. He's about six feet four and weighs about two hundred sixty pounds. His name is Damon Fortney, and he has a ranch about twenty miles southeast of Denver. He fell off the roof of his barn and broke nearly all of his ribs. His wife is visiting relatives in Missouri. Fortunately some neighbors saw him fall and brought him to the hospital."

"I see," Breanna said.

"Apparently Mr. Fortney's body does not respond properly to morphine or laudanum, so the doctors who are tightly wrapping his broken ribs — a slow and extremely painful process — are doing so with little pain control. I was up there a while ago, and he is in excruciating pain. Sometimes he seems to be out of his mind."

Breanna frowned. "My heart goes out to him. Without anything to kill the pain or even ease it, he has to be suffering horribly."

"That he is, Breanna."

When they had finished their discussion, Breanna left the office and began mounting the stairs toward the second floor.

Suddenly Breanna heard the rancher crying out again, but this time it was even louder. She realized he must be in the hall on the second floor.

Just as Breanna topped the stairs, she saw the wild-eyed man, obviously in severe pain, and he looked to be out of his mind. He was running hard toward the stairs, only a few steps away — and he was headed straight toward Breanna. Panic bubbled up inside her. She took a deep, shuddering breath while trying to avoid him, but he was coming too fast and was already too close. The large, wildly distraught man slammed violently into Breanna, and the impact lifted her off her feet and sent her flying through the air. She slammed hard on the stairs about halfway down, then tumbled head over heels until she hit the floor.

She lay motionless at the bottom of the stairs, her body crumpled and unconscious.

Damon had lost his balance from the impact with Breanna and also rolled down the stairs. When he hit the floor barely three feet from Breanna, he stood up and staggered out the main door of the hospital, seemingly unaware of his surroundings.

Outside, he took a few steps, collapsed, and hit the ground unconscious.

Moments later, as two doctors were picking up the unconscious Breanna, three male orderlies were outside working to pick up the patient. Only a few minutes passed before Dr. Carroll and several nurses, including Annabeth, were standing over the surgical table where Breanna Brockman lay unconscious.

As Dr. Carroll leaned over Breanna with an anxious look on his face, the nurses looked on, the same concern in their eyes. Dr. Carroll laid a hand on Breanna's forehead and asked Annabeth, "How did this happen? The orderly who came to get me said Breanna fell down the staircase at the front of the building. That's all he knew."

"I don't know all the details, Dr. Carroll, but evidently that man who had been screaming for quite a while went out of his mind, jumped off the table, and slammed both doctors to the floor. Then he ran out of the room into the hall. Apparently he headed for the staircase, where he collided with Breanna, who had just reached the top of the stairs. She was knocked all the way down to the first floor."

Dr. Carroll began making a thorough examination of Breanna's condition, from her bleeding head to her battered, swollen knees. He swallowed hard and turned to nurse Jean Barber to find an orderly. "Tell him to hurry to the federal building and advise Chief Brockman of what has happened to his wife and that I will personally perform surgery on her."

"Yes, Doctor."

Then Dr. Carroll turned to Annabeth and nurse Sarah Newton. His voice quivered. "Please prepare Breanna for surgery. I must begin as soon as possible."

A hush fell over the room as the two nurses began prepping the patient.

Dr. Carroll gently touched Breanna's limp right arm, bowed his head, and closed his eyes. "Dear Lord, You are the Great Physician, and I need Your help. Please take these hands of mine and help me to do my job perfectly. In Jesus' precious name, amen."

"Amen," Annabeth whispered. Her eyes were filled with tears as she looked down at Breanna. "I — I don't know if you can hear me, but just in case you can, you couldn't be in better hands. The Lord is guiding Dr. Carroll, and the Great Physician is in control of it all. You'll be fine, my sweet friend. I just know it. Keep that Breanna Brockman spirit up. God is holding you in His strong arms."

Annabeth wiped the tears from her cheeks, leaned over her unconscious friend, brushed a curl of blond hair from her forehead, then placed a tender kiss on her cheek.

Dr. Carroll wiped his own tears. "Bless

you, Annabeth. You ladies go ahead and finish prepping. I need to get started."

SEVENTEEN

At the federal building, Chief Brockman and Deputy Langford were finally discussing the subject the chief had brought him to his office to talk about. When they had arrived at his office, two Logan County sheriff's deputies from Sterling, Colorado, had been there and had taken up quite a bit of time.

When the deputies had gone and the chief had called Whip back into his office, he quickly brought up the Zarbo brothers and let Whip know what he was thinking.

"I agree, Chief," Whip said. "Since Lee Zarbo came to Denver, Todd and Chice are probably on their way here as well. Those brothers stick together. What crime or crimes do you suppose they're planning to commit here in Denver?"

John leaned back in his desk chair. "Well, it will be robbery for sure. But where they'll commit their robbery is hard to say. It wouldn't surprise me if they hit one of the banks."

"I agree. And who knows what else they have in mind since Denver is the biggest city anywhere near here."

"You're —" John's comment was interrupted by a knock. He knew it would be his deputy, Mike Allen. "Come in, Mike!"

Whip turned in his chair and looked toward the door. Deputy Allen stepped inside, obviously very upset. Beside him was a hospital orderly, Tim Dubois, whom John knew well. Tim also looked troubled.

John frowned and rose to his feet. "What's wrong?" the chief asked.

Mike pulled his lips into a thin line. "Tim has some bad news, Chief."

"What is it, Tim?"

Tim's voice shook and cracked. "Chief Brockman, Dr. Carroll sent me to let you know that your wife has been injured at the hospital." He quickly told Brockman how Breanna had been violently knocked down the stairs by a patient out of his mind with pain. Dr. Carroll was operating on Mrs. Brockman right away.

John's rugged features were salt pale and clenched in anxiety. "What part of her body is injured, Tim? How bad is it? Is her life in danger?"

"I don't know, Chief. All I know is that she is severely injured and unconscious and that Dr. Carroll is performing surgery and expects you to come to the hospital immediately."

"Of course." John grabbed his hat. "I'll go right now."

Whip's face showed extreme concern as well. "Can I go with you, Chief?"

"You sure can." He looked at Mike. "Are any other deputies in the building at the moment?"

"I know Roland is, Chief. I just saw him in the hall. I know he's got some paperwork to do before he'll be leaving."

"Okay. Let Roland know what has happened. Tell him that I need him to go to the ranch and bring Paul, Ginny, and Meggie to the hospital so they can be with their mother."

Mike nodded. "Got it, Chief. I'll make sure it's done."

"Thanks. Would you also have Roland go to Pastor Bayless's office before going to the ranch and let him know what happened."

"I sure will, Chief."

"And tell Roland to be gentle with Paul and the girls and try not to overly alarm them."

Mike nodded again and hurried toward the door. Over his shoulder, he said, "I'll make that clear to him, Chief."

"And thank Roland for me, please."

Mike disappeared through the door and made a right turn down the hall.

John looked at Whip and Tim. "Okay, fellas. Let's go. Let's just go on foot since the hospital is only a few blocks away."

The two lawmen and the orderly jogged to the hospital, weaving among pedestrians. Some of the people stopped to watch the three running men, and a few even called out to them, but the chief, his deputy, and the orderly kept up their pace, not taking time to stop and explain why they were running. John was praying in his heart the entire way, asking the Lord to take care of Breanna.

When the three men arrived at the hospital, they bounded up the stairs to the second floor.

As they climbed, Tim Dubois said, "Nurse Barber told me that Breanna is in surgery room six. When we get to the door, I'll peek in and ask Dr. Carroll if you two can come in. I didn't think to tell you, Deputy Langford, that your wife is one of the nurses helping Dr. Carroll."

"I figured she might be."

"Amen! What a blessing," John said.

They topped the stairs quickly, hurried down the hall, and soon drew up to the closed door of surgery room six.

Looking at the two lawmen as he took hold of the door handle, Tim said, "Wait right here." He entered the room and closed the door behind him.

Whip laid a gentle hand on his nervous chief's shoulder. "She's going to be all right. The Lord will take care of her."

John nodded, looking at Whip admiringly. "I'm sure trusting Him to take care of her, Whip."

No more than two minutes had passed when the door swung open and Tim stepped into the hall, pulling the door closed. "Chief, Dr. Carroll is glad you're here. He told me he'll be finished with surgery in about a half hour. I asked what kind of surgery he's doing, but he said there was no way he could explain it while concentrating on what he's doing. He said to tell you and Deputy Langford to go to the waiting room across the hall. He'll send for both of you as soon as he's finished."

"All right," John said. "Thanks for your help, Tim. Will you tell Dr. Carroll that Whip and I will be in the waiting room? Also tell him that Deputy Jensen is on his way to let Pastor Bayless know about Breanna being in surgery and then will go to the ranch and bring Paul, Ginny, and Meggie to see their mother."

"I sure will, Chief."

John and Whip made their way across the hall to the waiting room. No one was there at the time. Sighing deeply, John sat down on an overstuffed chair, and Whip sat down on one next to him. John lowered his face into his hands, trying to calm himself, and felt Whip's hand on his shoulder.

His face still in his hands, John prayed aloud, "Dear Father in heaven, I know You have a plan for each of Your children's lives, and for whatever reason You have allowed this to happen to my precious Breanna. I submit to Your judgment. Please hold her in the hollow of Your powerful hand, and guide Dr. Carroll's hands as he performs the surgery. I ask it in Jesus' wonderful name. Amen."

"Amen," Whip echoed, squeezing the chief's shoulder tenderly.

Just over a half an hour later, Whip was listening with interest as John told him about how he and Breanna had met and fallen in love and been married at First Baptist Church on June 4, 1871.

At that moment, the door of the waiting

room came open, and nurse Sarah Newton stepped in. John and Whip knew Sarah well. "Chief Brockman, Dr. Carroll has finished the surgery and sent me to tell you that you can come into the surgery room now. Breanna came through the surgery all right but will be under the effect of the ether for a while yet. Dr. Carroll will explain exactly what happened to her and the details of the surgery."

John nodded. "Thank you so much."

Sarah smiled. "Of course. Well, I must be going. I have to go down to the first floor."

"Since you're going down there, Sarah," John said, "will you do me a favor?"

"Certainly."

"Would you alert the people at the front desk that one of my deputies is bringing Paul, Ginny, and Meggie to see their mother so they can direct them to the right room?"

"I'd be glad to, Chief Brockman." Sarah paused before heading through the door. "You and Deputy Langford can go to the surgery room now."

As Sarah vanished from their sight, John turned to Whip. "Would you mind waiting in the hall to intercept my children when they arrive? I don't want them to just come in without my talking to them first. If you'll let me know they're here, I'll come out and talk to them. Once I've heard about the surgery from Dr. Carroll and seen Breanna for myself, I may have some things to tell them."

"Sure, Chief."

"Thanks, Whip. I appreciate it."

When they reached room six, John took a deep breath and entered, closing the door behind him. Whip leaned against the wall outside the door and waited.

As John made his way past the curtains that hung from the ceiling, partially covering the area where Dr. Carroll had done the surgery, he saw the doctor standing over Breanna as she lay on the operating table. John noted that she was breathing but her eyes were closed, indicating that she was still under the effect of the ether.

Annabeth was standing over Breanna on the other side of the table. Tears filled her eyes when she saw John, and she gave him a weak smile.

Dr. Carroll had heard the door open and close. His back was toward John at first, but then he turned to look at him. "Hello, brother-in-law."

John walked carefully toward the table and greeted Annabeth softly. Then he looked at Dr. Carroll. "Looks like she's still under the anesthetic."

"Yes. She will be for a while yet."

John looked down at his beloved wife and caressed her cheek lovingly. Then he looked back at the doctor. "What surgery did Breanna need, and what is her prognosis?"

Dr. Carroll took a deep breath. "You know the details of her fall, I presume."

"Yes. Tim Dubois gave me those."

The doctor swallowed hard. "Well, John, her right hip is dislocated, and I had to do surgery to set it." He went on. "You can't tell because of her hair, but she has a big bump on the side of her head where she hit either one of the stairs or the floor. But more seriously, the muscles around her spine are swollen and pushing hard against it. There is also deep bruising in and around her spine."

While Dr. Carroll continued to explain, John's eyes remained fixed on his wife's beautiful face. He then looked at the doctor and frowned, but before he could speak, Dr. Carroll choked up and tears flooded his eyes. "John, I — I'm not sure — I'm not sure she'll be able to walk again."

As those words left the doctor's lips, a deep shuddering racked John's entire body. He looked at his brother-in-law. "Sh-she may never walk again?"

Dr. Carroll's features crinkled and whitened. "That's right. I just can't say for sure right now. It doesn't look good. I'm so sorry this had to happen, John, but please know we will continue to give her the very best care."

John's deep voice trembled as he held back threatening tears. "I know you will, Matthew. I know you will."

The doctor laid a hand on John's shoulder. "I'm sorry I can't be encouraging about it, but Breanna took a real beating on those stairs. She's in God's hands. While I'm making sure she gets the best of care, I'll be asking Him to heal her."

John leaned over the still form of his beloved wife, took hold of her hand, kissed her brow, and said softly, "I'm here, sweetheart. You're going to be all right. When our pastor learns of this, he will be leading the church to pray for you. So many people will be praying for you."

Though Breanna lay absolutely still, a tiny smile formed on her lips.

When Annabeth saw it, her eyes widened and she put a hand to her mouth.

John looked at his brother-in-law. "I think she heard me, Matt. Did you see her little smile?"

"I . . . I did, John. I've seen this kind of thing a few times. Somehow an unconscious patient sometimes reacts to the voice of a loved one. Just keep talking to her. Somehow beyond even the understanding of medical experts, she knows you're here."

"Then I want to pray over her right now," John said.

"Great," the doctor said. "Lead us, John."

John bowed his head, as did Dr. Carroll and Annabeth. Still holding Breanna's hand, John asked the Lord to heal his dear wife and make it so she would be able to walk as well as before.

Just as John closed the prayer in Jesus' name, the door opened, and Whip entered. Hurrying up to the bed, he looked at Breanna, then his wife, then John. "Chief, your children are here."

"Thank you, Whip. You stay here. I'll go talk to Paul, Ginny, and Meggie." He looked down and saw that the faint smile was still on Breanna's lips, though she was still unconscious. He patted Breanna's hand. "I'll be right back, honey. Our precious children are out in the hall, and I need to talk to them."

As John rushed toward the door, Whip came close to Annabeth and put his arm around her.

John closed the door behind him and

folded all three children in his arms. Deputy Jensen smiled at him, and John managed to smile back.

Still holding his children tightly, John told them about their mother's fall and what Dr. Carroll had told him about her injuries. When they heard that their mother might never walk again unless the Lord healed her by His power, they wept, clinging to their father.

John tried to encourage them by saying that the Lord answers prayer and that together he and the three of them would do a lot of praying. All three agreed, wiping tears.

Deputy Jensen said, "Chief, when I stopped by Pastor Bayless's office, he wasn't there, so I knocked on the door of the parsonage. Mrs. Bayless came to the door and told me that the pastor was doing some marriage counseling with a couple in town. But she said she would tell him about Breanna when he returned and that both of them would come to the hospital as soon as possible."

"Thank you."

"Chief," Deputy Jensen said, "I need to go to the office and let the other deputies know about Mrs. Brockman's condition. Some of them came in just before I left the office, and they are very concerned about her."

"I'm glad they care about her. You head on back."

"Yes sir."

Ginny looked up into her father's eyes. "Papa, can we go in and see Mama now?"

Paul and Meggie nodded their heads.

"I'll go in and ask your Uncle Matthew if it's okay. You wait right here."

When John entered the room, Dr. Carroll was still standing over Breanna, who was still sedated. Whip and Annabeth were standing together on the other side of the bed. As John moved up beside the doctor, he noticed that Breanna's smile had vanished. He looked at the doctor. "Paul, Ginny, and Meggie want to come in and see their mother. Is that all right?"

"Tell you what," Dr. Carroll said. "Let's get her out of this surgery room and into a regular room. She'll be waking up soon, and it would be better if she can be conscious for a little while before she has everyone around her."

"I'll get orderlies and have them bring a padded cart, Doctor," Annabeth said. "We'll have Breanna in her room shortly."

"That will be good, Annabeth. Room 218."

"Oh, good. A *single* room."

"Yes. I don't want her having another patient with her."

Annabeth looked at her husband. "I'll be back with the orderly in a few minutes, honey."

"I'll be here," Whip replied.

Dr. Carroll turned to John. "You know where the waiting room is near room 218, don't you?"

John nodded. "Sure do."

"Okay. After we get Breanna to her room, I'll send Whip to the waiting room to let you know when you and the children can come and see her. I want her to be awake a little while before everyone joins her."

"Fine," said John. "I'll take them there right now."

When John went back to the hall, he found Pastor Bayless and Mary talking to the children. John thanked the Baylesses for coming. Then the pastor asked John to tell them the details about Breanna's injuries.

John explained everything about Breanna's injuries and that Dr. Carroll was concerned Breanna might never walk again. The pastor said he wanted to go to prayer for Breanna immediately. Heads were bowed right there in the hall, and with people passing by, the pastor led his wife, the three

Brockman children, and their father in prayer, asking God's healing hand to be upon Breanna.

John thanked the pastor, then told the group that Breanna was going to be taken from the surgical room to a regular hospital room. As he led the small group to the waiting room down the hall, he explained that Dr. Carroll wanted them to wait until Breanna had regained consciousness, which he expected to happen quite soon.

They sat down in the waiting room. As John and the Baylesses visited about Breanna, they were unaware that the orderlies wheeling a cart past them were actually carting the unconscious Breanna, followed by Dr. Carroll, Annabeth, and Whip.

They quickly entered room 218, and Dr. Carroll and the orderlies carefully lifted Breanna onto the bed. The orderlies left with the empty cart, and Dr. Carroll stood over Breanna on one side of the bed, with Annabeth and Whip on the other.

At that moment, Breanna began to stir.

"Look!" Annabeth whispered. "She's waking up!"

EIGHTEEN

Everyone's eyes grew wide as they looked down at Breanna. She tilted head back and forth, heart-rending moans and pain-filled sounds escaping from her mouth.

Dr. Carroll and Annabeth leaned over Breanna, both of them speaking to her in soft voices while Whip looked on, thanking God that Breanna was coming out of the anesthetic.

It took a few minutes for Breanna to understand what her brother-in-law and her dear friend were saying to her, but as her mind began to clear, she smiled at them, and with a thick tongue, said, "M-Matthew! An-Annabeth! I — I'm so glad to see you."

"We're so glad to have you waking up, Breanna," Dr. Carroll said.

Annabeth squeezed her hand. "We sure are!"

Whip leaned down. "Hello, Breanna.

Remember me?"

Breanna blinked heavy lids and smiled. "Of course I do, Whip."

Dr. Carroll leaned ever closer. "Breanna, Annabeth is going to wash your face. When she's done, some others in the waiting room across the hall want to see you."

Annabeth went to the sink at the rear of the room, where she collected a small water pitcher and washcloths and towels.

Breanna's lips quivered as she focused on the doctor. "J-John? P-P-Paul? Ginny? M-Meggie?"

"Yes," Dr. Carroll said. "Also Pastor Bayless and Mary."

Breanna's eyes were clearing quickly. "Oh, I want to see all of them."

The doctor smiled. "You will, dear, as soon as Annabeth washes your face. It will help to make your mind even clearer."

Dr. Carroll and Whip watched as Annabeth worked. Dr. Carroll turned to Whip a moment later. "She's ready. You can go get her family and the Baylesses."

A minute later, John led the rest of the family, along with the pastor and his wife, toward the bed where Breanna lay. After John and all three children tenderly greeted and kissed Breanna, Pastor and Mrs. Bayless said hello as well.

281

Dr. Carroll pulled John aside. "I don't want to interrupt your time with her, but I need to examine her more thoroughly in one area. I need to do so in private with Annabeth's help. If all of you will go to the waiting room for now, once the examination is done, you can come back to Breanna and spend more time with her. It will only take about twenty to thirty minutes."

John nodded. "Of course." He gathered the group.

When they had filed out the door, Dr. Carroll began his examination. When finished, Dr. Carroll looked at Annabeth on the opposite side of the bed and slowly shook his head. What the doctor had found was not good. The nurse blinked back her tears.

"Breanna," he said softly, looking down at her, "I — I'm afraid I have some disturbing news."

Breanna frowned as she studied his pinched face.

Dr. Carroll cleared his throat gently. "Breanna, there is some paralysis in your body from the waist down. It is from the bruising and swelling pushing against your spine. I am hopeful that the paralysis will ease when the swelling goes down and that with God's healing, the paralysis will completely disappear at some point so you can walk again."

Tears of frustration filled Breanna's eyes. "Th-this is quite a lot to take in, Matt," she said in a shaky whisper.

"I know it is, but you know I'll help in any way I can, and if the Lord wills, you *will* walk again one day."

Breanna wiped the tears from her cheeks. "I — I can't imagine not being able to walk. How would I ever be able to care for my family? How — how could I ever carry on my nursing career?" At that point, Breanna began to weep.

After Breanna wiped her tears, her brother-in-law took hold of both of her hands and said, "I'm so sorry this awful thing has happened to you, dear, but I would be wrong not to tell you right now. However, let's not give up. I am convinced that with prayer and proper care, you will walk again. It may be a long and difficult recovery, but remember that with God, *all* things are possible."

As Breanna listened to Dr. Carroll's encouraging words, her tears stopped and a peaceful calm entered her heart. "It's okay, Matthew. I know that the Lord has a plan for my life, and for some reason, He allowed this to happen. I know it won't be easy, but by God's matchless grace, I can have victory. One of my favorite Bible verses is Psalm 28:7. 'The LORD is my strength and my shield; my heart trusted in him, and I am helped.' All I can do right now is trust the One who is my strength and my shield to help me."

"Bless your heart, Breanna," Dr. Carroll said. "You are such a blessing. I know that God will be glorified through your life and your willingness to accept His almighty will."

Dr. Carroll squeezed Breanna's hands tenderly, then bent over and placed a kiss on her pale cheek.

"I'll let your family and the others in for a while, but then I want you to rest. You have undergone serious surgery, and you need to recover." He paused. "I'm going to give you some laudanum right now. By the time the Baylesses and your family leave, it will have begun to kick in and help ease the pain."

"Thanks, Matthew. I appreciate all you've done for me."

"My privilege, sweet sister-in-law. I want you to know that I'm here for you no matter what."

Breanna's smile widened. "You're the best, Matthew. Thank you."

John Brockman, the children, Whip, and

the Baylesses were pleased to see Annabeth come out. "All right, Dr. Carroll says you can come back to Breanna's room. He said it would be best to stay for no more than a half hour, because Breanna needs to rest."

John nodded. "We understand. We'll not stay any longer."

When the group entered the room, they gathered close around the bed. John bent down and kissed Breanna again, and his children did the same, followed by Mary Bayless. The pastor took hold of her hand and held it tenderly.

"Let me tell all of you where we're at with Breanna's injuries right now," Dr. Carroll said. He went on to explain that Breanna's legs were totally numb. She had no feeling and, of course, could not walk. Hoping to encourage them, Dr. Carroll said that once the swelling of the muscles around her spine had gone down, he'd know whether she might be able to walk again.

Breanna looked around at the group. "I'm trusting the Great Physician, my Lord Jesus, to heal me so I can walk again and be all that I should be as a wife and mother and to still be able to work in this hospital as a nurse."

Annabeth moved close to Breanna and took hold of her hand. "You are so brave,

Breanna. I'm proud of you."

"Me too," Mary said, taking a step closer to the bed on the other side.

John was next to speak of Breanna's bravery, followed by his children. Then Pastor Bayless spoke his part on it and was followed by Whip Langford.

John looked down at his lovely wife. "See, honey? You are such an example for all of us."

"That she is!" said Dr. Matthew Carroll.

Breanna blushed.

"I have something to tell everyone," John said, looking at the group. He told them about Lee Zarbo, who refused to reveal where his brothers were, and the date that Judge Dexter had set for his execution.

"Well, at least that takes care of a third of what's left of the Zarbo gang," Whip said. "I'll be glad when we catch the last two."

"Yes. They're a menace to society." John paused. "But I am going to the jail to try to lead Lee to the Lord."

"Well, amen," Pastor Bayless said.

The others agreed that it would be wonderful if Lee Zarbo got saved before he hanged.

Pastor Bayless looked at Breanna. "I'll be telling the entire congregation on Sunday about your injuries and asking them to hold you up daily in prayer."

Breanna smiled. "Thank you, Pastor. A little while ago, I told Matt and Annabeth that I know the Lord has some reason for allowing this to happen, but by His matchless grace, there can be victory for me. I quoted a portion of one of my favorite Bible verses, Psalm 28:7. 'The LORD is my strength and my shield; my heart trusted in him, and I am helped.' All I can do right now is trust the One who is my strength and my shield to help me."

The pastor smiled. "Glory!"

John looked down at his wife. "Sweetheart, that is indeed a wonderful Scripture. I know it's one of your favorites. In my devotions this morning, I was reading Psalm 121 and noted one verse there especially. The psalmist wrote in verse 2, 'My help cometh from the LORD, which made heaven and earth.' Those two verses tie together marvelously, don't they? 'My heart trusted in him, and I am helped,' then, 'My help cometh from the LORD, which made heaven and earth.' "

"That's *beautiful,* Papa!" Ginny exclaimed.

"Amen!" Pastor Bayless chimed in. Then the rest of the group spoke of how the combination of those two verses spoke to their own hearts.

"Let me share a couple of other verses in

the Psalms that I have claimed many times when I desperately needed the Lord to hear and answer my prayers," John continued. "In Psalm 143:1, David wrote, 'Hear my prayer, O LORD, give ear to my supplications: in thy faithfulness answer me, and in thy righteousness.' Then there's a verse that just thrilled my heart when I found it — it ties beautifully with the one I just quoted — Psalm 66:19, which says, 'But verily God hath heard me; he hath attended to the voice of my prayer.' Isn't that terrific?"

Everyone spoke their agreement.

"As I said," John went on, "I have claimed these two verses many times when I was desperate. What a wonderful God we serve!"

Though the laudanum was taking effect and Breanna's eyes were drooping, she looked up at her husband. "I will be claiming those exact verses when I bring my supplications to the Lord regarding my paralysis."

"I'll do the same thing in my prayers for you, Breanna," Mary Bayless said.

Dr. Carroll could see Breanna's dull, drooping eyes. "All right, everyone," he said, "as you can see, Breanna needs to get some rest." He turned to John. "You may stay quietly for as long as you want and come and go as you desire, but she will be sleeping for several hours now."

The doctor looked at the others. "You all look like you could use something to eat and some rest as well."

"I believe you're right, Doctor," said the pastor.

Before they left, both the pastor and his wife spoke lovingly to Breanna, vowing to pray regularly for her. Whip also said goodbye, then kissed his wife's cheek and hurried out the door. Breanna's children hugged her and told her they loved her. John did the same. "All right, children, let's let your mother rest so the Lord can begin healing her."

As they walked to the door, John paused and turned back. "Look at that," he whispered to his children.

Annabeth was standing over their mother, who was already asleep, a peaceful look on her beautiful face.

That evening at the Brockman ranch, while Ginny and Meggie prepared supper, they talked of the things they would do to help their mother and care for her when she came home. At one point, as they were setting the table, Meggie looked at her sister and asked in a small voice, "Mama *will* be all right, won't she, Ginny?"

Ginny smiled. "Our mama is a strong lady, honey. By God's grace, she will be as good as new!"

Meggie nodded. "Thank you, Ginny. I needed to hear that."

Ginny gave her little sister a hug. "We will all do our part for Mama, honey, and I *know* that the Lord will do *His* part!"

Todd and Chice Zarbo were at their camp several miles north of Denver, waiting for their brother, Lee, to show up. They were concerned that Lee hadn't returned to the camp yet. Later, when darkness had fallen and the moon was shining brightly, the time came to slip into their bedrolls for the night. They were very concerned that Lee was missing.

Standing over his bedroll, Chice looked at his older brother in the moonlight. "Todd, my shoulder's feeling better. If Lee doesn't show up by morning, we should go to Denver to find him."

Todd was standing beside his own bedroll a few feet away. "I agree. I sure hope our little brother hasn't gotten himself into trouble and been snatched by the law."

Chice bobbed his head, sucking air through his teeth. "I sure hope that hasn't happened." He looked at their horses, which were tied to nearby trees. "Let's water the horses and get some sleep."

The Zarbo brothers watered their horses at the adjacent brook, then slipped into their bedrolls for the night. It took them quite some time to fall asleep.

Sleep was a long time coming for John Brockman. Even then, at one point, he awakened to find himself reaching across the bed for Breanna. When he felt only the empty mattress and sheet, he was struck with the reality that his dear wife was in the hospital, bearing grave injuries. John prayed, once again seeking God's grace for Breanna, for his family, and for himself.

As he tried to go back to sleep, John thought about how he and the children could make things easier and more convenient for Breanna when she came home. Within a few minutes, he had devised a plan to turn the parlor into a cozy bedroom for Breanna. As he was mulling this plan over, sleep finally overtook him.

When John woke, just as the sun was rising, he agreed with himself that the plan he had devised should be carried out. He got dressed, went downstairs to the parlor, and started putting his plan into action.

Moments later, while rearranging furniture, John saw a sleepy Paul looking at him from the parlor door.

"Papa, what are you doing making all this noise at this hour?"

John smiled at him. "Oh, I'm sorry if I woke you, son. Guess I didn't realize just how early it is. I got an idea in the middle of the night to make this room into a temporary bedroom for your mother. As you know, the couch is quite comfortable to sleep on. She won't be able to navigate the stairs to the second floor for some time, and this way she can get the rest she needs day and night. It will also have her close to the rest of the family in the daytime."

"Okay . . . but why did you move the couch close to the big window?"

"Because I want her to be able to see the sky and the sunlight during the day. I'm going to sleep on the floor right here by the couch at night so she won't be alone."

This time Paul smiled. "You sure are smart, Papa. Let me help you put the chairs and tables that were by the big window where the couch used to be."

Soon the girls were awake too, and they joined in to help fix up their mother's new room. When everything was in place, John and the children looked around and examined their handiwork.

"Papa," Ginny said, "this is perfect for Mama. She's going to love it because it will keep her close to all the activity in the house, and when she wants rest and privacy, all she has to do is ask one of us to close the door."

"We'll take good care of her, Papa," said Meggie. "You can depend on us."

"That's for sure, Papa," said Paul.

John grinned. "Thanks, kids. I know I can count on you."

After shaving and eating a hurried breakfast, John rode his big black horse toward town earlier than usual. He had a Bible in his saddlebag, and after going to his office to check in, he planned to go to the county jail to try to lead Lee Zarbo to the Lord. But his first stop after the office would be the hospital, to check on Breanna.

When he eventually entered Breanna's room, he found nurse Elsie Widner sitting on a chair beside her bed.

Elsie stood and placed a forefinger to her lips. John could see that Breanna was asleep.

In a low whisper, Elsie said, "Chief Brockman, your wife had a rather restless night, but as you can see, she is now sleeping comfortably."

John smiled and whispered, "I won't bother her now. When she wakes up, please tell her I was here and I'll be back later."

"I'll tell her," said Elsie.

Chief Brockman entered Sheriff Carter's office with his Bible in hand.

The sheriff rose to his feet. "Good morning, Chief. What can I do for you?"

"I'd like to talk to Lee Zarbo in one of the private meeting rooms."

Carter eyed the Bible in John's hand. "Certainly. I'll go to his cell and tell him you want to talk. You can wait in the meeting room, and I'll bring him to you."

After the chief was seated, the sheriff went to Lee's cell and looked at him through the bars. "Lee, chief U.S. marshal John Brockman wants to talk to you privately."

Lee stepped up to the bars with a cynical look on his face. "I don't want to talk to him."

Sheriff Carter scowled at him and spoke through set teeth. "You can go quietly for your talk with Chief Brockman, or I'll have a couple of my deputies pick you up and carry you."

Lee squared his jaw. He knew he really had no choice. "Okay, okay, Sheriff. Though I have nothing but disgust for the man who put me in this jail, I'll talk to him."

A few minutes later, the chief U.S. marshal

and the convicted outlaw who was scheduled to hang in one week sat down at the table facing each other. Lee Zarbo flinched when he saw the Bible in Brockman's hand.

There was a burning hatred in Lee's eyes. "Whaddaya wanna talk about?" he snapped.

John opened his Bible. "Lee, a week from today, you are going to die. You need to receive God's Son, the Lord Jesus Christ, as your Saviour, lest you burn in the flames of hell."

Lee jumped to his feet and spit in Chief Brockman's face. "I don't want anything to do with you, with that Bible, or with Jesus Christ!"

As John wiped the spittle from his face and attempted to keep a grip on his temper, Lee reached for John's Bible. "I'm gonna tear it up!"

John snatched his Bible out of Lee's reach and stood up.

Lee stepped around the table and lunged at him, grabbing for the Bible in the chief's left hand.

With his right hand, John unleashed a powerful punch that slammed against Zarbo's jaw with the force of a thunderbolt. The outlaw hit the floor flat on his back and was out cold.

One of the deputy sheriffs, Brandon

Moore, came bolting through the door, having heard the shouting and commotion. "Chief!" he gasped. "What happened?"

John held up his Bible. "He tried to grab my Bible and said he was going to tear it up."

"Oh, yeah. I heard him say he was going to tear something up. Guess he had it coming!"

Lee began to regain consciousness. When his head had cleared, he sat up, flicked a glance at the sheriff's deputy, then looked angrily at the chief U.S. marshal as he struggled to his feet, rubbing his jaw.

Deputy Moore looked on as Chief Brockman tapped his Bible. "Will you listen to me, now, Lee? You need to be saved."

Wrath was evident in Lee's eyes as he stepped toward Brockman and spit in his face again. "I told you, I don't want anything to do with you, that Bible, or Jesus Christ!" Lee looked at the deputy. "I want to go back to my cell."

"All right," Moore said. "I'll take you back right now." He looked at John Brockman. "Chief, will you stay here for a few minutes? I want to talk to you."

John nodded. "Of course."

"I'll be right back."

John watched the two men as they went

out the door. Lee Zarbo cast a hateful look
back over his shoulder.

NINETEEN

Less than five minutes after Deputy Moore had left to return Zarbo to his cell, Moore reentered the private room and found Chief Brockman sitting at the table reading his Bible.

John closed the Bible. "Did Lee Zarbo try to escape from you on the way back to his cell?"

"No sir. All he did was mutter about how much he hates *you*."

John shrugged. "Lots of outlaws hate me."

As Moore sat down opposite him, John asked, "So what do you want to talk to me about?"

Moore adjusted himself on the chair nervously, "Well, sir, as I told you, Sheriff Carter sent me to wait outside the door while you were talking to Lee Zarbo."

"Yes."

"The sheriff wanted me outside so if any trouble started, I could help you."

298

John nodded.

"Well, sir, when I overheard you tell Zarbo that he needed to receive the Lord Jesus Christ as his Saviour lest he burn in the flames of hell, it really got to me. I'm going to die someday too. Chief Brockman, I've heard about the need to be saved before, but I don't know how to get saved. I don't want to go to a burning hell when I die. I want to go to heaven."

John smiled. "Bring that chair around here beside me, and I'll show you straight from the Scriptures how to be saved."

Brandon Moore moved quickly and sat next to the chief U.S. marshal moments later. John opened the Bible and carefully took the young deputy through the gospel of Jesus Christ and the plan of salvation. After nearly an hour, Brandon Moore received the Lord Jesus Christ as his Saviour.

Brandon was wiping tears of joy from his eyes when John showed him the Scripture regarding his first step of obedience to the Lord after being saved — to be baptized. John then invited Brandon to come to First Baptist Church the next morning to present himself for baptism.

"Oh, I want to do that!" Brandon said. "Since I have tomorrow off, I'll definitely be there, Chief."

John told Brandon he'd meet him in front of the church just before ten o'clock for Sunday school time. John then laid a hand on Brandon's shoulder and prayed for him, asking the Lord to bless him in his new life with Jesus in his heart. Brandon was wiping at his tears as the chief U.S. marshal left the jail.

As John headed for his office, he rejoiced over Brandon Moore's salvation. At the same time, he was heavy-hearted over Lee Zarbo's rejection of Jesus Christ.

Todd and Chice Zarbo rode into Denver just after ten o'clock that morning, wondering what had happened to their brother. As they rode slowly along the main street, searching both boardwalks, Chice suddenly pointed to the right. "Todd! Look over there. It's Buck Skidmore!"

Todd caught sight of the man instantly. "Well, sure enough. Let's pull over and talk to him."

Buck was in his early sixties. When the Zarbo brothers and some other outlaws — including Buck — had been pulling robberies together in Nebraska seven years before, a couple of the male bank customers had pulled their guns, and Todd had saved

300

Buck's life by cutting both men down.

Soon afterward, Buck — who had never killed anyone as an outlaw — was caught by the law and sent to the Nebraska State Penitentiary for five years.

As the two riders guided their horses up close to the boardwalk, they caught Buck Skidmore's attention. Buck's jaw dropped open as he recognized the riders. "Hey! Todd . . . Chice."

The two Zarbo brothers quickly dismounted, and Buck stepped off the boardwalk and shook their hands. "Great to see you boys."

Both brothers noticed that Buck had a rolled-up newspaper stuck under his belt.

"Buck," Todd said, "you were released from prison about two years ago, weren't you?"

"Sure was."

"What are you doing here in Denver?"

"Well, when I got out of prison, I came here to start a new life. Since coming to these parts, I've lived in a mountain cabin some twenty miles west of town. However, I recently received an inheritance from an uncle in Kansas. I bought a nice house right here in Denver, and since then, I've been trying to sell the cabin."

Chice grinned. "Well, Buck, you'll sell it

one of these days. I'm just glad to know about your inheritance."

"Yeah, me too," Todd said.

With a break in his voice, Buck said, "You two must be here to visit Lee."

Both brothers' mouths fell open.

While Chice gasped for words, Todd said, "What do you mean, Buck? You mean you've seen him?"

Buck shook his head. "No, but I just found out that Lee is locked up in the county jail." He took the rolled-up newspaper from under his belt. "I read about it right here in this morning's edition of the *Rocky Mountain News.*"

Buck opened the newspaper, turned around, and stepped between the Zarbo brothers so they both could see the paper. He showed them the article on Lee's arrest by chief U.S. marshal John Brockman. The article included a photograph of Lee Zarbo taken by a reporter. The article also went into detail about Lee being a part of the Zarbo brothers' murderous gang. Judge Ralph Dexter had set a date for Lee to be hanged.

Todd sucked in a sharp breath. "July 21! That's a week from today."

"Oh no . . . ," Chice said.

Todd's cheeks flushed as he growled like

an angry dog. "I'm gonna kill that Chief Brockman!"

Buck shook his head. "You saved my life once, Todd. Now let me save yours."

"What do you mean?"

Buck looked him square in the eye. "You try to kill Brockman, it'll be your last day on earth!"

Todd seethed with anger. "What're you talking about? I've cut down a lot of hotshot lawmen in my day."

"Not this one . . . Let me explain, okay?"

Chice looked on, as Todd nodded to Buck. "Okay."

The silver-haired man looked steadily at Todd Zarbo. "Have you ever heard of a tall, rugged man of the West who was more than lightning fast and deadly accurate with his gun, a man called the Stranger?"

"Yeah. I've heard a lot about that guy. He was challenged many a time by some of the top gunfighters all over the West, but not one could ever outdraw or outshoot him."

"I've heard the same things about the Stranger," Chice said. "Some people even called him John Stranger."

Buck nodded and set his jaw. "That's true, Chice. A lot of cocky gunslingers tried to make names for themselves by challenging the Stranger, feeling sure they could outdraw him. Well, let me tell you. A lot of men tried, and a lot of men died."

Todd then looked at Buck. "What's this John Stranger got to do with that big shot federal marshal who arrested Lee?"

"Let me ask you something," Buck said. "What does this newspaper say the federal marshal's first name is?"

Todd glanced at the paper again. "John."

"Yeah," Buck said. "He's also known as John Stranger."

Todd Zarbo shook his head.

Buck could see the powerful effect of his statement on the Zarbo brothers. "That's why I said earlier I wanted you to let me save *your* life this time. If you try to kill Chief Brockman, he will drop you dead in your tracks. It'll be your last day on earth."

Todd stiffened his neck and squared his shoulders. "I won't challenge him to a quick draw. I'll find another way to kill him."

Buck shook his head. "Todd, even if you tried to sneak up on Chief Brockman and shoot him in the back or shoot him from some hidden place, you would still get killed."

Todd snarled. "Oh yeah? Well —"

"A normal human being has five basic senses," Buck interrupted. "You know — sight, hearing, smell, touch, and taste —

but John Brockman has a sixth sense that has kept him alive despite the outlaws who have tried to kill him in every way imaginable."

Since neither Zarbo brother responded, Buck continued. "I've heard some people say that Brockman's sixth sense is a gift from God because Brockman walks close to Him."

Buck peered at the pale, shell-shocked faces of his old outlaw pals. He then fixed his steady gaze on Todd. "Got the picture, my friend?"

Todd was deep in thought but did not answer. He couldn't make a sound. His voice was caught in his throat.

Chice saw the state his brother was in. "Buck, my brother has the picture, all right, but I can see that he is even more stunned than I am to learn who the chief U.S. marshal that arrested Lee really is."

Todd finally found a portion of his voice and laid a hand on Buck's shoulder. In a humble tone, he said, "Buck, thanks for telling me who Brockman really is. I've also heard of the Stranger's sixth sense. If I had tried to kill him, I no doubt would have ended up dead."

After a few seconds of silence, Chice said, "T-Todd, we have to do *something* to keep

Lee from being hanged."

Todd nodded. "We'll have to come up with a way to rescue Lee from the law and from the gallows."

"We will . . ."

Todd turned to Buck, his voice stronger. "I need to ask you something."

"Sure."

"Would you let Chice and me stay at your mountain cabin? It's best that we not stay here in town. Somebody might come along and recognize us."

"Well, Todd, since you saved my life some time ago, I'll do anything for you. Of course, you and Chice can stay at my cabin."

Todd's brow furrowed. "Buck, do you mean that? *Anything?*"

Buck had folded the newspaper again and was holding it in his left hand. He squeezed the paper, causing it to give off a crinkling sound, and with an affirmative tone said, "Yes, Todd, I mean exactly that. *Anything.*"

"Good. I just thought of a way to save Lee from hanging. Buck, do you know if Chief Brockman has a wife?"

"Yes, he sure does." Buck looked confused. "Why do you want to know? And what's that got to do with me saying I'll do anything for you?"

Chice's eyes were fixed on his brother as

306

Todd turned to Buck. "If Chice and I could abduct Brockman's wife and secretly keep her captive at your cabin, I could send a message to Brockman and tell him to set Lee free before next Saturday or we will kill his wife. We'll need to use your cabin to keep Mrs. Brockman hostage until the big shot chief marshal sets Lee free. Okay?"

Buck immediately had an uneasy feeling, and the thought of John Brockman's wife being abducted made his flesh crawl. However, he knew he dare not cross the Zarbos.

"Since Brockman won't know where we're holding his wife," Todd continued, "he will certainly see to it that Lee is set free."

Chice chuckled. "Hey, I like that idea."

Buck didn't like the idea of the Zarbo brothers abducting Chief Brockman's wife at all, but he felt relief when he realized what he could show them in the newspaper he was holding in his hand. He opened the newspaper again. "There's something else here in this edition you need to see."

Todd and Chice looked on as Buck turned to a different page. "Let me read this article to you."

Both men stood beside him as before so they could get a look at the article while Buck read it to them.

They learned that the chief's wife, Breanna, was presently a patient in Mile High Hospital, where she was employed as a nurse. Mrs. Brockman was paralyzed after taking a fall down the stairs at the hospital. When Buck finished reading the article to them, he said, "You two would have a tough time trying to abduct her from the hospital. She can't even walk."

The Zarbos looked at each other, and Todd said, "He's right about that. There's no way we're gonna be able to grab her." He then turned to Buck. "Do you know if the Brockmans have children?"

Buck felt his flesh crawl again, but knew he must tell the man who had once saved his life the truth. Buck rubbed his jaw. "The Brockmans have a son who is fifteen years old, a daughter who is thirteen, and an adopted daughter who is nine. The family is written up in the *Rocky Mountain News* quite often."

"Then you would know their names?" Todd asked.

"Well, uh . . . yeah," Buck replied nervously. He didn't like the direction this conversation was going.

"So?"

Buck didn't want to tell him, but he feared what Todd might do to him if he refused to give him the names of the Brockman children. Trying to cover his nervousness, he said, "The boy's name is Paul. The older girl's name is Ginny, and the adopted girl's name is Meggie."

Todd nodded, then looked at Chice. "I want to abduct Ginny and keep her at Buck's cabin."

"Sounds good to me," Chice agreed, grinning wickedly.

Buck felt his spine tingle, and his heart skipped a beat. He started to say that he didn't want them abducting any of the Brockman children, but he knew how violent Todd and Chice could be when they became angry, and he feared what they might do to him. He remained silent.

"Chice, I believe that if we're holding Brockman's real daughter rather than the adopted one, he'll be more apt to do what the message commands. When the big chief gets the message warning that he must set Lee free immediately or his daughter will be killed, I have absolutely no doubt that he will comply right away."

"You betcha!" Chice said.

"Buck, you think it'll work?"

With his stomach feeling as if it was lined with broken glass, Buck still attempted to cover his nervousness. "I have no doubt, Todd."

"That's the way I see it." Todd grinned. "Let me ask you something else."

"What's that?"

"Where do the Brockmans live?"

Still fearful for his own safety, Buck told them, his mouth dry. "They have a ranch a few miles west of Denver."

"I'd like to see it," Todd said.

"Me too."

"Well, whenever I take you to my cabin, you'll see it," Buck said. "We'll have to ride right past the Brockman ranch."

"Tell you what, Buck," Todd said. "I'd like you to take us to your cabin as soon as possible. We'll take a good look at the Brockman place as we ride past. Can you take us now?"

"I can do that. I keep my horse in a stable just a block from here. You can lead your horses and walk with me to the stable. Then we can ride together to my house here in Denver."

Chice frowned. "Why do we need to go to your house first?"

"Because I need to take some medicine before we head into the mountains."

"What for?" both men asked together.

Buck rubbed his chest. "I've developed heart trouble, and my doctor put me on the medicine to ease the chest pains."

310

"Oh," Todd said. "Sorry to hear about that."

"Me too." Chice said.

While the Zarbo brothers led their horses along the street, Buck walked between them. Todd and Chice brought up some of the robberies they and Buck had done together in Nebraska. When the Zarbo brothers chuckled and talked freely about people they'd killed during some of the robberies, Buck felt his muscles go tense. But he told himself he was thankful he'd never taken a life during his outlaw days.

When they arrived at the stable, Buck went into the office and then walked to the corral and got his horse. He bridled and saddled his bay stallion in the barn and soon rode onto the street where the Zarbos were waiting in their saddles and led them away.

At Mile High Hospital, Dr. Carroll looked up from the desk in his office and saw Annabeth come through the open door. As she approached the desk, a wide smile creased her face.

The doctor chuckled. "Well, what are you so happy about, Annabeth?"

"Damon Fortney awakened from his coma about an hour ago, Dr. Carroll, and he is now talking quite clearly. Isn't that good news?"

Dr. Carroll smiled. "It certainly is. Has his memory returned?"

"He is still quite confused about some things. He only remembers falling off the roof of his barn. He is still in a great deal of pain due to so many broken ribs, but thankfully, as you said, none of the broken ribs punctured a lung. That is quite obvious now."

Rising from his chair, Dr. Carroll said, "I'll go check on him and determine his condition now that he is out of the coma. That coma was a blessing actually. It has given his injuries some time to heal."

As the doctor stepped around the desk to head for the door, Annabeth stopped him. "Just a minute, please, Doctor. I want you to know that I just told Mr. Fortney about knocking Breanna down the stairs and the injuries she suffered."

"Oh?"

"Of course, he doesn't remember a thing about it, but when I told him that she may never walk again, tears streamed down his face. When I explained the seriousness of Breanna's injuries, he insisted that he be taken to her room to see her. He wants to apologize. But I told him I'd have to check with you first."

"It sounds like it's going to be very painful for him emotionally if he doesn't get to see Breanna and apologize."

"I'm sure you're right about that."

The doctor rubbed his jaw. "I'll take Mr. Fortney to Breanna's room. Will you go check on Breanna and see if she's awake?"

Annabeth nodded. "Of course."

"Thank you," Dr. Carroll said. "In the meantime, I'll go get a wheelchair and come back here. You can meet me here and tell me if Breanna is awake."

Annabeth nodded. "See you shortly."

TWENTY

Annabeth arrived back at Dr. Carroll's office about ten minutes later and saw him coming down the hall toward her pushing a wheelchair.

"Breanna is awake, Doctor, but I only chatted with her for a moment. I didn't tell her that Damon Fortney had come out of his coma and was asking to be brought to her room so he could talk to her."

"You did the right thing, Annabeth. Mr. Fortney should be able to spring this pleasant deed on Breanna on his own. I'll head on down to Mr. Fortney's room and see if I can grab an orderly on the way to help me get him in the wheelchair. If you want to drop by Breanna's room in a little while, feel free."

Annabeth smiled. "I'll do that."

She watched Dr. Carroll walk down the hall toward Damon Fortney's room, then turned and went to look in on a patient in a nearby room.

Along the way, Dr. Carroll spotted one of the young hospital orderlies coming out of a patient's room. "Hey, Dale! I need some help."

Dale Robins looked up at the oncoming chief administrator and waited until he drew up. "What can I do for you, Dr. Carroll?"

"You know who Damon Fortney is, don't you?"

"Oh, yes sir," Dale nodded his head a little. "The rancher who went out of his mind and knocked poor Mrs. Brockman down the stairs."

"Well, now that he is out of his coma and has been told what he did to Mrs. Brockman, he wants to apologize to her. I need you to come help me get him in this wheelchair so I can take him to Mrs. Brockman's room."

"Be glad to," Dale said. "Let's go."

Within a few minutes, the doctor and the orderly entered Mr. Fortney's room and found the gray-haired rancher lying on his bed, wide awake and clear-eyed.

After greeting the patient, who was eying the wheelchair quizzically, Dr. Carroll told Fortney that Nurse Langford had shared Mr. Fortney's desire to talk to Breanna Brockman and apologize for knocking her down the stairs. He was here to wheel him to Mrs. Brockman's room.

Damon Fortney's face glowed with delight, and his lips curled in a smile. "Oh, thank you, Dr. Carroll! I just have to see her and apologize."

"All right, Mr. Fortney. I must warn you that when Dale and I move you from the bed and to the wheelchair, you're going to experience some pain in your ribs."

"I know, Doctor," the rancher replied, "but I just gotta do it."

Dr. Carroll smiled. "Okay." He nodded at Dale as they agreed on a plan for moving Mr. Fortney. Ever so gently, they helped him to sit up in the bed, then lifted him into their arms. A low groan escaped his tightly clamped lips as they placed him in the wheelchair.

Letting out a gasp, the rancher looked at Dr. Carroll. "I don't mean to be a baby, Doctor, but I've never had anything in my life hurt as much as these broken ribs."

Annabeth entered the room just then. Dr. Carroll nodded at her and looked down at the rancher. "That's quite all right, Mr. Fortney. Now, let's just give you a few minutes to sit here, and maybe some of the pain will ease up."

Fortney nodded, then looked at Annabeth.

He managed a faint smile. "Hello, Mrs. Langford. Nice to see you again."

"You too." Annabeth looked at the doctor. "I thought I'd stop by and see if you had already gone to Breanna's room. I'll just walk down with you."

"Fine," Dr. Carroll said.

"Dr. Carroll," the orderly asked, "is it all right if I go now? I've got some work to finish up."

"Of course, Dale. Thanks for your help."

"My pleasure, sir."

Annabeth turned her attention to the patient and saw that he was licking his very dry lips. She walked to a nearby table where a pitcher of water sat with a glass beside it and filled the glass with water. Handing Fortney the glass of water, she said, "Here you go, Mr. Fortney. This will help your dry mouth."

The rancher smiled and quickly drank all the water in the glass. He handed the empty glass to Annabeth and looked at the doctor. "Okay, Doctor, I'm as ready as I can be to talk to Mrs. Brockman. I hope she understands that I was crazed with pain and didn't know what I was doing when I knocked her down the stairs."

Dr. Carroll smiled kindly. "Oh, you can be sure that sweet lady indeed understands what you were going through. It has all been explained to her. Being the proficient nurse she is, I guarantee you she understands. So if you're ready, let's go."

The rancher nodded. "Yes. Let's go."

Dr. Carroll pushed the wheelchair through the door into the hallway with Annabeth behind him. As they started down the hall toward Breanna's room, she moved up beside him. At the slight jarring of the wheelchair, Fortney groaned and quickly placed his hand over his mouth to stifle it. Dr. Carroll slowed the wheelchair.

The rancher looked up over his shoulder. "It's okay, Dr. Carroll. Just keep on pushing it. Let's get to Mrs. Brockman."

Breanna was lying in her hospital bed, talking to her sister, Dottie, who was seated on a wooden chair next to the bed.

Dottie was in the middle of a sentence when the door opened. Annabeth walked in with Dottie's husband pushing a wheelchair with a wide-awake Damon Fortney sitting in it. The sisters looked at each other with pleasant surprise as Dr. Carroll brought the wheelchair to a halt on the opposite side of the bed from where his wife was sitting.

Dr. Carroll smiled at Dottie. "Hello, sweetheart."

"And hello to *you*."

Dr. Carroll looked down at Breanna. "As you can see, Mr. Fortney has come out of his coma. Annabeth was with him when he regained consciousness, and she quickly learned that the only thing he remembers is falling off the roof of the barn. When Annabeth told him about his knocking you down the stairs and the harm it caused, including the fact that you may never walk again, he insisted that he be brought to your room so he could talk to you."

Breanna set her big blue eyes on Damon Fortney and smiled. "I'm just so glad to see that you're doing so much better, Mr. Fortney. What did you want to talk about?"

With tears in his eyes, the man said, "Mrs. Brockman, as nurse Annabeth told you, I don't remember the incident on the stairs at all, but I want to tell you how sorry I am for what I did. From the depths of my heart, I apologize."

Breanna reached her hand out to him. "Thank you for your apology, Mr. Fortney, but I know what you did was not your fault. I understand how the pain you were in had you out of your mind. Dr. Carroll and Annabeth have kept me up on your condition and the fact that you were in a coma. I'm just relieved you're out of the coma."

Fortney looked at Dr. Carroll. "You said that she may never walk again. Is there some hope that she *will* be able to walk?"

Dr. Carroll's face went pale. "Only if God does a miracle."

The rancher broke into sobs and looked at Breanna. "Oh, I'm so sorry it is this serious. Please, please forgive me."

At that moment, Pastor Bayless entered the room through the open door with his wife at his side. They had both heard the sobbing man asking Breanna's forgiveness from outside the room.

Breanna was now weeping as well. "Mr. Fortney, please listen to me. I do not blame you for what happened. But if it will make you feel better, then I will say it. I *do* forgive you."

Tears spilled down the rancher's cheeks. "Oh, thank you, Mrs. Brockman. Thank you for your forgiveness."

"You are welcome, Mr. Fortney."

Wiping tears from his eyes, Fortney smiled at her, then glanced up at the couple that had just come in.

"Mr. Fortney," Breanna said, "this is my pastor, Robert Bayless, and his wife, Mary, of First Baptist Church here in Denver."

The rancher smiled at them. "I am glad to meet both of you."

The pastor extended his hand, and as Fortney weakly met his grip, Pastor Bayless said kindly, "Mr. Fortney, Mrs. Brockman has explained to me the kind of pain you were in at the time you ran into her. She has held no ill will toward you for her injuries."

"Pastor Bayless, her forgiveness will always be a treasure to me."

Mary Bayless looked down at Fortney. "That's sweet."

Leaning down a little, Pastor Bayless looked into the rancher's eyes. "Mr. Fortney, if you feel up to it, I'd like to talk to you later about another kind of forgiveness. May I do that?"

Looking a bit perplexed, the rancher said, "Of course, sir. I'd be glad to hear it."

The others in the room smiled at each other, knowing exactly what the pastor had planned.

"Mr. Fortney," Dr. Carroll said, "since you've talked with Mrs. Brockman, I think it would be best to take you back to your room so you can lie down. I don't want you getting too tired. I'm sure Pastor Bayless will help me lift you out of the wheelchair and get you in the bed."

"I sure will," said the pastor.

As Dr. Carroll grabbed the handles of the

wheelchair, Damon Fortney reached out a shaky hand and placed it on Breanna's on the edge of the bed. Tears misted his faded blue eyes. "Again, ma'am, I am so sorry for the injuries I inflicted on you. Thank you, once again, for your forgiveness, and if I can ever do anything for you or your family once these ribs are healed, I'm at your service."

Breanna was touched by his words. "Thank you, Mr. Fortney. I appreciate your kind offer. In the meantime, you just get better. Then when you're able, please come to our ranch and see us. My husband and my children will be happy to meet you. Don't you worry about me. The Lord is in control of my life, and I'm safe in His loving care."

The rancher nodded silently, then squeezed her hand. "Thank you again for your forgiveness. I'll be seeing you as soon as possible."

As Dr. Carroll began pushing the wheelchair toward the door, Breanna said, "Bye, Mr. Fortney. Thank you for having Dr. Carroll bring you here to talk to me."

Fortney waved at her as he and the doctor made a turn and disappeared.

Pastor Bayless looked at Breanna. "We'll come back and let you know how it goes."

"Please do," Breanna said. "I'll be praying."

After Buck Skidmore took his medicine at his house, he and the Zarbo brothers mounted their horses and rode west out of Denver.

Soon the three men were riding past the Brockman ranch and saw a tall teenage boy and two girls standing in front of the ranch house.

Buck pointed to the boy. "That's Paul. Ginny is the bigger girl, obviously. Both girls have blond hair and blue eyes."

"As I already said, I believe Chief Brockman will be more apt to see that Lee is set free if his *real* daughter's life is in danger." Todd paused. "We'll find a way to successfully abduct Ginny."

Buck quivered at Todd's words, wishing he could talk him out of the kidnapping, but he knew that both Todd and Chice wanted their brother to live and they would do anything to see that Lee's life was spared. Buck would only endanger his own life if he tried to stop them.

At Mile High Hospital, Breanna lay on her bed with her eyes closed, praying in a whisper that the Lord would give Pastor

Bayless Holy Spirit power as he shared the gospel with Damon Fortney and tried to lead him to the Saviour.

Just as she whispered her "amen," she heard footsteps and looked up to see two couples enter the room — Fred and Sofie Ryerson and Wayne and Lucille Ryerson, members of their church. Fred and Wayne were brothers. When John had been traveling the West as the Stranger, he had helped out Fred and Sofie financially and had the joy of leading them to the Lord. Fred and Sophie had been instrumental in bringing Wayne and Lucille to the Lord, and now both couples lived on a farm just east of Denver.

As the couples approached the bed, Sofie said, "Hello, Breanna! We just had to come and see how you are doing."

Breanna smiled at her friend. "Well, in one way I am doing better."

"And what's that?" Lucille asked.

Breanna adjusted her head on the pillow. "You all remember that I told you the name of the man who knocked me down the stairs, Damon Fortney."

The four nodded.

"He had been in a coma ever since. Well, when he came out of the coma a little while ago, Annabeth was tending to him. She learned that he didn't remember anything about knocking me down the stairs. All he remembered was falling off the roof of his barn. Everything else was a blank."

Wayne shook his head. "Wow! Isn't that something?"

"Yes, it is," Breanna agreed. "So anyway, Mr. Fortney asked to be brought to me so he could talk to me. Dr. Carroll put him in a wheelchair and brought him to my room. The dear man wept and asked my forgiveness. During our conversation, Pastor and Mrs. Bayless came in and heard quite a bit of what Mr. Fortney said. When we were done talking, Pastor asked Mr. Fortney if he could talk to him about another kind of forgiveness, and Mr. Fortney said yes.

"Pastor and Mrs. Bayless are in Mr. Fortney's room right now, and the pastor is talking to him about his need to receive the Lord Jesus as his Saviour."

"Oh, glory to God!" said Fred.

"I sure hope the rancher gets saved," Wayne said.

Both women spoke their agreement.

Even as they were speaking, Pastor and Mary Bayless came into the room and were greeted by all four Ryersons.

"Pastor, I was just telling the Ryersons that you were with Mr. Fortney in his hospital room, talking to him about being saved. Did he receive Jesus as his Saviour?" Breanna asked.

Smiles immediately broke across the Baylesses' faces. "He sure did!"

Tears filled Breanna's eyes. "Oh, praise the Lord!"

Pastor Bayless smiled broadly. "As soon as Mr. Fortney is well enough, he is going to present himself for baptism at First Baptist Church. And, get this . . . he told Mary and me that when his wife comes home from Missouri, he wants to see her get saved."

Breanna and the Ryersons rejoiced together, giving praise to the Lord for this good news. They all agreed to be praying for Mrs. Fortney's salvation.

When the group grew quiet, more tears began to stream from Breanna's eyes. "Just seeing Damon Fortney saved as a result of this accident makes all my suffering worth it. Now he'll never suffer in the flames of hell!"

Mary leaned down and kissed Breanna's tear-stained cheek. "Sweetie, I appreciate your attitude so very much."

"So do I," the pastor affirmed.

Breanna's lips trembled. "I'm sure if the Lord saw fit that I should never walk again, it would be very difficult to bear, but if that's what it took to get that dear man saved, it's worth it. We never know how God is going to work in our lives and in the lives of others with whom we come in contact, but maybe some Christians who know the Fortneys have been praying that they would be saved. Since I apparently had a part in the answer to their prayers, I am very blessed."

Mary, Sofie, and Lucille were weeping.

"If the Lord sees fit to let me walk again, I will be most grateful to Him, but if not, as He said to the apostle Paul in 2 Corinthians 12:9 when he needed healing, 'My grace is sufficient for thee: for my strength is made perfect in weakness.' " Breanna took a short breath. "I believe that with all of my heart."

"Oh, Breanna," Mary said, "you are such a blessing to me!"

"She's a blessing to all of us." Pastor Bayless smiled down at Breanna.

The Ryersons spoke their agreement, and then the pastor said, "I want us to pray together right now, okay?"

Heads were bowed and eyes were closed as Mary held one of Breanna's hands while the pastor led them in prayer. His own voice shaking, Pastor Bayless asked the Lord to heal Breanna so she could walk again and asked that when Damon Fortney's wife arrived home from Missouri, they would be able to reach her with the gospel and see her open her heart to the Saviour.

Twenty-One

Buck Skidmore and the Zarbo brothers finally pulled up in front of Buck's cabin, which was located in the foothills of the Rocky Mountains.

As they dismounted, Chice said, "Looks like an okay cabin, Buck. A little old maybe, but it'll serve our purpose."

"Yeah," Todd said. "It's not very big, but it'll do as a place to keep our hostage."

Heading for the front porch, Buck said, "Let's go in right now, fellas, and I'll show you the interior of the cabin. Even though I'm living in my house in Denver, the cabin still has all its furniture."

When they stepped inside, Buck led them through the parlor and the kitchen to the two bedrooms at the rear. They were across a small hall from each other. One bedroom was a bit larger, and as the Zarbo brothers stood in the hall, looking back and forth, Todd pointed to the larger bedroom and

329

said, "I'll take this one."

Chice shrugged his shoulders. "Fine, big brother. I'll be comfortable in the smaller one. The beds are the same size. That's what matters."

Buck grinned. "Well, I'm glad you fellas are in agreement on that. Let's go back into the parlor."

As they passed through the kitchen, Todd looked around the room. "Looks like there's plenty of cupboards in here, Buck. The stove and kitchen table are good-sized. Looks like Chice and I will be comfortable. We'll have to find a way to keep Ginny Brockman tied up somewhere here in the cabin."

"Well, we can tie her to one of these wooden chairs at the table."

Todd rubbed his chin and looked at Buck. "Didn't I see a closet in the parlor?"

"Yes. I'll show you."

Buck led them back into the parlor and over to the door of a small clothes closet. He opened the door and let the Zarbo brothers look inside.

"Uh-huh," said Todd. "There's room enough in here for that girl." He stepped back and looked at the doorknob, noting the keyhole. "And it's got a lock. That's good. We'll keep Ginny locked up in here most of the time." He looked at Buck. "You got the key for this door?"

"Oh . . . sure," Buck said, already feeling sorry for Chief Brockman's daughter. He went to a small table by the couch, opened the drawer, and pulled out the key. He handed it to Todd, then reached into his pocket and handed him another key. "This one will lock both the front and back doors."

Todd grinned as he slipped both keys into a trouser pocket. "Great. Thanks."

"Let's go to the rear of the cabin, and I'll show you a couple of things," Buck said.

When the three men stepped out onto the back porch, Buck pointed to the corral on one side of the small barn. "You can keep your horses in the corral or the barn. There's still hay and grain in the barn. I'm sure you won't be here long, so there'll be enough." Buck also pointed out a feeding trough that stood next to a water pump with a metal water trough next to it.

Todd smiled. "Buck, ol' pal, we really appreciate you letting us stay here."

"Sure, Todd," Buck said with a grin. "It's the least I can do." He paused. "Well, we'd better head back to town."

Buck had Todd lock the doors. The three men swung into their saddles and rode back toward town.

When they arrived in Denver, they

stopped at a general store, where Todd bought paper, a small box of envelopes, and a pencil. They then rode on to Buck's house.

As they entered the front door, Todd turned to the others. "I'm gonna write the letter to Brockman now. Guess I'll sit down at the kitchen table."

"Mind if we look on while you write?" asked Chice.

"Not at all."

Todd headed for the kitchen. He sat down at the table, and both Buck and Chice stood over him and watched.

Brockman —

My name is Todd Zarbo. My brother Chice is with me. We have your daughter, Ginny, at a secret location. Since you captured and arrested our brother Lee, you must see to it that Lee is set free before noon on Wednesday or Ginny will die. You are to tell Lee to meet his brothers where he last saw us no later than three o'clock on Wednesday afternoon. If Lee shows up as directed, Ginny will be set free unharmed. However, if Lee has been followed, Ginny will die. If you do not see that Lee is released, YOU HAVE SEEN GINNY FOR THE LAST TIME!

As Buck looked at Todd's warning to the marshal, grief welled up within him, black and cold. He wished he had some way to keep Ginny Brockman from being kidnapped by the Zarbo brothers, but he knew that attempting to stop them would no doubt mean his own death.

Todd folded the paper, placed it in an envelope, and sealed it. He then wrote CHIEF U.S. MARSHAL JOHN BROCKMAN on the front. "Hey, Buck. How can we get this letter to John 'the Stranger' Brockman once we've abducted his daughter?"

Buck had to take a deep breath because of the fluttering in his heart. "Well, when Chief Brockman is at his office at the federal building, his big black horse is kept with all the deputies' horses in a small fenced area behind the building."

Todd nodded.

"When Ginny has been abducted and you and Chice have her at my cabin," Buck said quickly, "I could attach the envelope to Chief Brockman's saddle. He'll find it for sure. I guarantee you." Buck's heart was pounding in his chest now. He gritted his teeth and swallowed hard.

Todd stood up, shoved the chair back, and turned to Chice. "We'll hide in that forest on Brockmans' property near the house and outbuildings and keep watch. One way or another, we'll find a way to kidnap that thirteen-year-old girl."

Chice nodded. "Okay."

"When we do kidnap her," Todd continued, "we'll take her immediately to Buck's cabin. Then while I stay with Ginny, you can ride into town and let Buck know we have her so he can put the letter on Brockman's saddle."

Chice grinned. "Good."

"It's too late today to try grabbing Ginny. Let's do it on Monday since Brockman no doubt won't be in his office on Sunday anyway."

Feeling guilty for helping the Zarbos, Buck Skidmore wished for a way out of the situation but reminded himself that the only way out would be to die at the hands of those two killers. His mouth was dry, his tongue coated with a bitter metallic taste, and his pulse was throbbing in his temples.

In the Sunday morning service at First Baptist, after Pastor Bayless had made his usual announcements and had the ushers take the offering, he called Dr. Carroll to the platform and asked him to explain to the church Breanna Brockman's injuries.

Dr. Carroll stood in the pulpit and told

the story of how Breanna was injured and about her present condition and the possibility that she might never walk again. As he spoke, a solemn quietness fell over the room.

Dr. Carroll blinked at his tears as he asked the congregation to hold Breanna up in prayer daily. He gave them several Scriptures on the subject of prayer, encouraging them to claim them as they prayed for her.

As John Brockman and his children, along with Whip and Annabeth, wiped tears from their faces, Meggie, who was sitting next to her adoptive father, looked up at him. Through her tears she whispered, "Papa, with this many people praying for Mama, God will heal her. I just know it!"

John leaned over and kissed the top of her little blond head.

Pastor Bayless thanked the doctor for his clear explanation of Breanna's condition, then looked out over the congregation and said, "Let's have a special time of prayer for our dear friend Breanna Brockman right now." The pastor led in a touching prayer for Breanna's healing, praying especially that she would indeed be able to walk again.

After closing the prayer in Jesus' name, the pastor told the people about how the Lord had made a way for him to talk to Damon Fortney, the rancher who was responsible for the accident, and that he'd had the joy of leading Fortney to Jesus. Fortney was planning to come to the church for baptism when he was released from the hospital. Joyful praise filled the auditorium.

Ginny happily clapped her hands and looked at the others on her pew. "The Lord Jesus is the Great Physician, and He can do marvelous and wonderful things. I just know He will make it so Mama can walk again."

Meggie looked at her sister. "Yes! We must believe it."

"Amen," Paul said. "Our God can do it. He is the only one who *can*."

His children's demonstration of faith caused John to shed more tears. "Yes!" He wiped his eyes with a bandanna. "Praise the Lord; He is able to do it."

The people in the pews around them joined in and gave praise and glory to the Lord.

After a choir special, followed by a men's quartet singing Philip Bliss's great song, "Hallelujah, What a Saviour!" Pastor Bayless preached a powerful sermon on salvation, and at the invitation several adults and young people walked the aisle to be led to Christ.

Deputy Sheriff Brandon Moore went

forward as well and had the joy of testifying to the people that Chief Brockman had led him to the Lord at the county jail. There was much rejoicing in the crowd when Deputy Moore was baptized.

Before leaving the baptistry, Pastor Bayless looked toward the pew where John Brockman was sitting. "Chief Brockman," he said loud enough for all to hear, "since you led Deputy Moore to the Lord, I'd like you to stand with him in the vestibule when we close."

The tall, handsome chief U.S. marshal nodded, acknowledging that he would do so.

The song leader led the congregation in a song while the pastor prepared to come back to the platform. As they finished the second verse, Pastor Bayless appeared from a side door, stepped to the pulpit, led in a closing prayer and then dismissed the service.

When John reached Deputy Moore in the vestibule, they shook hands and then gave each other a manly hug. Brandon thanked John once again for leading him to the Lord.

John patted his shoulder. "The pleasure was mine, Deputy Moore."

"Not totally, sir! My sins are gone now, washed away in the blood of the Lamb.

What a blessing!"

When the people began to pass by and congratulate the deputy on his new life as a Christian, they also commended Chief Brockman for leading him to the Lord — and promised their continued prayer for Breanna.

John thanked them sincerely.

Paul, Ginny, and Meggie stood nearby with their aunt Dottie and uncle Matthew Carroll, and each time they heard the people tell their father they'd continue to pray for Breanna, all five thanked them.

Pastor and Mrs. Bayless looked on. After shaking hands with those who had received the Lord, the Baylesses asked Brandon Moore if he would come home with them for Sunday dinner. Moore gladly accepted.

John Brockman and his children were about to leave when Dottie turned to him and said, "Would you and the children come home and have Sunday dinner with us?"

"We'd love to have you," Matthew said.

John turned to the children. "Would you rather eat Aunt Dottie's cooking or go home and see what I can whip up?"

Paul laughed. "No, offense, Papa, but my vote is that we eat Aunt Dottie's cooking!"

"I'm with Paul, Papa," Ginny said. "My

vote is for Aunt Dottie's cooking."

Meggie giggled. "Ah . . . Aunt Dottie *is* a better cook than you, Papa."

John hugged all three. "Fine then. Let's get in the buggy and head for the Carroll Restaurant!"

Paul, Ginny, and Meggie applauded and lifted a cheer to Aunt Dottie.

John and the children climbed in the Brockman buggy while Matthew and Dottie climbed in theirs, and together both buggies left the church parking lot.

When they arrived at the Carroll house, Ginny and Meggie dashed to their aunt and volunteered to help with setting the table and the cooking.

Dottie smiled, hugged both of them, and turned to Paul and the men. "You gentlemen go sit on the front porch. Ginny, Meggie, and I will get dinner ready."

Paul laughed. "But only let them help with the cooking, Aunt Dottie, if you keep a sharp eye on them!"

Ginny made a face at Paul. "Meggie and I can both outcook *you!*"

Everybody laughed, even Paul.

The men chose to go to the parlor, and the girls went with their aunt to the kitchen.

When the meal was ready, Meggie ran to the parlor and announced that the food was on the table. Matthew, John, and Paul quickly followed Meggie to the dining room.

When everyone was seated, Matthew asked Paul to lead them in prayer. Then they passed the food around and began eating.

Everyone enjoyed the meal and the conversation immensely. They all had faith that the Lord would heal Breanna and make it so she could walk again.

John looked at his family around the table. "I read the psalms a lot, and in my devotions this morning, I came across a verse in Psalm 50 that really spoke to my heart. It's verse 15, where the Lord said to His own, 'And call upon me in the day of trouble: I will deliver thee, and thou shalt glorify me.' I had a good time of prayer after reading that promise, and my faith about Breanna being healed and able to walk again has been strengthened. And I tell you this . . . when God makes it so she can walk again, I certainly will glorify Him for it!"

"We *all* will," said Matthew.

"Yes!" Dottie exclaimed.

Paul, Ginny, and Meggie spoke their agreement.

After dinner, the Brockmans and the Carrolls went to the hospital to spend some time with Breanna. While they were gathered around her bed, John told her how the Lord had used Psalm 50:15 during his devotional time that morning to add strength to his faith for her full recovery. Tears filmed her eyes. "Glory to God!" she said.

Breanna was deeply touched when the group told her about all the people at church who had declared that they had been praying for her and would continue to do so.

When the evening church service was over, John and the children and the Langfords went to Mile High Hospital to see Breanna again.

When they were about to leave so Breanna could get her much-needed sleep, John asked Paul to lead in prayer for his mother.

Heads were bowed, and Paul held his mother's hand as he prayed for her. He told the Lord how encouraged he was after reading Psalm 107, which shows God's saved people on earth as they have troubles. He then quoted verse 28: " 'Then they cry unto the LORD in their trouble, and he bringeth them out of their distresses.' "

The adults and the girls whispered their praise to the Lord as Paul shared this teaching. Paul gleefully prayed, "Dear Lord, thank You that You are going to heal my mama! I so well remember verse 31 in that same psalm: 'Oh that men would praise the LORD for his goodness, and for his wonderful works to the children of men!' We love You, Lord. Thank You that You are going to heal my mama so she can walk again."

By the time Paul closed his prayer in Jesus' name, the Langfords and the Brockmans — including Breanna — were crying, deeply touched by Paul's prayer.

That night, after John Brockman had gone into the children's bedrooms to say good night, he headed into his bedroom. As he started to unbutton his shirt, he heard a tap on the door.

Rebuttoning his shirt, he walked to the door and opened it. He found Ginny standing there with a sweet look on her face, and he couldn't repress a smile. "What can I do for you, honey?"

"I didn't come for you to do something for me, Papa. I just wanted to tell you something."

John stooped over a bit. "Well, all right. What is it?"

Her eyes glistened with tears. "Papa, I know with all that has happened, you are carrying a big load on your heart for

Mama."

Ginny wrapped her arms around her father and hugged him tightly. "I just wanted to say I love you so much, Papa."

John returned her hug and held her close.

After a moment, Ginny eased back in her father's arms. "Papa, when we bring Mama home, I want you to know that Paul, Meggie, and I have agreed that we will see to her every need."

John nodded. "I'm not surprised at the agreement you three have made, sweetheart. I appreciate so much that I can depend on you kids to help take care of your mama."

"We will do all we can to bring as much joy and happiness into our wonderful mama's life, Papa. She is so precious to us, and believe me, we will see that she wants for nothing!"

John kissed the top of her blond head. "I appreciate that, Ginny. I'm placing a lot of responsibility on you, but I know that you are very capable of handling it well."

Ginny smiled up at her tall, ruggedly handsome father. "I've made out a list of responsibilities for all three of us kids, and Paul and Meggie have seen the list. Paul will do the heavy housecleaning, along with his normal outside duties. Meggie and I will take care of the other household chores and

Mama's private care. So it's all arranged, and I hope she can come home soon. I just know she will do worlds better when she's here in the home she loves so much."

John smiled down at her. "Sounds like you've thought of everything, honey, but if and when you need my help, all you have to do is let me know."

Ginny lifted her arms and stood on her tiptoes. John bent down again, and she hugged him around the neck. "I love you, my special Papa," she whispered in his ear.

"I love you too, my special little daughter," he whispered back.

Ginny then asked if they could pray together and if she could lead. John was a bit surprised his daughter wanted to lead in prayer, but he was also pleased. They bowed their heads, and when Ginny prayed, John was amazed at how well she did. When she said "amen," he hugged her again, telling her how very much he loved her.

A few minutes later, John doused the lantern, crawled into bed, and thanked the Lord for Ginny's tenderness. He also thanked the Lord for Paul and Meggie and for his dear wife.

Though John was tired to the bone, sleep was a long time coming. Lying in the big bed, he missed Breanna so very much and rolled over to her side of the bed. Placing his face into her pillow, he could still detect her sweet scent.

As he lifted his head slightly, tears filled his eyes and ran down his rugged cheeks. "Oh, Breanna, darling," he said in a shaky voice, "my heart always has a big empty spot when we're apart.

"Dear Lord," he prayed, "please answer all of those prayers coming to You from myself, my family, and our friends concerning Breanna. Please give my sweet love her strength and health, and if it could be Your own perfect will, please let her walk again."

John paused a moment. "Lord, I want Your perfect will to be done in Breanna's life. I — I know that no matter what the outcome, Your grace is sufficient for all of the needs of my precious wife and children and for myself."

He took another raspy breath. "Lord, Psalm 124:8 says, 'Our help is in the name of the LORD, who made heaven and earth.'" With those words of promise still in his mind, John hugged Breanna's pillow close to his heart. Slowly, life-sustaining sleep crept into his weary body, his mind now at peace.

TWENTY-TWO

Before dawn on Monday morning, Todd and Chice Zarbo rode onto the Brockman ranch, tied their horses deep in the forest, and settled at the edge of the trees. They peered toward the ranch house, which was quite close. There was a bit of moonlight left in the west, and they could see that all was still around the house. No lantern lights were shining through any windows yet. Everyone in the Brockman house was still asleep.

Soon the moonlight was gone, and a faint light began to appear on the eastern horizon.

A short time later they saw movement at a couple of windows on the second floor. The chief U.S. marshal and his children were up, preparing for the day.

Chice chuckled and looked at his brother. "They have no idea what a surprise we've got for them, do they?"

"They sure don't, brother, but what we're going to do today will result in Lee being released and missing the noose."

The faint light on the eastern horizon became long lines of bright pink, which lasted only a short time and then began to recede as the morning brightened. A bank of fleecy clouds in the north was turning a rose color, and in every direction blue sky began to appear.

Only minutes later, in the eastern sky, a golden light gathered and slowly brightened until it was like fire. The rosy bank of clouds in the north turned a bright pearl color, and in the east appeared a great circle of gold. A few minutes later, an intensely bright disk appeared and rose swiftly, blazing out of the dark shadows on the rolling hills, giving color to the great sweep of the land.

The Zarbo brothers waited patiently among the dense trees. About two hours after sunrise, they saw the tall, broad-shouldered form of chief U.S. marshal John Brockman go out the back door of the house. He made his way quickly to the corral, then into the barn. A few minutes later he appeared leading his big black stallion. The horse was bridled and saddled. Brockman led him through the corral gate and closed it behind him. He swung into the

347

saddle and rode away as his three children waved from the front porch.

The Brockman children went back inside, alone.

Speaking in a low voice, Chice asked his brother, "Should we just go up to the house, knock on the door, overpower the teenage boy and the younger girl and capture Ginny?"

Todd kept his eyes on the house. "If we have to, we'll do that, but maybe if we wait a little while, the circumstances will make it easier."

Chice nodded. "Okay."

Less than fifteen minutes later, they saw Paul, Ginny, and Meggie come out the back door of the house. Ginny was carrying a watering pail.

The Zarbo brothers were close enough to hear the three young people talking. They heard Meggie say she was going to help Paul with the morning chores at the barn and corral.

While Ginny's brother and sister headed that direction, she started watering the flower gardens at the side of the ranch house, which put her out of view of the barn and the corral.

Todd grinned at his brother. "Perfect! As soon as the other two go inside the barn, we'll grab her."

Chice chuckled in a low tone. "You were right, big brother. We waited, and it's gotten easier!" He glanced at the barn and saw Paul and Meggie go inside. "They're in the barn. Let's go grab Ginny right now!"

While Ginny watered the flowers, she was praying for her mother's full recovery. Suddenly she heard the sound of horses' hooves thumping on the ground behind her. Looking over her shoulder, she saw two strange men approaching, leading their horses by the reins. A trickle of fear ran along her spine as she straightened herself to face them.

Forcing a smile, Ginny gripped the handle of the watering pail. "If you have come to see my father, he isn't here. He has already gone to his office in Denver."

The men dropped the reins and stepped up close. "Well now, little lady, that's just how we planned it," the older man said. "We aren't interested in seeing your father." He spit a brown stream of tobacco that splattered close to Ginny's feet and then lunged for her. "We came here to take you with us."

Ginny dropped the watering pail on the ground and opened her mouth to scream when Todd quickly stuffed a dirty bandanna into her open mouth, stifling the sound. She gagged at the stench of the bandanna. Her eyes were wide with fear as she searched the yard for a glimpse of her brother or sister. But they were nowhere in sight.

Holding the terrified child tight in his arms, Todd said, "You are to obey everything we tell you, girl, or we'll *kill* you!"

Ginny's heart was pounding with terror.

While Todd held Ginny tightly and prevented her from screaming, Chice bound her wrists behind her back with a short length of rope. He then took a small gunnysack out of one of his saddlebags. "Ginny, I'm gonna cover you with this sack while I take you on my horse."

A frown lined the thirteen-year-old's brow. Working against the bandanna that Todd was holding in place in her mouth, she looked at Chice strangely.

Chice understood. "You're wondering how we know your name."

"Mmf-mmf."

Chice grinned. "Well, you'll just have to keep wondering. You're probably also wondering why I'm gonna cover you with this gunnysack."

Ginny managed a nod in spite of the fact that Todd was holding her head rather tight.

"Well, it's because I don't want anybody who knows you to see you with me. And let me tell you this. My brother is gonna take that bandanna out and tie it as a gag over your mouth right now. If you try to cry out to *anybody,* I'll choke you to death. You hear me?"

Ginny had to wait for Todd to finish tying the bandanna behind her neck. Then, eyes wide, she looked at Chice and nodded.

"Good," he said. "If you want to live, you'll do whatever my brother and I tell you. Got it?"

Ginny nodded again.

"I want a promise from you, kid!" Chice snapped.

Ginny looked up at him questioningly.

Chice showed his teeth as he said roughly, "You'd better promise to sit still when you're in the saddle with me and keep absolutely quiet."

Terrorized, Ginny nodded and made a frightened and affirmative "Mm-hmm."

Chice then quickly covered Ginny with the gunnysack from her head to her waist. As he tightened it around her, he could feel her whole body trembling. "Now, you stand still, girl," he said. "I'm gonna mount up, and my brother is gonna pick you up and put you in front of me in the saddle. Understand?"

Beneath the gunnysack, Ginny made a

muffled, "Mm-hmm."

Chice put his left foot in the stirrup and swung into the saddle. Todd then picked up the trembling thirteen-year-old girl and lifted her up to his brother. Chice took hold of her and placed her in the saddle in front of him. Todd mounted his horse, and the Zarbo brothers rode away from the Brockman ranch with the horrified Ginny Brockman as their helpless captive.

While the kidnappers were riding away with Ginny, Paul and Meggie were working together in the barn. Paul, of course, was doing most of the work and at the moment was repairing two broken steps on the ladder that led from the barn floor up to the second level, where the hay was kept.

Meggie was scattering some straw on the barn floor with a pitchfork when she heard her brother draw a quick breath and say, "Ow!" She turned, looked at him, and saw him pulling a splinter from the thumb on his right hand. "You all right, Paul?"

"Nothing serious. I need to go to the house and get my leather gloves, or I'm gonna get more splinters working on these two steps."

Meggie leaned the pitchfork against the nearby wall. "I'll go get your gloves for you. They're in your bedroom in the dresser drawer, aren't they?"

"Yes, but you don't have to go after them. I'll do it."

"But you can still do something on those steps with that hammer if I go after the gloves, right?"

"Well, yes. I can pull some more nails."

"Okay." Meggie headed for the barn door. "I'll be right back."

When Meggie drew near the ranch house, she decided to go around to the far side where Ginny was watering the flower gardens and see how she was doing. When she rounded the corner of the house, she spotted the watering pail on the ground near one of the flower beds, water trickling from its spout.

Meggie figured Ginny must be inside. She entered the house and hurried upstairs to Paul's bedroom, then took the leather gloves from the dresser drawer. She went to Ginny's bedroom and looked inside. Ginny was not there.

Meggie hurried down the stairs, glanced in the parlor, then glanced in the dining room and the kitchen. When she entered the kitchen and there was still no sign of big sister, she called out loudly, "Ginny! Ginny-y-y!"

Silence.

Meggie hurried back outside and ran to the side where Ginny had been watering. The watering pail still lay on the ground. The nine-year-old dashed completely around the house, running her gaze in every direction, but Ginny was not to be found.

Meggie was getting worried now. She ran to the barn and dashed inside. Paul was standing by the ladder that led to the hayloft, hammer in hand. He could tell by the look on his little sister's face that she was upset. "Meggie, what's wrong?"

She dashed up to him. "I can't find Ginny! The watering pail is on the ground. She wouldn't just go off somewhere and leave it like that. I searched through the house, and she isn't there. I'm scared, Paul."

A dreadful unease penetrated Paul's senses. "Let's go look together."

As they ran toward the house, both Paul and Meggie let their eyes roam all around them. They went inside, and while they were going through their home upstairs and downstairs, they both called Ginny's name loudly.

They left the house and rushed back to the corral. They searched the sheds and even the barn. By this time, panic had gripped them. They ran toward the ranch house again and made their way through the yard, turning in circles, frantically calling out Ginny's name, surveying the property around the house carefully.

When they had covered the entire area around the house, including the small outbuildings, Meggie looked at Paul through tears. "We've got to find her!"

Paul agreed, and together they went into the nearby forest, then out onto the fields of the ranch, but still there was no sign of Ginny.

They decided to go back to where Ginny had been watering. When Paul set his eyes on the watering pail on the ground, he couldn't tear his tortured stare away from it.

Meggie looked at Paul with horror-filled eyes. "Paul, where can she be?"

Paul shook his head in utter despair. "Meggie, I don't know. It's as if somebody took her. But I didn't hear the sound of horses or a wagon. This is really strange."

"She wouldn't have any reason to go walking somewhere without telling us, would she?"

"I can't imagine Ginny doing that. Let's take another walk in the forest. The trees could have kept us from seeing her easily."

Together Paul and Meggie dashed into the forest and made their way deeper than they had gone before. As they passed two large cottonwood trees, Paul looked at the soft ground around their trunks. "Look there, Meggie! Hoofprints! I'd say a couple of horses were standing here." Then he noticed hoofprints leading away from the spot and pointed them out to Meggie. "Let's follow these."

Meggie stayed close to Paul's side as they followed the obviously fresh hoofprints. Within a few minutes, the prints began to fade into the foliage that covered the ground. And soon, where the ground was harder, they disappeared altogether.

Paul took hold of Meggie's hand and stopped. "No more prints here, honey," he said, disappointment showing on his face. "There's no way to know whose horses they were and whether they had something to do with Ginny."

Fear beat through Meggie like the frantic wings of a bird. Breaking into sobs, she wailed, "Oh, Paul! Something bad has happened to Ginny! I just know it!"

Paul folded her into his arms and gritted his teeth as the horror of it all became a solid, palpable thing inside him. "Meggie, we must go tell Papa that Ginny has disappeared!"

When the kidnappers arrived at Buck Skidmore's log cabin with Ginny Brockman, still covered with the gunnysack, they both pulled rein. Todd dismounted, stepped up to Chice's horse, and lifted his arms. "Let me have her."

Chice lowered the still-trembling Ginny into his brother's arms. "Okay, Todd, I'll ride to town right now and see to it that you-know-who puts the envelope on that saddle immediately."

Todd nodded at Chice, knowing it was best that Ginny not hear Buck Skidmore's name. He placed Ginny's feet on the ground and lifted the gunnysack off her. Both of them watched as Chice galloped away.

Todd knew that Chice would ride like the wind to Denver. He would tell Buck that they now had Ginny Brockman as their captive and that Buck could put the envelope on John Brockman's saddle at the federal building.

It was just after ten o'clock that morning when Paul and Meggie arrived at the federal building in the Brockman family buggy.

The chief U.S. marshal was at his desk

when there was a knock at the door. Looking up, he called, "Come on in, Darrell!"

When the door came open, John was surprised to see Paul and Meggie dash past Deputy Dickson. Both of them skidded to a stop in front of his desk as he rose from his chair. Taking a look at the horrified panic on their faces, John asked, "What's wrong, kids? What are you doing here?"

Deputy Dickson stepped up beside them. "Chief, Paul and Meggie insist on talking to you right away."

"All right."

Deputy Dickson hurried out the door and closed it behind him.

Paul and Ginny started talking at the same time, and their combined voices were nothing but a garble. John couldn't understand a word. Lifting his palms toward them, he interrupted. "Hold it, hold it! One at a time, please."

Meggie drew a trembling breath and tried to speak, but her words ran together and made no sense.

John looked at his son. "Paul, what is she trying to tell me?"

Meggie was now sobbing. Paul was making an effort to get control of his voice as well.

John put an arm around each of them and

led them to the sofa near the office window. He grabbed a wooden chair that was close by, placed it in front of them, and sat down. Meggie was still sobbing. Something was seriously wrong. Trepidation filled his rapidly beating heart as he looked at his two terrified children. "Paul, tell me what's wrong."

Gulping down the raw alarm that was threatening to strangle him, Paul stammered, "P-Papa . . . it-it's G-Ginny!"

John's eyes widened. "What about her?"

While Meggie attempted to bring her sobbing under control, Paul told his father that Ginny was missing. He explained that Ginny had been watering Mama's flower gardens beside the house while he and Meggie were working together in the barn. When he got a sliver, Meggie ran to the house to get his gloves and realized Ginny was gone.

Paul went on to tell his father that he and Meggie had looked all through the house, the barn, the sheds, and the outbuildings, as well as the fields and the forest, and they could not find her. He told him about the hoofprints that appeared to have been made by two horses in the forest, but when they tried to follow the hoofprints, they soon disappeared where the ground turned harder.

His heart pounding with fear, John said,

"We'll go back to the ranch together, and I'll look the place over myself. You came in the buggy, didn't you?"

Paul nodded.

"All right. I'll ride Blackie, and you two can go back in the buggy."

"Okay, Papa. We'll go out and wait in the buggy while you get Blackie."

"I'll meet you out front in a few minutes. And . . . ah . . . it's best that you not tell Deputy Dickson what has happened. Just tell him that I'll let him and the other deputies know later and that the three of us are going home right now."

"Sure." Paul was already on his feet. Meggie was standing at his side, wiping tears from her eyes.

Paul and Meggie hurried out the door and John stepped into the hall and headed for the rear of the building. He ran to the small corral where his big black horse was kept. As he walked up to Blackie, he noticed something white sticking out from under the front of the saddle. Frowning, he took hold of it. It was an envelope bearing his name.

John tore open the envelope and took out the letter. He squared his jaw and bit down on his lip as he read the ransom note. His eyes lingered on the words, "You must see to it that Lee is set free before noon on Wednesday or Ginny will die."

John's heart pounded in his chest. A sharp hissing sound filled his ears as his breath escaped through gritted teeth. He could feel the veins in the side of his neck pulsing. Words from the ransom note echoed through his head: *If you do not see that Lee is released, YOU HAVE SEEN GINNY FOR THE LAST TIME!* He thought of how ruthless and cold-blooded the Zarbo brothers were and wondered if they would keep their word to return Ginny unharmed even if Lee *was* released.

The chief hurriedly led Blackie to the front of the federal building, a mixture of alarm and anger stirring in his heart. He drew up to the side of the buggy, where Paul and Meggie were already on the driver's seat.

He held up the letter, explaining who it was from. The envelope had been attached to his saddle. He told them what the letter said.

Paul and Meggie were terrified.

John quickly took them back to his office and told the three deputies on duty — Darrell Dickson, Barry Sotak, and Whip Langford — that Ginny had been kidnapped. He showed them the letter.

The deputies were stunned, and Barry asked the chief what he was going to do.

Right now John needed to show the letter to both Sheriff Carter and Judge Dexter . . . and he made clear that he wanted Paul and Meggie to stay there with the deputies while he was gone.

The deputies said they would keep Paul and Meggie safe.

John told them he would return as soon as he had seen the sheriff and the judge. Then he would take Paul and Meggie to the hospital so they could be with him when he told their mother what had happened to Ginny. "I hate to break this horrible news to Breanna when she is lying paralyzed in that hospital bed, but I can't keep it from her. She has a right to know."

"Yes, she does," Whip said. "May I go along with you, Paul, and Meggie to see Breanna?"

"You sure can."

"I know it will help Breanna if Annabeth is at her side when she hears this," Whip said softly.

"You're right, Whip. We will make sure to take your dear wife to Breanna's room." He then opened his arms to Paul and Meggie and hugged them good. "I'll be back soon. We'll take Uncle Whip with us to see your mother."

Paul and Meggie sobbed as they watched their father hurry out of the building, carrying the horrible letter with him.

As a deeply disturbed John Brockman left the federal building and walked swiftly toward the offices of Sheriff Carter and Judge Dexter, his mind went back to the night before, when precious Ginny had talked to him, showing her love, tenderness, and compassion for him in the burden he was carrying for her mother.

Tears surfaced in John's eyes. "Dear Lord, please protect our sweet Ginny, wherever the cold-blooded Zarbos are holding her, and by Your power, please see to it that she is set free unharmed."

John arrived at Sheriff Carter's office and stepped up to the front desk. "Hello, Alfred. Is Sheriff Carter in his office? I need to talk to him about something urgent."

"He is, Chief Brockman, but Judge Dexter is with him at the moment."

"I see." The chief nodded. "I actually need to talk to both of them. Would you mind stepping in there and telling them I'm here with an incredibly urgent matter?"

"No problem. Be back in a moment."

A few minutes later, the deputy came out

of the sheriff's office. "Chief Brockman, they said to come on in."

The men took one look at John's face as he walked in and knew something was wrong. They invited him to sit down with them around the small table.

John quickly broke the news of Ginny's abduction by the Zarbos, explaining it in detail. He then read the letter that had been left on his saddle.

When John finished, Judge Dexter rubbed his chin. "Chief, you know what a deadlock is, I'm sure."

John nodded. "Yes. A struggle that neither side can win. An inescapable situation. An impasse."

"Right," the judge said. "Chief, it looks like you've got a deadlock here. For you and Breanna, if we don't release Lee Zarbo, his brothers will kill Ginny. For Todd and Chice Zarbo, if their brother is not released and doesn't escape the noose, he will die."

"That is exactly right, Judge," Sheriff Carter said solemnly. "And there's more to the deadlock. If the Zarbo brothers hurt or kill Ginny, they'll only further condemn themselves and have the law after them . . . especially John."

Judge Dexter nodded vigorously. "I wouldn't want John after me."

The judge looked at the Stranger. "Chief, unless the Zarbos' hiding place can be found and Ginny rescued right away, I will give the order for Lee Zarbo to be released, hoping that the Zarbos will keep their word about sparing Ginny's life."

John Brockman looked into the judge's eyes. "Thank you for your willingness to try. As rotten as the Zarbos are, I can't be sure they'll keep their word and spare Ginny's life even if Lee *is* set free." He sighed. "First I'll do all I can to find out where the Zarbos are holding Ginny. I'll have to do it before Wednesday morning."

John squared his jaw. He pounded his right fist into his left palm with fiery determination. "With God's help and guidance, I will find Ginny and rescue her!"

TWENTY-THREE

Paul and Meggie sat in the front office of the chief marshal's talking with their uncle Whip, who was trying to encourage them in the face of their sister's abduction. As he was speaking to them in a tender tone, the front door opened, and they saw the chief walk in.

Paul and Meggie saw the mask of anger across their father's rugged facial features and that his eyes were filled with resolve. Whip could see it too.

Meggie gasped softly at the look in her father's eyes. She had never seen him like this before.

Whip stood up as his boss drew near.

John caught the consternation in little Meggie's eyes. He met the stares of Paul and Whip and then scooped Meggie into his arms, his countenance softening a bit. He squeezed her tight, then eased her back a little and looked down into her troubled eyes. "Honey," he said, "it's going to be all right. The Lord will see to it that we get our Ginny back unharmed, and the evil men will be prosecuted for kidnapping her and threatening her life."

Meggie wiped away the tears that were welling up in her eyes and gave her beloved adoptive father a weak smile. "I — I know the Lord can take care of Ginny, Papa. I guess I'm just a scaredy-cat."

John patted her cheek. "That's okay, sweetheart. I know you love Ginny. Has something else bothered you?"

Meggie nodded and looked down at the floor. "Yes, Papa. I've been worried that that those bad men who took Ginny might come back for Paul and me."

John hugged her again and glanced at Paul. "Honey, you have nothing to worry about. You and Paul will *never* be left alone until Ginny is safe and those men are in prison!"

A small smile creased Meggie's face. "Oh, thank you, Papa. I just know those bad men don't stand a chance with you after them!"

"The Lord helping me, you're right about that! Let's take Uncle Whip with us now to see your mama and tell her what has happened to Ginny. And remember, I'm depending on you and your brother to help her through this."

"We'll do our best to comfort and encourage Mama," Paul said.

"And if I can help in this matter," Whip said, "I'll do my best, Chief. Let's go."

A short while later, John, Paul, Meggie, and Whip entered the hospital. As they walked down the hall toward Breanna's room, Whip paused. "Let's stop at the nurses' station, and I'll find out where Annabeth is. I want her to be with Breanna when you tell her about Ginny."

"I'd like that," John said.

Whip asked the nurse on duty where his wife was and learned quickly that she was in Breanna's room, tending to her.

"The Lord is already working on Breanna's behalf, Chief."

"He sure is."

Annabeth was standing over Breanna's bed when the four of them entered the room. Breanna looked at the foursome, and a big smile started to emerge on her lips. But when she noted the gravity of their faces — and that Ginny wasn't with them — her smile faded.

John walked quickly to her side, and the children followed. Annabeth could tell something wrong, as could Breanna, who frowned. "John, I can tell that all four of you are upset. What's wrong? Where's Ginny?"

John leaned down and took one of her hands in his. Determined to be strictly honest with his dear wife but as easy on her as possible, John told her that Ginny had been kidnapped by Todd and Chice Zarbo. He gave her all the details, including what was said in the letter.

Annabeth gripped her husband's hand, biting her lips.

Breanna's eyes filled with horror, and she quickly placed her free hand over her gaping mouth to stop the wail that was about to come. Slowly, she lowered her hand, and her eyes misted with tears as she began to sob. "Oh, my poor baby!" she gasped. "John, you must find her before those wicked men harm her!"

The others looked on, their hearts pounding, as John squeezed Breanna's hand. "Darling, I didn't want to tell you about this at all, but I felt that you have a right to know."

"You've got to find her and rescue her, John!"

Desperately seeking to calm her fears, John said quietly, "I plan to do *exactly* that, my sweet. I know this is a terrible blow for you, especially in your weakened condition, but with the Lord's help, I *will* find her, and those Zarbo brothers will be punished. I promise you."

Gulping down her tears, Breanna offered her husband a tentative smile. "I know you'll do everything in your power to rescue Ginny, darling, and with God's help, and by His grace, you'll succeed."

Tears continued to stream down Breanna's face, but knowing that her precious heavenly Father was in control brought a measure of peace.

John told the group about Judge Dexter's use of the word *deadlock* in this grave situation, along with Sheriff Carter's comments about it.

John then picked up Breanna's Bible off the nightstand. "Honey, I want to read you Pastor Bayless's main text for the sermon he preached Sunday evening. I didn't tell you when we were here after the service because you were so tired."

"I'd like to know what he preached about."

Flipping pages, John said, "It was on the subject of prayer."

The others looked at each other and smiled, recalling the pastor's dynamic sermon on Sunday night.

John found the page he wanted and looked down at Breanna. "It's in Psalm 102. The first two verses, where the psalmist says, 'Hear my prayer, O LORD, and let my cry come unto thee. Hide not thy face from me in the day when I am in trouble; incline thine ear unto me: in the day when I call answer me speedily.' "

"I vaguely recall those verses," Breanna said. "They're marvelous, aren't they?"

"They sure are." John said. "In his sermon, Pastor Bayless showed from these verses how we Christians should approach the Lord in prayer when we are in trouble, and since it's natural to want His help in a hurry, we should call on Him in the manner written here by the psalmist. It was really a good sermon, and it was very encouraging."

"It sure was," spoke up Paul. "I've thought a lot about these verses and Pastor's sermon when I've been praying for Ginny since I learned that she was abducted."

The Langfords and Meggie each told how they had done the same thing.

Breanna looked up at John. "Those two verses tie in well with Psalm 50:15. 'And call upon me in the day of trouble: I will deliver thee, and thou shalt glorify me.' "

John smiled. "Yes, they *do* tie in well together. We can claim them for both the rescue of Ginny and for your health."

The others spoke their agreement.

John flipped pages again. "Listen to this. David said in Psalm 143:1, 'Hear my prayer, O LORD, give ear to my supplications: in thy faithfulness answer me, and in thy righteousness.' " Flipping more pages, he said, "Keep in mind that supplications are our prayers to our wonderful Lord. David said to the Lord in Psalm 28:2, 'Hear the voice of my supplications, when I cry unto thee.' Then he said in verse 6, 'Blessed be the LORD, because he hath heard the voice of my supplications.' Isn't that wonderful?"

Everybody spoke their agreement. Then Breanna said, "John, I remember that passage well. Read the next verse. Verse 7."

John dropped his eyes to the page once more and read, " 'The LORD is my strength and my shield; my heart trusted in him, and I am helped: therefore my heart greatly rejoiceth; and with my song will I praise him.' "

"Tremendous!" Whip said.

"Isn't it though?" Breanna said. "Everybody keep that phrase of David's in mind: 'My heart trusted in him, and I am helped.' Now, John, turn to Isaiah 41:10, where God speaks to His saved people. I just read it this morning and was applying it to myself.

Now I plan to apply it to Ginny. Everybody note the word *help*."

John flipped the pages, found the passage, and read it aloud: " 'Fear thou not; for I am with thee: be not dismayed; for I am thy God: I will strengthen thee; yea, I will help thee; yea, I will uphold thee with the right hand of my righteousness.' "

"Mama, what does *dismayed* mean?" Meggie asked.

"It means discouraged, honey. God says we are not to be discouraged because He is *our* God, and He is going to help us. He is going to help us get Ginny home safely because He is our God!"

Meggie clapped her hands. "Yes! Yes!"

John flipped more pages, found the passage he wanted, and said, "Breanna, indeed we have help coming to get Ginny rescued."

He handed the Bible to Meggie, and said, "Honey, look here in Psalm 121, and read what the psalmist said about where his help comes from."

Holding the Bible carefully, Meggie set her eyes on Psalm 121:2, and read it aloud with excitement in her voice: " 'My help cometh from the LORD, which made heaven and earth.' Yes! Oh, yes! Our help comes from the God, who made heaven and earth. I'm glad you showed us this verse, Papa. We are going to have my sister back safe. Thank You, Lord Jesus, thank You!"

John wiped his own tears as Meggie placed the Bible back in his hands. He closed the Bible, laid it on the bed stand, and said, "Judge Dexter told me that unless the Zarbos' hiding place can be found and Ginny is rescued right away, he'll give the order for Lee Zarbo to be released and then hope the Zarbos will keep their word about sparing Ginny's life."

The others exchanged glances.

"As cold-blooded and wicked as the Zarbos are, I have serious doubts that they would let Ginny live, even if their brother was released."

"Me too, Chief," Whip said.

"Since Ginny would still be at the mercy of the Zarbos even if Lee was released and escaped the noose, and since they are such merciless outlaws and killers, we've got to ask the Lord to help us find where Todd and Chice are keeping Ginny and rescue her. Let's bow our heads together right now, claim these powerful verses we have just discussed, and thank the Lord that since He knows where Ginny is being held hostage, He will help us find her and bring her safely home!"

While Meggie and Paul together held one

of their mother's hands and John held the other, he led in prayer. John brought all the Scripture passages to the Lord, asking Him to reveal Ginny's whereabouts in His own way so she could be rescued and Todd and Chice Zarbo could be arrested.

As John Brockman led his family and the Langfords in prayer, Buck Skidmore was back at his house in Denver taking his heart medicine. He was having severe chest pains and was afraid he might die.

As the thought of death filled his mind, he felt oppressive guilt about having helped Todd and Chice Zarbo abduct Ginny Brockman, though it was possible he would've risked his own life had he refused to help. Buck told himself that he could not die with this on his conscience. Despite his chest pains, he would go to the federal building and talk to Ginny's father. Clutching his chest, Buck left the house, saddled his horse, and rode down the street toward the downtown area.

Buck pulled up in front of the federal building, tied his horse to the hitch rail, and entered the marshal's office. When the silver-haired man asked to see chief U.S. marshal John Brockman, Deputy Allen told him that Chief Brockman was at the hospital at the moment. Suddenly the office door came open, and the chief entered with Paul and Meggie at his side, as well as Deputy Langford.

Deputy Allen told his boss that this man had just come in to see him.

John stepped up to Buck Skidmore, who rubbed his chest and asked if he could talk to the chief alone.

"All right, Mr. Skidmore," John said. "Come with me into my office." He told the others to wait in the front office.

When both men were seated, John noticed that Buck was rubbing his chest in a circular motion. "What is it you wanted to see me about, Mr. Skidmore?" he asked, though his mind was wandering to his daughter and the danger she was in.

"First, Chief Brockman, let me tell you about myself."

"All right."

Buck then explained his outlaw background and told the chief of the years he had done time in the Nebraska State Penitentiary. John was listening, but his mind was also on Ginny and the peril she was facing. He was picking up on what Buck was saying, but he was also trying to figure out how he was going to find Ginny and rescue her.

Buck filled the chief in on his move to the Denver area after getting out of prison and his purchase of a cabin in the nearby foothills. He explained about his heart trouble and that he now lived in Denver.

But then he *really* caught John's attention when he told him that his outlaw past included robberies with the Zarbo brothers and how Todd had once saved his life. Then he admitted that it was he who had placed Todd Zarbo's letter on John's saddle that morning.

John could hardly believe what he had just heard. "So you're telling me that you were in on the kidnapping of my daughter!"

Buck nodded, his face flushed. "Yes sir. And to get it off my conscience, I want to tell you where they're holding her. I'm so ashamed that I had a part in Ginny's abduction, and I want to make it right."

John's heart began pounding. He jumped to his feet. "Well, tell me! I've got to get to Ginny fast!"

Buck stood up and quickly told John that he still owned the cabin in the foothills and it was there that the Zarbo brothers were holding Ginny. Rubbing his chest again, Buck said, "Chief Brockman, I'll take you to the cabin myself."

John marveled at God's goodness. *While I*

was still praying for God to show me where Ginny is, He was already working in this exoutlaw's heart, preparing the answer to my prayers! Thank You, dear Lord!

"Buck, I'll take some of my deputies along so we can surround the cabin."

Less than a half hour later, John rode away with Buck Skidmore on one side of him, Whip on the other, and a dozen deputies following on their horses. Waiting at the office, Paul took Meggie aside, and they prayed together, thanking the Lord that their father now knew where Ginny was and was on his way to rescue her.

As the chief and his deputies rode toward the mountains and neared Whip's home, Whip spoke above the rumble of galloping hooves and offered to stop at his place to grab his gallant wolf, Timber. John agreed.

It was early afternoon when John, the other lawmen, and the former outlaw Skidmore drew near Buck's cabin. Whip's big gray wolf, Timber, was staying close beside Whip and his horse, waiting for instructions from his master, sensing that something important was happening.

When John drew rein in the woods with the cabin in view, he directed the dozen deputies to quietly dismount and surround the cabin on foot, staying low so they

378

wouldn't be seen, and to have their guns ready. As he, Buck, and Whip dismounted, John told Buck to stay close to him and Whip. In turn, Whip told Timber to stay close to him.

Inside the cabin, Todd Zarbo was tying the frightened Ginny to a wooden chair in the kitchen near the stove while Chice looked on with a smirk on his face.

When Todd had finished tying the knot in the rope, he said, "Okay, Chice, let's go outside and water the horses."

Ginny watched them go out the door and, with tears in her eyes, said in a low voice, "Please, dear Lord, do a miracle and let me get away from those bad men."

Outside, as the Zarbo brothers were walking toward the small corral where their horses were kept, they talked about how good it was going to be when Lee was set free.

Their conversation was suddenly interrupted as a loud male voice shouted, "Todd! Chice! Stop right there, and get your hands in the air!"

Both men recognized authority in the voice. They swung around and saw a chief U.S. marshal and their friend Buck standing there. Their eyes filled with hatred as they realized that Buck had obviously led the chief marshal to the cabin.

At the same time, they saw men wearing badges closing in on them from every side, with cocked guns aimed at them. They immediately raised their hands over their heads. On the chief marshal's right side, they saw a deputy with a large gray wolf beside him. They swallowed hard as the deputy gave the wolf a command and the animal charged toward them, growling fiercely. The beast skidded to a halt in front of them, his sharp teeth bared as he continued to growl with a fiery look in his eyes.

Cold chills ran down the brothers' spines. "We don't have a chance of escape," Todd said. "We're gonna hang, just like Lee."

Chice gritted his teeth as the circle of armed deputies closed in on them. "If we went for our guns, we could die right here with bullets cutting us to ribbons, but I'd rather hang."

Todd took a short breath. "Since it has to be one or the other, I'll take the noose too."

Inside the cabin, unaware of what was happening outside, Ginny wriggled and strained against the rope that held her to the chair as she wept and continued to ask the Lord to deliver her.

Suddenly the door swung open. She could

hardly believe her eyes. Through her tears, she recognized her father and Uncle Whip. More tears — but happy tears — rushed to her eyes as her father dashed to her.

"It's okay, sweetheart," John said as he began untying the rope.

"Oh, Papa," she said in a quivering voice, "I'm so happy to see you and Uncle Whip! How did you find me?"

John threw the rope aside and gathered Ginny into his arms. "I'll tell you later, honey. Right now I need to get you back to Denver so your mother and brother and sister will know you're all right." John kissed her cheek and ran a hand over her arms and back. "Did they hurt you in any way?"

"No, Papa," she said. "They didn't hurt me, but they sure did scare me when they told me if you didn't let their brother out of jail, they would kill me. I did a lot of praying, Papa, and praise the Lord, He answered me."

"We all prayed for you, sweetheart," said John, holding her tight. He looked upward and said, "Thank You, Lord! Thank You!"

"Well, Chief, the deadlock is over!" Whip said. "Praise the Lord!"

John joyfully agreed. When he and Whip stepped out of the cabin with Ginny, Todd and Chice Zarbo — now handcuffed and

on their horses — looked on with unbeliev-
able terror in their eyes, their faces pinched
and pale. They could almost feel the nooses
around their necks.

The dozen deputies were also in their
saddles and were ready to take the captured
outlaws to Denver, where they would be
locked up in the same jail as their younger
brother. John told the deputies they could
take the Zarbos and put them behind bars.

As the deputies and their captives galloped
away, Whip swung into his saddle and told
the chief that he would leave Timber off at
home and join him at the hospital. Then he
galloped away with the big gray wolf running alongside him.

Buck told John he was going to ride
directly to his house in Denver and trotted
his horse eastward.

John put Ginny on his horse with him and
told her they would go to his office, get Paul
and Meggie, then go to the hospital to let
their mother know that she was all right.

Ginny loudly praised the Lord for her
escape from the outlaws who would have
killed her if she had not been rescued.

John lifted his voice in a powerful "amen"
and told Ginny how he had learned where
she was being kept. As they rode away,
Ginny thanked the Lord for Buck Skidmore.

■ ■ ■ ■

It was a wonderful moment when Paul and Meggie saw their father come through the office door with Ginny at his side. Many happy tears flowed as big brother and little sister hugged Ginny while giving thanks to the Lord for answered prayer.

In her hospital room, Breanna was lying very quietly on her bed, eyes closed, her mind going over many precious memories of Ginny while an ongoing prayer graced her lips. Hearing the door creak, Breanna opened her eyes, then squealed when she saw John leading her precious Ginny by the hand into the room. Behind them were Paul and Meggie.

Ginny dropped her father's hand and rushed to her mother, who immediately embraced her and cried, "Ginny! Oh, Ginny!"

Ginny pressed her face against her mother's shoulder. They wept and rejoiced together as John, Paul, and Meggie looked on.

Finally their emotions calmed, and Breanna took Ginny's lovely face between both of her hands. "Are you all right, sweetie? Did they hurt you?"

Sniffling, Ginny replied, "They didn't hurt me. I'm all right, Mama. I'm just fine now that I'm back with my family. God is so good!"

"Yes, He is, dear." Breanna tousled her daughter's hair. "Indeed, He is!"

The two of them smiled as they looked into each other's eyes.

At that moment, Whip and Annabeth walked into the room together. They embraced Ginny, while John told Breanna about Buck Skidmore, filling her in on every detail of how the Lord had answered prayer in leading him, Whip, and the deputies to Buck's cabin. There they had broken the deadlock, bringing the Zarbo brothers to justice.

With tears running down her cheeks, Breanna praised the Lord that Buck Skidmore had done the right thing by coming to John and telling him where Ginny was being held.

Holding Breanna's hand with Ginny at his side, John said to Breanna, "I haven't told Whip yet, but tomorrow I'm going to take him with me to Buck Skidmore's house and try to lead this ex-outlaw to the Lord."

A big smile spread over Whip's face. "Great, Chief! I'd love to go with you!"

Breanna looked up at her husband. "I'll be praying for Buck."

"So will I!" Ginny said. "I'm just thankful to the Lord that He made Mr. Skidmore willing to do what was right. I want him to be saved. I know it was the Lord who answered prayer and caused Mr. Skidmore to do what he did to bring Papa, Uncle Whip, and those deputies to rescue me! Praise the Lord!"

TWENTY-FOUR

On Tuesday morning, John took Paul, Ginny, and Meggie to the hospital so they could spend time with their mother. Then, with Whip at his side, he went to Buck Skidmore's house. Bible in hand, John intended to give Buck the gospel and try to lead him to the Lord.

When Buck answered their knock, he smiled, even though he was clutching his chest. He welcomed the two lawmen inside.

Buck led them into the parlor, eying the Bible in Chief Brockman's hand, and they sat down together.

Though Buck was patting and rubbing his chest, he gladly listened as John read Scripture after Scripture on the subjects of sin, hell, salvation, and heaven. John then showed him the gospel, which incorporated the bloodshedding death of God's only begotten Son on the cross of Calvary, His burial, and His resurrection from the dead three days later.

Buck told John he had never doubted that the Lord Jesus Christ was the virgin-born Son of God, nor His crucifixion, death, burial, and resurrection. He said he just had never understood about Calvary and the Lord's death on the cross, as well as His rising from the dead three days later — but he still did not doubt it.

John went on to lay out the plan of salvation plain and clear. Then he led Buck, still clutching at his chest, in repentance of his sins, to call on the Lord Jesus Christ, receiving Him into his heart as his Saviour.

"Thank you, Chief Brockman," Buck said, "for caring about my soul and for coming to show me how to be saved from going to hell."

Before John could reply, Buck suddenly grabbed hard at his chest, his face pinching in pain, collapsed, and fell off the over-stuffed chair. He hit the floor hard.

John and Whip dropped to their knees beside him, knowing the problem was with his heart.

"Let's pick him up and carry him to his bed, Whip. Then you can stay with him while I go for a doctor."

As they picked Buck up, he was breathing stiffly, his eyes closed. While hurrying him toward his bed, Whip asked, "How about you stay with him, Chief, and I'll go get a doctor?"

"That's fine," John replied as they moved through the open bedroom door.

As they laid the new Christian on his bed, Buck opened his eyes and looked up toward heaven. His breathing eased, and with his eyes still looking upward, he smiled broadly, released one last breath, and closed his eyes.

John put his fingers on both sides of Buck's neck and looked at Whip. "No pulse." He leaned down and placed an ear over Buck's mouth. After a few seconds, he straightened up. "He's not breathing. He's gone, Whip."

"Yeah!" Whip said. "To heaven! Did you see that smile on his lips as he was looking up toward heaven?"

John nodded. "I sure did."

"Chief, he must have gotten a glimpse of the face of his Saviour as his soul slipped from his body. That's what made him smile, don't you think?"

Smiling, John replied, "Yes, Whip. That has to be why he smiled like that. He saw the Lord Jesus, who was taking him to heaven."

Both men wiped tears from their eyes and agreed that they should take Buck's body to one of Denver's morticians.

When Buck's body had been cared for, John and Whip went to the jail. There they tried to talk to Todd and Chice Zarbo — who were sharing a cell — about salvation. Whip gave them his own testimony of salvation, telling them about his past as an outlaw. John opened his Bible and began reading to them about the death of the Lord Jesus Christ on the cross. Both Zarbo brothers angrily railed at the two lawmen, telling them to get out. They didn't want to hear any "Bible stuff."

John warned them of the burning hell that they were going to if they died without Jesus as their Saviour, but they angrily cursed at him, telling him to go away.

John and Whip left the jail sadly and returned to the hospital. Dr. Carroll and Annabeth were in Breanna's room with her and the children.

John joyfully told them what happened at Buck Skidmore's house. They were all sad to learn of Buck's death, but they rejoiced that before he died, he asked the Lord Jesus to save him.

Whip then told them of the way Todd and Chice Zarbo had treated him and John when they went to the jail and tried to give them the gospel.

Ginny shook her head sadly. "When they die, they'll wish they had let you talk to them."

On Wednesday, July 18, Breanna lay in her hospital bed with just a sheet over her. It was midafternoon and a very hot day. The window was open, and occasionally a stray breeze blew into the room, making it a bit more comfortable.

Breanna's eyes were closed as she prayed for her loved ones and for herself. "Lord, my husband and children need me to be healed so I can walk again. You know how active I've been in my adult life, both in nursing and in being a wife and mother. I don't mean to complain, heavenly Father, and if it is Your will that I never walk again, then use this in some way to glorify Yourself. Please help me to be content if it is Your will, and help me to know the peace that the apostle Paul wrote about in Philippians 4:7: 'the peace of God, which passeth all understanding.' "

Breanna paused as a stiff breeze came through the window and ruffled the sheet that covered her. "Please, dear Lord, give me Your sufficient grace, and deliver me from Satan's attacks. Discouragement is the devil's greatest weapon among believers.

Please rebuke Satan in my life. While I am paralyzed — and if I never walk again — help me to accept Your will with an open, loving heart and spirit, and when I become dismayed and disheartened, help me to always look to You, and You alone. I love You, Lord. My desire is that You will still use me for Your glory. In Jesus' precious name I pray. Amen."

Just as the "amen" came from Breanna's lips, she became aware of the door opening. Her hand quickly fluttered over her eyes and cheeks, dispelling any trace of tears.

She looked up to see an unfamiliar woman standing in the open doorway, wringing her hands nervously. Breanna smiled warmly at her.

"Mrs. Brockman, may I come in?"

Breanna smiled again. Her voice was soft and encouraging. "Of course. What may I do for you?"

Taking slow, measured steps into the room, the woman drew up beside the bed, staring at Breanna. She fixed her eyes on what she knew were the lifeless legs covered by the sheet. Looking back into Breanna's eyes, she said softly, "Mrs. Brockman, I'm Barbara Fortney, Damon's wife."

"I see."

As Barbara Fortney continued, tears

welled in her eyes and ran slowly down her cheeks. "I just got home from Missouri. I received a letter while there written by Dr. Matthew Carroll, as dictated by my husband, telling me about how he had fallen off the barn and the damage his body had suffered. I just spent over an hour with Damon, and he told me about how he knocked you down the stairs here in the hospital and seriously injured you, especially your legs." Taking a handkerchief from her dress pocket, she dabbed at her tears.

Breanna reached out her hands and clasped Barbara's. "Thank you for coming, Mrs. Fortney. It's a pleasure to meet you."

Barbara looked deep into Breanna's eyes. "I'm so sorry that my husband did this to you, though he doesn't remember it. Damon feels so horrible because it's his fault, and he is so upset that you can no longer walk." She squeezed Breanna's hands. "Is there anything I can do for you? I will do *anything!* I will help you with your housework and anything else you need."

Breanna smiled kindly at the distraught woman. "Mrs. Fortney, it was an accident, nothing more. Your husband asked me to forgive him, and I did. He was out of his mind with pain. And as for me, I have a husband and three children who can help me when I get to go home. I'm just praying that this paralysis in my legs will soon be gone and that I'll be up and about doing my regular housework." Letting go of the woman's hands, Breanna said, "Please sit down here on the chair beside the bed. I'd really like to talk to you about a very important matter."

Barbara pulled the wooden chair a little closer and sat down. "Before you bring up the important matter, I want to tell you that Damon just told me that he is a Christian now and that he wants me to become one too. He said you're a Christian. Would you help me?"

A smile lit up Breanna's face. "Dear Mrs. Fortney, that is the *exact* important matter I want to talk to you about!"

"I *do* want to become a child of God!"

"I have a Bible right here on the bed stand. I will be more than happy to show you how to be saved."

With eagerness in her eyes, Barbara said, "I am ready to listen."

After some forty minutes of reading Scriptures on the subject of salvation to Barbara Fortney, Breanna had the joy of leading her to the Lord. She then showed Barbara that the first step of obedience after receiving Jesus as her Saviour was to be baptized. Barbara replied that she wanted to do that.

Breanna explained that Dr. Carroll's wife, Dottie, was her sister and that both of the Carrolls were Christians and members of Denver's First Baptist Church as well. She said Barbara should go to Dr. Carroll's office and tell him that she had just been saved and that she wanted to go to First Baptist on Sunday morning and be baptized.

Barbara leaned over, kissed Breanna's cheek, and thanked her for leading her to the Lord. Then she hurried away.

Ten minutes later, Dr. Carroll entered Breanna's room and told her that Barbara Fortney had come to him and that he and Dottie were going to take her with them to church on Sunday morning. Barbara was planning to go forward at invitation time with Dottie at her side, give her testimony about how Breanna had led her to the Lord, and be baptized. Breanna was thrilled and joyfully praised the Lord.

On the following Saturday morning, July 21, 1888, all three Zarbo brothers were hanged on the Denver gallows.

On the following Monday, July 23, Dr. Carroll allowed Breanna to leave the bed in her hospital room at times and sit in a wheelchair. Annabeth took Breanna for rides through the hospital to get her out of the room she had occupied for so long. She was taken to visit Damon Fortney, and they praised the Lord together for Barbara's salvation.

On Wednesday, August 1, Breanna was allowed to go home, and the wheelchair went with her. So did her sister, Dottie, who stayed in the Brockman home to look after her.

On Monday evening, August 6, the Brockmans, Carrolls, and Langfords ate supper together at the Brockman home. They were joyfully talking about how the Lord answered prayer in so many marvelous ways to free Ginny from the Zarbos and to make Breanna well enough to leave the bed, ride in the wheelchair, and finally come home from the hospital.

The subject of Breanna being able to walk again came up, and Dr. Carroll told them that it still didn't look good.

Breanna was sitting in her wheelchair at the table between Ginny and Meggie.

When her uncle Matt made that statement, Meggie looked around the table and said, "Two weeks from today, August 20, is my tenth birthday. I have been asking the

Lord to give me a special birthday present
— that my mama will be able to walk again."

Meggie's words touched everyone at the
table, especially Breanna. Leaning over in
her wheelchair, Breanna put her arm around
Meggie, squeezed her tight, and with tears
in her eyes said, "Thank you, sweetheart,
for praying that way."

That night, when John and Breanna were
in the rearranged parlor, preparing for a
good night's rest, Breanna was sitting in the
wheelchair in her nightgown while John
turned down the covers on the sofa for her.

Breanna looked up at him. "Darling, I
have something to tell you. I didn't bring it
up while our guests were here or in front of
the children because I didn't want anyone
to get high hopes only to possibly have them
dashed, but I feel I should tell *you*."

John looked at her, a slight frown on his
brow. "What is it, sweetheart?"

"Well, just yesterday morning I began having some feeling in my feet and legs."

John's face lit up. He stopped what he was
doing, hurried to Breanna, bent down, and
wrapped his arms around her. "We need to
tell Matt! If you still have feeling in your
feet and legs in the morning, is it okay if I
go to his office and tell him?"

Breanna hugged him back. "Yes. It's okay."

■ ■ ■ ■

The next morning, John entered Matthew's office and told him of the feeling being back in Breanna's feet and legs. The doctor was delighted to hear it and told John he would give him a cane to take home. If the feeling grew stronger, John should hold Breanna on her feet a little each evening while she attempted to walk with the cane. Elated, John took the cane home that afternoon, smuggled it into the closet in their bedroom, and told Breanna what Matt had suggested they do.

During the week and a half, John and Breanna secretly did as the doctor had suggested. Each night, Breanna did better and her legs grew stronger, and John and Breanna praised the Lord together for answered prayer.

By the time the nearly two weeks had passed, she was actually walking on her own with the help of the cane. Tears of joy and gratitude toward the Lord streamed down Breanna's cheeks as John held her in his strong arms. She looked up at him excitedly. "Oh, John, praise the Lord! I can walk! I can walk! I'm still a bit unsteady, but I'm getting stronger every day!"

John and Breanna agreed to keep this to themselves until Meggie's birthday because of the special birthday present the sweet child was asking the Lord to give her.

Still holding his beloved wife in his arms, John kept his voice low so as not to be heard by the children. "Oh, hallelujah! Thank You, dear Lord, for this miracle as an answer to our prayers!"

On Monday, August 20, a birthday party for Meggie was held at the Brockman home. During the birthday dinner in the dining room, which was to precede the party in the parlor, Breanna sat in her wheelchair as usual.

The Carrolls were there, as well as the Langfords and the Baylesses. As far as anyone except John knew, Breanna was still confined to her wheelchair.

As everyone sat around the table enjoying the scrumptious meal prepared by Dottie Carroll, Breanna looked at her precious family and friends. *They are all so special to me,* she mused. *Thank You, dear Lord, for my loving, faithful family and friends.* A small smile graced her lips.

Eagerly anticipating her surprise present for Meggie's birthday, Breanna's heart pulsated and her smile enlarged, causing her eyes to shine brightly.

When it was time to go to the parlor for the party, Breanna looked at John and asked loudly for everyone to hear, "Darling, will you carry me up to our room so I can rest a little bit?"

"Of course, sweetheart," John replied, knowing Breanna's plan. "I sure don't want you getting too tired."

As John took hold of the handles on the back of the wheelchair, Breanna turned to Meggie, patted her arm, and said, "I'll be at the party in a little while, honey. But you should go ahead and open your presents."

Meggie shook her head. "No, Mama. I want you there when I open my presents. I'll just wait till you get your rest. Then when Papa brings you down to the parlor, I'll open them."

Breanna smiled and patted her arm again. "All right, little birthday girl. I'll be back as soon as I can."

Everyone around the table was smiling at Meggie as John wheeled Breanna out of the dining room. They all made their way down the hall to the parlor. Everyone sat down, with Meggie sitting by a stack of brightly wrapped birthday presents.

Some twenty minutes later, everyone was pleased when John's voice called down the hall that he and Breanna were back.

All eyes darted to the parlor door and widened quickly when they saw Breanna enter the room — *walking!* The cane was in one hand, and John was steadying her by holding her other hand.

Paul, Ginny, and Meggie rushed to their mother, smiling broadly, their arms open wide to hug her.

"Easy! Easy!" John gently admonished them.

The three excited children drew to a halt a few feet in front of her. Then Breanna stopped and said, "I want hugs!"

One at a time, they each gave her a delicate, heartfelt hug as their father continued to steady her. Tears misted Breanna's eyes.

Everyone else was on their feet, staring in stunned silence, hardly able to believe their eyes.

When the hugs were over and the Brockman children were standing at their father's side while he continued to hold their mother's hand, Breanna looked first at John and her children, then at the others, and said, "Thank you all for praying for me. Remember Psalm 28:6? 'Blessed be the LORD, because he hath heard the voice of my supplications'? Yes, and the voice of *your* supplication too! It is only through God's abounding love and grace that I am walking again. As Psalm 121:2 says, 'My help cometh from the LORD, which made heaven and earth.' May all the glory go to Him who loves us and gave Himself for us on the cross!"

As happy tears were shed around the room, John guided his wife to a comfortable chair and helped her to sit down. Meggie went back to the stack of unopened birthday presents and stood beside them, looking at her mother.

Breanna smiled brightly at Meggie and said, "Okay, birthday girl, let the party begin! Open your presents!"

Meggie smiled at her mother, then peered around the room at the others' faces. "I already got the special birthday present I wanted most!"

She then looked toward heaven and said, "Thank You, Lord Jesus! I know I will like all these presents in the packages, but this is my favorite birthday present. *My mama is walking!*"

The employees of Thorndike Press hope you have enjoyed this Large Print book. All our Thorndike, Wheeler, and Kennebec Large Print titles are designed for easy reading, and all our books are made to last. Other Thorndike Press Large Print books are available at your library, through selected bookstores, or directly from us.

For information about titles, please call:
  (800) 223-1244

or visit our Web site at:
  http://gale.cengage.com/thorndike

To share your comments, please write:
Publisher
Thorndike Press
295 Kennedy Memorial Drive
Waterville, ME 04901